A Conspicuous Woman

Tabitha & Wolf Historical Mystery Series

Series

Book Thirteen

Sarah F. Noel

Also by Sarah F. Noel

Tabitha & Wolf Historical Mystery Series

A Proud Woman

A Singular Woman

An Independent Woman

An Inexplicable Woman

An Audacious Woman

A Discerning Woman

An Indomitable Woman

An Intrepid Woman

A Patient Woman

An Enigmatic Woman

A Valiant Woman

An Anointed Woman

The Continental Capers of Melody Chesterson

A Venetian Escapade

Mischief In Morocco

The Amsterdam Enigma

ACKNOWLEDGMENTS

I want to thank my wonderful editor, Kieran Devaney and the eagle-eyed Patricia Goulden for doing a final check of the manuscript.

To Leslie Wadler, dedicated reader and Tabitha & Wolf Wordle player.

Foreword

This book is written using British English spelling. e.g. dishonour instead of dishonor, realise instead of realize.

British spelling aside, while every effort has been made to proofread this thoroughly, typos do creep in. If you find any, I'd greatly appreciate a quick email to report them at sarahfnoelauthor@gmail.com

CHAPTER 1

October, 1898

"Jeremy, is this melodramatic suspense really necessary? At my age, surprises are rarely a good thing. At the very least, I may require smelling salts." The dowager's acerbic comments were made as Wolf led her and Tabitha to the front door in Chesterton House. Wolf doubted the dowager had ever needed smelling salts, and didn't take her complaints seriously.

Instead, he replied, "All will be revealed, Lady Pembroke, as soon as Talbot opens the door."

The butler appeared to be in on the secret; Tabitha thought she even caught a slight quirk of the lips from the normally inscrutable man. She nervously wondered what on earth Wolf was about to reveal. Tabitha had noticed her husband acting quite secretively over the past few days, but she trusted him too much to worry; she had been confident that whatever he had planned, she'd learn about it soon enough. That they needed to go outside to see the surprise was interesting. However, again, she wasn't overly concerned.

"Ready, milord?" Talbot asked, his hand on the doorknob, ready for the grand unveiling.

"Indeed, Talbot!" Wolf exclaimed with an unusually theatrical flourish.

The butler opened the door, and Wolf urged Tabitha and the dowager to step outside. On the road in front of Chesterton House, they were confronted by... well, what exactly were they confronted by? The two women were dumbfounded.

The contraption before them resembled a carriage, but no horses were attached. More specifically, it looked like a landau, complete with carriage lamps and wooden coachwork. Polished brass lamps sat on either side of a narrow seat, and a kind of lever protruded where a sensible person might expect reins. The whole contraption seemed to balance precariously on four enormous bicycle wheels

Wolf ran down the steps to stand beside the contraption, positively radiant. "Beautiful, is she not?"

Neither the dowager nor Tabitha responded for a moment; they were too stunned by the machine before them.

Finally, the dowager remarked, "Whatever this is, it looks like the outcome of an unfortunate marriage between a hansom cab and a kitchen stove."

As much as Wolf was tempted to question how many kitchen stoves the dowager had seen in her lifetime, he kept that thought to himself and answered, "This is an automobile, a motor-car. More precisely, a six-horse-power Daimler Wagonette, with twin cylinders, front-mounted engine, shaft drive. The very latest word in progress." Before he had time to consider the wisdom of his words, Wolf continued, "I have heard that the Prince of Wales himself is planning to order the same car."

"Ha!" the dowager exclaimed triumphantly. "Bertie! One need look no further than the Prince of Wales as evidence of how foolhardy the use, let alone the purchase, of such a contraption is. When has that man ever been a model of sound judgment?"

Given the dowager's well-known disdain for the heir to the throne, Wolf realised too late the bad judgement of such a boast

Wolf noticed that Tabitha still hadn't commented on his new purchase. He turned to his wife with a look of such boyish, hopeful exuberance that she tried to temper her initial shocked reaction. The truth was that, in the more than a year since Wolf inherited the earldom, he had rarely, if ever, indulged himself in any way that reflected his new wealth and status. Left to himself, he wouldn't even be dressed in the fine tailoring and fashionable accessories he was wearing. It was only at his valet's insistence that he didn't wear clothes barely finer than his old thief-taker outfit. If he had finally indulged in some extravagance, Tabitha reflected that she needed to be careful in her choice of words.

After spending a moment studying the machine and considering how to respond, Tabitha folded her hands before saying in a measured tone, "I will concede it is... impressive. But does it not seem rather exposed? There is nothing between you and the road. Or the sky. Or whatever unfortunate object you might collide with."

Placing a proud hand on his automobile, Wolf attempted to reassure Tabitha. "It only looks perilous. "The balance is remarkable, the mechanism steady. I promise you, it is far less dangerous than it appears."

"One can only hope!" the dowager interjected caustically. "Because if we are to go by its appearance, then you have just purchased a deathtrap. If Providence had intended us to travel in open tin cans, it would not have provided horses."

While Wolf had anticipated some reservations about his purchase, he had to work hard not to let his disappointment show. He was so excited about his new motor-car and wanted Tabitha at least to share that excitement. Instead, she was eyeing the machine as if it were a dangerous wild beast, ready to attack her loved ones.

Wolf cast around for the best words to reassure his nervous wife. "A Daimler man came down from Coventry to show me how the motor-car works. He was a clever fellow, extremely precise about oil and the like. After an hour or two, he declared I had 'the makings of a motorist'."

The dowager raised her eyebrows sceptically. "Jeremy, dear, do you really imagine that a representative from this Daimler company would even tell a customer otherwise?" Tabitha wanted to be supportive; she really did, but she agreed with the dowager's words, even if she wouldn't have said as much out loud.

Looking at her loving husband, as happy as a child with a Christmas stocking full of treats, Tabitha realised that, just as she wished not to be wrapped in cotton wool and be allowed to make decisions for herself about how much danger she was prepared to face, she also had to grant

Wolf the same freedom. She considered how reluctant they both had been initially to use the telephone that the dowager had installed at Chesterton House without their permission more than a year ago. Now, neither she nor Wolf could imagine functioning without it, and they always became irritated when they stayed somewhere without access to the technology.

Tabitha did her best to infuse her voice with an enthusiasm she didn't feel and said, "Well, I am glad that you received some formal training and am sure you will be appropriately cautious when out in this motor-car." Despite her best intentions, even to Tabitha's ear, her words struck less of an enthusiastic note and more one of reluctant acceptance. Even so, Wolf appreciated her attempt to be supportive and gave Tabitha an appreciative smile.

"Now that we have seen this thing, may we return to the drawing room so I can finish my tea?" the dowager asked with one of her signature sniffs. "I was already quite parched when you called us out here, and now I fear I may expire if I am unable to have at least a sip or two soon."

Both Tabitha and Wolf were familiar with the dowager's penchant for hyperbolically claiming martyrdom of some sort. They shared an amused, if resigned, glance before agreeing to return to the drawing room.

When they were all seated again and the dowager had taken her first life-saving sips of tea, Wolf felt it was time to reveal the second part of his surprise. "I have another, related piece of news," he announced with some trepidation.

"Surely not, Jeremy," the dowager said, with the weary patience of a saint enduring the most grievous of biblical trials. "I was almost inclined to ask for brandy in my tea, such was the stress-inducing nature of the unveiling of your machine. I am not sure my nerves can handle much more in a single afternoon."

Determined to be as supportive a wife as possible, Tabitha said, "Hush, Mama. Wolf, what is your other news?" The dowager's pout made her disapproval at being shushed quite clear; nevertheless, she said nothing more.

"Well, the man from Daimler told me about a motor-car run taking place in a couple of weeks. It goes from London to Brighton. It follows the route of the Emancipation Run of 1896," Wolf explained.

"And what would that be?" the dowager asked.

"Well, apparently, before then, a person waving a red flag had to walk sixty yards ahead of a vehicle. An Act of Parliament two years ago abolished this rule and increased the speed limit from 4 mph to 14 mph. The 1896 run was to celebrate the emancipation from these restrictions."

As he'd expected, the dowager's response was to raise her eyebrows and remark, "And this is considered a good thing Jeremy?"

Tabitha's concern was more practical. "So, in two weeks, you are going to drive your motorcar all the way to Brighton, having only just learned how to use it? Do you believe that is wise, Wolf?" Unspoken were her feelings on hearing that Wolf would be going to Brighton

While she felt secure in her husband's love, Tabitha was unable to forget that his first great love, the beautiful and manipulative Lady Arlene Archibald, lived in Brighton and had tried to seduce Wolf during their previous visit. She had failed, and had even admitted this failure to Tabitha, acknowledging that she was no longer the love of his life. Nonetheless, Tabitha disliked the idea of Wolf visiting there alone. Perhaps Lady Archibald would decide to try her luck again using her not insignificant feminine wiles.

There was no doubt Wolf would refuse to let Tabitha drive with him. In truth, she had no wish to do so. Nonetheless, surely, he wouldn't argue against her taking the train to Brighton to meet him there at the end of the rally

She voiced this suggestion only to have Wolf shoot it down immediately. "Tabitha, I thought we had agreed that you were not to exert yourself. It is a miracle that you and the baby are well after the horrors at Stonehenge. Why tempt fate with such a trip?"

Tabitha controlled herself enough not to say the first thing that came into her head. Instead, she took a moment to reflect on how terrified Wolf had been when he rescued her from almost being a human sacrifice during a Druid ritual reenactment the previous month. Of course, he wasn't the only one who had been scared; for some time, Tabitha had been unable to shake the fear that her ordeal had affected her miraculous pregnancy.

After taking a moment to collect herself, Tabitha said gently, "Wolf, I know you are worried about the baby; I am as well. However, I refuse to take to my bed for the next four months, and Dr Pauls agrees. I cannot imagine that taking the train the short distance to Brighton and then relaxing in a luxury suite at The Grand is something that will be harmful to me or the baby?" Tabitha smiled at Wolf; she hoped reassuringly.

Never one to be left out of an adventure if she could help it, the dowager chimed in, "And I will accompany Tabitha to ensure her well-being."

Wolf wasn't convinced that the dowager's presence would make the trip less stressful for Tabitha, but he knew when he was outnumbered. "I insist that Bear travel with you as well," was the most he felt able to impose on his wife.

"Will he not be driving with you?" Tabitha asked.

Laughing, Wolf answered, "I cannot imagine Bear squeezing his frame into that motor-car comfortably. Certainly not for hours. I asked Langley to accompany me, but it seems he has a surprising fear of automobiles and is otherwise engaged. So, I will be driving alone."

"Surprising fear? I am pleasantly surprised to find Maxwell so sensible!" was the dowager's final comment on the topic.

CHAPTER 2

I t was a chilly, but sunny and crisp November morning. Tabitha buried her gloved hands deeper into her mink muff and consoled herself that at least Wolf wouldn't be driving in the rain, or worse.

A crowd had gathered along Whitehall Place, pressing against the railings outside the Hotel Metropole to watch the spectacle. Policemen shouted, engines sputtered, and gentlemen in goggles and dust-coats posed for photos beside their gleaming machines.

Tabitha and the dowager stood at the edge of the throng, observing the seeming chaos of it all.

"Good heavens!" the older woman murmured, surveying the line of motorcars. "It looks like the gates of Bedlam."

Tabitha smiled faintly, though her heart gave a nervous flutter as she searched for Wolf among the crowd. Finally, she caught sight of his Daimler, gleaming dark green against the morning light, its brass fittings shining as they should after the hours of elbow grease Madison had put in polishing them.

"Do try not to fret," the dowager said, misreading her silence. "If the machine explodes, at least he will be in distinguished company. Half the peerage seems to be here and determined to immolate themselves before luncheon."

The dowager did have a point; it seemed that Wolf was in fine company with his new hobby. As Tabitha looked around, she noted two viscounts, a marquess, and at least one duke. Given how much the new motor-car must have cost, it was no wonder that only a select few chose to be in the vanguard.

What surprised Tabitha more than excessive representation by Britain's aristocrats was that it seemed that not all the drivers were men. In the distance, she saw two women hovering around a red car. Given their outfits, more refined, couture-like versions of the men's, it seemed they were also driving to Brighton. One of the women was tall and willowy with dark hair, and the other was shorter and more curvaceous with blonde hair that, even from that distance, Tabitha could see was as golden and shiny as the sunlight on the polished brass of their car.

Tapping the dowager on her arm, Tabitha drew her attention to the women.

"Heaven help us," the dowager exclaimed as if witnessing the fall of civilisation. "Those women cannot possibly be planning to join these men in their folly."

"Based on their outfits, I imagine they might," Tabitha replied. Part of her was as horrified as the dowager, but another part envied the women's independence and willingness to fly so blatantly in the face of convention.

"The moment women begin doing men's foolish things, I fear we are approaching the end of civilisation!" the dowager said rather hyper-bolically.

Tabitha was well aware of the dowager's views on women's rights, particularly suffrage. Of course, the woman held those rather regressive views about her own gender, while still believing herself more intelligent and competent than the Prime Minister and all his cabinet. She held this belief regardless of which party was in power and which men ran the country.

As Tabitha continued to observe the two women drivers and wonder what kind of woman had the self-confidence and courage to drive a car from London to Brighton, the taller of the two turned. No! Surely her eyes were deceiving her. Tabitha's heart sank. She squinted and focused on the elegant figure of the woman and was quite sure: it was Lady Arlene Archibald.

At that moment, the dowager announced, "Why, I believe one of those women is dear Lady Archibald. How delightful. We must go over and greet her."

Among the many things that discombobulated Tabitha about the beautiful, charming Lady Archibald, not the least was that the dowager had taken to her so quickly. Initially, this preference seemed to stem from a delight in tweaking Tabitha's nose about the beautiful woman whom Wolf had courted in his youth. However, there was little doubt that the dowager genuinely enjoyed Lady Archibald's sharp wit and admired her willingness to engage in social combat, especially when this was directed toward Tabitha.

Moreover, there was little the dowager enjoyed more than confounding expectations. It hadn't been unrealistic to expect the usually snobbish dowager to look down her nose at the woman whose dark skin tone might suggest a variety of parentages, including southern European, but was actually due to a Caribbean mother. Given this, the dowager had been positively gleeful at Tabitha and Wolf's surprise at her warm embrace of Lady Archibald.

"We must go and say hello," the dowager said, already beginning to walk in Lady Archibald's direction.

There was nothing Tabitha would have liked more than to have a good excuse not to follow the dowager, but she couldn't think of any reason why she would not abide by social etiquette and at least be polite. She had met Lady Archibald nearly a year ago, which now seemed almost a lifetime, and was before Tabitha and Wolf had declared their love for each other. Now, they were married and expecting a child. Tabitha had no sensible reason for feeling insecure.

Arlene had broken Wolf's heart over a decade ago. When they met again in Brighton, Lady Archibald made it quite clear she wanted to pick up where they left off years earlier, but Wolf had firmly rejected her advances and chosen Tabitha.

Tabitha knew all this rationally, yet she was unable to stem the flood of emotions that washed over her as they approached the glamorous woman, who turned towards them with a smile that didn't quite reach her mesmerising, almond-shaped, green eyes.

"Why, what a surprise. What are you doing here, Lady Pembroke?"

While this question might have been directed to either Lady Pembroke, as Arlene extended her hand and made eye contact, there was no doubt that her greeting was not meant for Tabitha. Finally, as if she hadn't noticed Tabitha standing there, Arlene shifted her gaze and said, "And the other Lady Pembroke; twice over now I hear." Then, she laughed at her own wit.

"Lady Archibald. What a surprise," Tabitha replied, trying to keep the vinegar out of her tone. "Will you be driving?"

"Well, for this rally, I shall be the passenger. My dear friend, Miss Isabella Hartwell, will be the driver." With this, Arlene directed their attention to the blonde woman, who had moved slightly away and was talking to a uniformed man who seemed to be a mechanic. They were standing next to what, even Tabitha recognised, was an impressive motorcar.

Where Wolf's Daimler was sleek and elegant, this bright, cherry-red machine was built for boldness rather than beauty; boxy, powerful, and brash. The seats were upholstered in pale cream leather, quite impractical but undeniably lovely, and every curve of its body suggested the finest craftsmanship, with no expense spared.

Lady Archibald saw Tabitha's admiring glances and said, "It's a Panhard et Levassor. Shipped from Paris. She's the choice of serious motorists and the most fashionable Europeans."

The mechanic said something, and Miss Hartwell laughed before replying. The sound carried easily above the hum of the crowd, bright and unmistakably American.

"Bella, let me introduce you to some friends," Arlene called out.

The other woman turned, and Tabitha got a full view of the most beautiful face she had ever seen. Isabella Hartwell possessed the kind of appearance that novelists were forever inventing; her features were perfectly formed, including a rosebud mouth, a porcelain complexion, and large, deep blue eyes framed by almost unnatural-looking, thick, long dark lashes. Rarely did Tabitha lack self-confidence in her own looks. However, staring at the almost angelic face of Miss Hartwell, Tabitha felt she might as well have been a carthorse standing beside a purebred Arabian mare.

It would have been all too easy to develop an instant dislike for Isabella Hartwell, both because of her striking looks and her friendship with Arlene. Then, she smiled, and unlike Arlene's greeting, it was a warm, welcoming grin that genuinely lit up her eyes.

Leaving the mechanic, Isabella approached and held out her hand to Tabitha. "Well, any friend of Nene's is a friend of mine," she said.

Nene? Who was Nene? The question was answered when Lady Archibald's insincere laugh tinkled again, and she said, "Oh, Bella, you are silly. You are the only person who calls me by that nickname."

"Am I? Oh well. Any friend of Lady Arlene Archibald's is a friend of mine. Is that better?" This was said with such open, light-hearted pleasantness that Tabitha had to wonder how the two women ever became friends.

Then, Miss Hartwell asked the question Tabitha had hoped to avoid: "Are you here to cheer on a particular driver?"

Without permitting Tabitha to stall or respond in any way at all, the dowager said, "Yes, Lord Pembroke is driving."

Arlene raised her eyebrows. "Wolf has a motor-car? When did this happen?"

Reluctantly, Tabitha explained, "It is a new purchase. This will be his first significant drive, besides practising around Mayfair."

Tabitha hoped that her anxiety wasn't evident in her voice, but the smile hinting at mockery she received in reply from Arlene dashed that hope. "There is no need to worry, Lady Pembroke. Motor-cars are the way of the future. I am convinced there will come a time when London is full of them." While the words themselves were harmless enough, the derisive tone in which they were said made Tabitha want to scream.

It seemed she was the only one who heard anything underlying Lady Archibald's seemingly innocuous words.

Isabella nodded in agreement as the dowager said, "You know, I believe you are correct. I have been thinking much the same thing myself ever since Jeremy surprised us with his delightful new purchase." Tabitha turned to look at the dowager and shot her a look of disbelief, which the old woman chose to ignore.

Arlene said pointedly, "I won't bother Wolf now. We'll have more than enough time at the starting line and when we reach Brighton."

Tabitha was not proud of how happy she felt to answer brightly, "Yes, we really must all catch up in Brighton. Mama and I are getting the train down as soon as you are all on your way." She knew it was petty and childish, but she was incapable of not taking pleasure in the sulky look of disappointment that came over Lady Archibald's face at this news.

CHAPTER 3

Tabitha stood and watched Wolf as he happily observed the mechanic Daimler had sent to help him tune the car and prepare for the drive. He was a tall young man in oil-stained gloves with the patient expression of someone familiar with assisting wealthy men enjoy their new toys.

"The Daimler people insisted on sending one of their men," Wolf explained. "A formality, apparently."

"And this young man cannot travel with you?" Tabitha asked, trying to keep the anxiety out of her voice.

Wolf hesitated before answering. The truth was that Daimler had made just such an offer, but Wolf had turned them down. In an act of hubris he hoped he wouldn't later regret, Wolf decided he didn't want to play at being a driver while someone else did all the real work. While this had made sense to him when he'd politely declined Daimler's offer, Wolf realised that if he said this aloud to Tabitha, it might not sound as reasonable as he hoped.

So, instead, he told a white lie. "Apparently, at this point, Daimler does not have enough mechanics to provide one to drive with every owner of one of their cars."

There was a kernel of truth to this statement; the Daimler representative had indeed mentioned that their motor-cars were becoming so popular that they were beginning to suffer from a shortage of trained mechanics capable of servicing them. They had then offered to send one such mechanic to help at the start of the run. Wolf chose to infer from those two statements that, had he agreed to have the mechanic accompany him, the stated lack of manpower might have been given as a reason to back out of the offer.

Fortunately, Tabitha didn't question his statement, and Wolf hoped the mechanic was too far away and too busy with the motor-car to overhear their exchange.

There had been few things that truly excited him about inheriting the earldom. He often found the great responsibility now resting on him for the livelihood and well-being of many servants and tenants overwhelming. Certainly, he found the trappings of his rank and wealth, such as the fancy clothes and the constant kowtowing, absurd and embarrassing. Wolf didn't care about the houses, the membership to exclusive clubs, the thousands of acres of land he now owned, or anything else he'd inherited.

However, being able to purchase the Daimler Wagonette was something he never would have considered as a thief-taker, and he was genuinely enthusiastic about it. As such, he wanted to enjoy it to the fullest.

As he noted the mechanic performing some final tuning to the motor-car, Wolf expressed his own worries. "Are you sure it is wise to have Rat, the twins, and Melody travel to Brighton?" While he had given up hope of dissuading Tabitha from making the trip, Wolf still hoped he might prevail when it came to the rest of the entourage.

Tabitha looked at him in exasperation. "Wolf! We have discussed this already. It was one thing not to take Melody to Salisbury; there was little she would have enjoyed about a cathedral town. However, Brighton is an entirely different matter; you know how much fun she had playing on the beach and watching the Punch and Judy show. I cannot imagine going without her. And if she is to come, then it seems quite unfair to leave the other children out."

Wolf sighed; he knew Tabitha was right, of course. With Langley preoccupied with the affairs of the House of Lords, Rat was probably left to his own devices and feeling rather bored. The boy had enjoyed all that

Brighton offered just as much as his sister had. Moreover, Wolf understood that Tabitha felt strongly that if the O'Leary twins were to share the nursery with Melody, they shouldn't be treated as the poor relatives and needed to be given the same opportunities as the little girl.

He decided to try once more, albeit half-heartedly. "It is only that, of course, it is not just the children. It is the extra servants, not to mention the dog. I simply worry that it is too much for you to manage alone."

"I will not be alone; I will have Mama, Bear, and most importantly, Mrs O'Leary, who is the most capable person I know." Tabitha realised that including the dowager in a list of positives for the trip rather than obligations and responsibilities was rather a stretch.

Having delivered her tart reply to Lady Archibald, Tabitha had promptly left the group, determined to enjoy her upper hand for as long as possible. However, the dowager had insisted on remaining behind to speak with Arlene and Miss Hartwell. Tabitha had chosen to make the most of the dowager's absence and delay pointing out the women to Wolf. Again, she knew it was both petty and pointless; he would undoubtedly notice them at some point on the trip to Brighton. Nevertheless, Tabitha hoped to delay that discovery for as long as possible.

Her wish was dashed when the dowager returned to stand beside Tabitha and immediately informed Wolf of their unexpected encounter with Lady Archibald and her friend.

"Arlene is here and participating in the run?" Wolf asked in surprise. The last time he had seen his erstwhile love, she had hinted that she might retire to the country to live a quieter, less conspicuous life. Being one of the only women participating in the motor-car run didn't seem to align with that plan.

As Wolf asked this, he looked around, trying to spot Arlene. Tabitha wasn't sure how she would have expected or hoped he would behave upon receiving this news, but she was irritated by his reaction. "Really, Wolf! I am sure you will have a chance for a tête-à-tête with the charming Lady Archibald at some point. Do you not have more important things to focus on at the moment?"

Whatever Wolf might have replied, he was saved from it by the dowager. "Perhaps Tabitha has a point, Jeremy. I have always said that nothing breaks a man's concentration like the sudden reappearance of the woman who once addled his wits."

Tabitha shot her a look of irritation; while, at least superficially, this comment seemed intended to support Tabitha's position, its tone and the smug look on the dowager's face that accompanied it suggested its real intention was to rankle her further.

Hoping to change the subject somewhat, Wolf asked, "And who is this Miss Hartwell driving the car?"

The dowager was happy to pass on the titbits of information she had managed to learn after Tabitha had left. "It appears this Miss Isabella Hartwell is the daughter of an American industrialist. He owned something called Hartwell Ironworks." Then, in a rather conspiratorial voice, the dowager continued, "Apparently, she is in Britain as a guest of the Duchess of Marlborough!"

Wolf's ploy had succeeded; Tabitha was distracted. "The Duchess of Marlborough?"

"Indeed! Perhaps Miss Hartwell is yet another of those American heiresses bought at auction to prop up a failing title. I am told the duchess is a charming young woman, but, of course, one can hardly expect refinement to be hereditary when one's fortune comes from railroads. To say nothing of being an American!" The dowager had never been shy about expressing her views of Americans, decrying their style and taste, as well as their speech, manners, and particularly their attempts to claw their way into the British nobility.

Of course, it was difficult to come up with a group of people the dowager didn't look down her nose at. Certainly, she had only negative things to say about the Scottish, the Welsh, and the Irish, not to mention her views on continentals. While her opinions on the working class were complicated and contradictory, she had complete disdain for people of her own rank and status. Perhaps her least favourite were the middle classes, particularly those she viewed as striving parvenus. Tabitha did wonder whether this was how she viewed all Americans.

For her part, though not personally acquainted with the Duchess of Marlborough, Tabitha had read and heard enough to form an opinion. She knew Consuelo Vanderbilt was one of the famous "dollar princesses," American heiresses whose fortunes had rescued more than one crumbling

English estate. Yet there was also something tragic about it: an arranged marriage driven by ambition rather than affection. Of course, this was not so different from Tabitha's own marriage to Jonathan, so she felt some sympathy for a young woman whose beauty and grace had been exchanged for a title and an influx of cash into her father's accounts.

Was that the reason Isabella Hartwell was in England? To secure herself an aristocratic husband? Having met the lively and seemingly independent young woman, Tabitha found that somewhat hard to believe. Making a spectacle of oneself by defying all social conventions and driving in a motor-car run otherwise entirely composed of men didn't seem like the behaviour of a husband-hunting ingenue.

Tabitha was torn; she was curious about Miss Hartwell and would have liked to further their acquaintance. However, she had no desire to spend more time with Lady Arlene Archibald than absolutely necessary, and that wish far outweighed the other. She was hopeful they might spend the three days they planned to be in Brighton without encountering Arlene.

Even as this thought entered her mind, Tabitha wondered whether Wolf had planned to call on his former love. Certainly, he hadn't mentioned any such plans, but perhaps that was because he anticipated Tabitha's reaction. Still, she was unable to imagine him doing so behind her back, so maybe he was planning to skirt the issue altogether.

Tabitha did feel a little guilty about the bind in which she had likely put her husband. It wasn't that she didn't trust Wolf, quite the opposite. It was rather that she didn't like or trust Lady Archibald and considered Wolf a little naive when it came to the woman's intentions and her willingness to use her many charms to get what she wanted.

CHAPTER 4

The motor-car run was scheduled to start on the hour. There were twenty minutes remaining, but already the excitement was palpable. The pavements bustled with eager onlookers: gentlemen in top hats craned for a better view, shop clerks leaned from windows, and children excitedly darted between the motor-cars. Reporters made their way through the crowd with notebooks and cameras at the ready. Clearly, the event was destined to be front-page news for every newspaper present.

A discordant chorus of chugging engines, rattling chains, and the occasional explosive, fuel-filled cough of a misfiring engine filled the air with sounds and smells that Tabitha found almost overwhelming.

The line of vehicles stretched the length of the street, each one a curiosity in its own right: sleek Daimlers and boxy Panhards beside contraptions that looked scarcely more advanced than farm machinery. Someone's engine emitted a sharp hiss and a puff of smoke, prompting delighted applause from onlookers who seemed to imagine it part of the show.

Tabitha stood a little apart, gloved hands clasped, while the dowager beside her grew increasingly impatient. The older woman's expression suggested she was weary of waiting for the run to begin.

"Surely, we need not stay any longer, Tabitha," she complained. "We have come and shown our support and will be at the finish line when Jeremy has completed his personal Odyssey. Is that not enough?"

It took all of Tabitha's self-control not to snap irritably. She had suggested that the dowager not accompany her for precisely this reason. Yet, fearful of missing out, the woman had insisted she be included in the outing, even though it had involved leaving her bedchamber far earlier than was usual.

Instead of pointing this out, Tabitha suggested, "Mama, why do you not wait in the carriage? I intend to stay until the start of the run."

Tabitha observed the dowager weighing her options. There was little she hated more than the insinuation that she was too old and fragile for an activity. On the other hand, she was cold and bored and would prefer to wait in the relative warmth of the Pembroke carriage.

Before she had the chance to make her decision, they heard raised voices coming from the direction where they had seen Lady Archibald earlier. At least one of those voices was a woman's. Then, across the line of motorcars, the sound of the woman's raised voice, followed by the unmistakable crack of a slap. Heads turned at once.

"I think that is Arlene," Wolf said. "What is going on?" He immediately hurried to the source of the commotion. The dowager had no wish to miss what was unfolding and followed him. Tabitha wasn't sure what to do, but finally shrugged and followed.

By the time they reached the red French motor-car, a considerable crowd had gathered to view the ongoing spectacle.

Wolf pushed his way through to Lady Archibald, who was standing almost toe-to-toe with a rotund, florid man whose face was contorted into a nasty sneer. He was holding his cheek, and the obvious conclusion was that Arlene had just slapped him.

"You presumptuous creature," Arlene hissed. "If you ever address me again in such a manner, I'll do worse than that."

"Arlene." Wolf was already by her side, his stride quick, his expression unmistakably furious. He placed himself between the two. "What has this man said to you?"

"Nothing fit for a lady's hearing," she said, trembling but defiant.

The man inclined his head and attempted a laugh, though his colour betrayed him. "Heaven help me! Does no one have a sense of humour anymore? It was merely a misunderstood jest, that's all."

Wolf's voice was low but carried clearly. "I believe you insulted Lady Archibald."

"Lady Archibald, is it?" the man said, saying her title with just enough irony to suggest he doubted her breeding and right to be in his company. "All I said were some words of admiration. If Lady Archibald," and again, he said her title with undisguised mockery, "chooses to take offence at being invited for a private dinner, that is hardly my fault."

The murmurs grew louder as the crowd's excitement at the melodrama intensified. Several journalists were scribbling already.

"You will apologise," Wolf demanded.

"I will not," the man said defiantly.

"Then let me be clear," Wolf snapped. "You are a disgrace. If you approach Lady Archibald again, you will answer to me."

The man's smile twisted. "Why, how very chivalrous of you. One might imagine you take your devotion to Lady Archibald rather personally." This was said with such blatant innuendo that the crowd gasped.

Tabitha reached for her husband's arm too late; he had already taken a step forward, his fists clenched.

Then, an icy voice rang out. "That is quite enough," the dowager declared, her tone slicing through the noise. "Sir, you will apologise to Lady Archibald or remove yourself before I summon someone to do it for you."

For a moment, no one moved. Then the man inclined his head stiffly. "My apologies, Lady Archibald. I meant no insult."

"You most certainly did," Arlene replied coldly.

The man spun around on his heel, muttering, "Overwrought women!" and stalked back toward his motorcar.

"Arlene. Are you alright?" Wolf asked anxiously. "I am so sorry you had to endure that boorish behaviour."

"He is hardly the first man to imagine he can take liberties with me that he would not with most women of rank, and he will not be the last." Arlene said this with such weary bitterness that, for a moment, Tabitha forgot her antipathy towards the woman. What must it be like to know that society's tolerance of your skin colour was a thin veneer at best?

"That is terrible," Tabitha said sincerely. Arlene gave her a resigned half-smile. Tabitha wasn't sure whether the gesture was a general comment on what had happened or a judgement on Tabitha's consolation. Whatever it was, she felt compelled to add, "Perhaps you should not take part in the run to Brighton. That dreadful man does not seem like someone who would take a public shaming lightly. I would hate for him to run into you when no one else is present," she added.

Miss Hartwell approached and placed her hand on her friend's shoulder. "We'll be fine. We won't let a bully like that ruin our plans." Arlene nodded her head in agreement.

For a moment, it seemed as if Wolf wouldn't be willing to accept that answer. Tabitha felt his muscles tense beneath her hand. She squeezed his arm. "Wolf, these ladies have made their choice. Why don't we return to your motor-car? The run will be starting shortly."

Arlene caught Tabitha's eye and held her gaze briefly, then offered a quick, tight smile. Reluctantly, Wolf allowed himself to be led away.

By the time they returned to the Daimler, it seemed the run was about to begin. Tabitha encouraged Wolf to put on his goggles and heavy motoring coat and get into his motor-car.

A sudden flurry of movement rippled through the crowd as a man in a bowler hat stepped onto a wooden crate near the starting line. He carried a small Union Jack with an air of theatrical importance. "Ladies and gentlemen," the man called, raising his voice above the engines. "Today we celebrate progress, courage, and the triumph of ingenuity over doubt! Two years ago, the Emancipation Run celebrated our freedom from the onerous restrictions put on these machines and proved they could conquer the road from London to Brighton. Today, we prove they can do so again, but even faster this time!"

Polite applause followed, mixed with laughter and the startled whinny of a passing horse. The man smiled, undaunted. "May all reach Brighton safely!"

He waved the flag, and a roar answered him. Amid cheers, smoke, and the sound of horns, one after another, the machines began to move forward, some smoothly, others more joltingly. The mechanic gave the starting handle a sharp turn and the Daimler's engine sprang to life with a throaty growl. Tabitha felt her heart twist as she watched it vanish down Whitehall, a disappearing blur of green and brass.

When she could no longer see even the dust that Wolf's motor-car had thrown up, Tabitha turned to the dowager. "Let us return home and gather the children. I would like to make the one o'clock train, if possible."

The Pembroke carriage slowly made its way through the crowd still gathered along Whitehall. Tabitha tried but was unable to quell the unease she had felt since Lady Archibald's unpleasant encounter. She found everything about the incident disturbing, including Wolf's reaction. Tabitha wanted to believe that her husband would have jumped just as passionately to the defence of any woman, but was that truly the case? She did not doubt he would have been chivalrous in protecting the honour of any wronged woman. However, would he have done so with the same intensity he'd shown that morning?

Tabitha must have been lost in her own thoughts for some time, because finally, the dowager leaned forward, placed a surprisingly gentle hand on her knee, and said kindly, "She has spent her life having to tolerate such rudeness and petty slights. Jeremy must have witnessed this more than once. Anyone who once cared for Lady Archibald would be outraged on her behalf."

Although she'd been gazing out of the window lost in contemplation, now, Tabitha looked into the dowager's face and saw a surprising depth of compassion and understanding. "Thank you, Mama," she said with a tentative smile.

CHAPTER 5

A small cheer rippled through the cluster of spectators pressed along the pavement as the motor-cars began moving forward. Someone waved a Union Jack, and another shouted, "Godspeed, sir!" One nearby vendor was roasting chestnuts, and another was selling pies. The atmosphere was reminiscent of the Guy Fawkes festivities that had taken place only the night before.

Wolf glanced at the motor-cars setting off around him. There were perhaps sixty entrants this year: French Panhards and Peugeots, German Benzes, and quite a few Daimlers like his own, even a few odd-looking tricycles and contraptions with tillers instead of wheels. His heart beat a little faster. Though he'd driven the Daimler for a couple of weeks, this was his first time navigating a crowd of other motor-cars. The idea of speed excited him, yet the possibility of an accident, a burst tyre, or a collision with a runaway horse, made his hands clammy inside his gloves.

It hadn't fully dawned on Wolf until this moment that there was a significant difference between his usual practice drives, mainly in the early morning to Hyde Park, along Rotten Row or on South Carriage Drive, and what he was now undertaking. He had taken a few longer drives through Kensington and Brompton, but those had been in the early hours. He had frightened and irritated some grooms and milkmen, and on one occasion, nearly collided with a rag and bone cart. However, what he hadn't encountered before were other motor-cars. Now, he was driving amongst many of them, which was rather intimidating.

As much as Wolf had dismissed Tabitha's concerns, especially those about him driving alone, as he briefly turned his head and saw the mechanic wave him off, he did wonder how wise this decision had been.

The procession of vehicles passed beneath the shadow of Admiralty Arch. Crowds lined both sides of Whitehall, craning to see the spectacle. Women waved handkerchiefs; boys darted dangerously close, only to be hauled back by anxious mothers. Policemen stood at intervals, attempting to maintain order.

Wolf kept the Daimler steady in second gear, wary of the erratic movements of the vehicles ahead. A steam machine to his left belched white vapour, momentarily obscuring his view. He honked the bulb horn, and the driver gave a vague salute before swerving back into line.

A horse-drawn omnibus crossed his path at the corner by Westminster Bridge, the driver shouting curses as he sharply reined in his horses. Wolf braked suddenly; the motor-car jerked but remained steady. His pulse pounded in his ears. The crowd roared with approval as if such chaos were part of the spectacle. He exhaled slowly, forcing his shoulders to loosen.

Once across the bridge, the air felt clearer, the road wider, the crowds thinner. The spectators were mostly clerks in bowler hats, errand boys, and maids performing their morning chores. They waved and shouted encouragement or, occasionally, derision. The Houses of Parliament fell away behind them, and the procession wound along the river, through Lambeth and Vauxhall.

Every turn demanded vigilance. The roads were narrow, with uneven surfaces and ruts left by years of horse traffic. Already, Wolf's arms ached from holding the steering wheel steady against the constant jarring. He had to brake sharply twice to avoid dogs that darted across his path. He found himself muttering a steady rhythm of curses and prayers under his breath.

By the time they reached Clapham, the line of motor-cars had started to spread out. The slower steam carriages fell behind, while the faster petrol-driven ones surged ahead, leaving faint trails of exhaust and dust behind them. Wolf began to relax enough to test his throttle. The Daimler responded easily, climbing from ten to fifteen miles per hour.

The wind tugged at Wolf's coat and stung his eyes despite the goggles. For the first time that morning, he allowed himself to smile; this really was fun. He had not expected the sensation to be so intoxicating. The roar of the engine beneath him, the tremor through the machine's seat, and the rush of air in his face were all so much more exhilarating than when he was tentatively getting used to the Daimler. Back then, he'd driven extremely slowly, unsure of himself and the motor-car. However, now that he was motoring along at a good clip, the unease of the crowded start faded behind the reassuring rhythm of the engine.

In Streatham, a wheelbarrow tipped over in the road, scattering cabbages. Wolf swerved, narrowly missing a cyclist who shouted curses at his retreating back.

"My apologies!" Wolf shouted over the wind, though he doubted the man heard. A policeman at the corner waved his truncheon and scowled.

Beyond Norbury, the streets thinned, houses giving way to hedgerows, and the road widened. The faint scent of manure and wood smoke replaced the heavy coal reek of London. Wolf dared another notch on the throttle. The engine deepened its growl, and the speed pressed him gently against the seat.

Wolf had been driving for just over an hour. The bustle and grime of the city had entirely faded now, and the air was free of smog. The Daimler's engine hummed confidently, and the road to Brighton stretched out clearly before him. Provided he encountered no mechanical issues. Wolf anticipated easily arriving in time for tea.

Hearing a sound quite close behind him, Wolf glanced back: a blue Panhard was gaining on him, its driver grinning beneath his goggles. The driver raised a hand in salute as he drew level and then surged past, his exhaust snapping like gunfire. Wolf felt a childish urge to chase him but resisted. The Daimler was robust, but not designed for racing. The mechanic had made a point of mentioning this several times that morning.

Wolf realised he hadn't seen Arlene yet. Given her position in line at Whitehall, he assumed she was some way behind him. He only hoped that the unpleasant gentleman was nowhere near her. He'd had to fight the urge to slow down and try to keep pace with her red Panhard. Lady Archibald wasn't his responsibility, and he knew that she wouldn't appreciate the condescension. Tabitha would definitely look askance at his taking on a protective role for his former love. Despite this, he resolved to look for Arlene when they arrived in Brighton to ensure there was no repeat of the earlier scene.

The next few miles passed in a blur of wind and motion. Wolf kept his eyes on the narrow strip of road ahead, avoiding stones and ruts, steering clear of the occasional horse cart whose drivers watched with wide-eyed suspicion as the procession roared past. A few waved, but most merely cursed the noise and the dust.

At Croydon, the first official checkpoint appeared: a line of bunting strung across the street, stewards noting numbers and times. Wolf slowed to roll past the desk, gave his name, and received a nod of acknowledgement. A cluster of local children cheered as he accelerated again.

By this time, Wolf had been driving for nearly two hours. The Daimler's engine had settled into a steady rhythm, and his hands confidently gripped the wheel. Occasionally, people stood by the road, waving hats and handkerchiefs, cheering as if the procession of motor-cars were a royal cavalcade rather than a line of sooty, sputtering machines.

After all the time holding the steering wheel, Wolf felt the strain in his arms and the numbness in his fingers as the cold November air bit through his gloves. He tried to ignore his physical discomfort and instead focus on the Daimler. The mechanic had been clear that every sound from the engine mattered: the rhythmic pop of combustion, the occasional clank of a loose chain. Any of these might herald disaster. Wolf had been warned to pay attention to them all.

Through Purley and Coulsdon, the road climbed steadily, winding between fields mostly lying fallow before winter. The Daimler's pace slowed as the incline increased. The engine knocked faintly. Wolf enriched the mixture and notched the spark back, coaxing her onward.

At the summit, he heard a sound that worried him and decided to stop to check the radiator. The mechanic in London had shown him a few basic things to do if trouble arose: how to tighten a fitting, clear a fuel line, or check the water level. Wolf set the brake, climbed down, and took his spanner from the tool tray, just in case. Finding nothing wrong, he threw the tool into the tool tray, meaning to stow it properly at Brighton. Wiping his goggles with his handkerchief, he took a moment to appreciate the view from his position.

From here, London lay behind him, a haze of smoke and stone fading into the distance. Ahead, the Downs revealed themselves in their full splendour on the clear, sunny day. Wolf felt an unexpected surge of pride; despite the reservations expressed by the dowager, Tabitha, and even Langley; he had driven out of the capital without wrecking himself or his motor-car, and the open road awaited.

As far as he could see, there was nothing wrong with the radiator. Wolf was relieved until he realised that he now had to restart the engine. He'd seen the mechanic do it and had then, with Madison's help, managed to start it himself for his morning drives. However, now he was in the middle of the countryside, with no one around to help. What would he do if he were unable to start it alone? Of course, he reasoned, other drivers would be along soon enough, but it would be humiliating to be caught out, unable to start his own motor-car.

Wolf took a steadying breath and grasped the starting handle, feeling the cold of the metal even through his gloves. After a moment's resistance, the tool kicked back viciously, jolting his arm. Muttering a curse, Wolf tried again, sweat beading under his cap despite the chill. The engine sputtered once, teasing him, then fell silent. He adjusted the choke and gave one final, determined swing. This time, the Daimler roared to life. Wolf grinned, triumphant and breathless.

By the time he descended into Redhill, the road had grown quieter as the field of competitors stretched across miles of countryside. The sun was higher, warming the chill from the air. Here and there, villagers gathered to wave, their expressions a mix of wonder and apprehension.

Wolf paused briefly outside a roadside inn to top up his fuel, retrieving a tin of motor spirit from the rear compartment. He used the small hand pump he carried to pour it into the tank. As he was pulling up, he saw another bottle-green motor-car drive past him.

A stable boy came out, wiping his hands on his apron. "What do you call that thing, sir?" he asked.

"A Daimler," Wolf replied with a proud smile.

The boy grinned. "Does she run as nice as she looks, sir?"

"Indeed, she does," Wolf said, tossing the boy a coin for his praise.

Wolf revved the engine again. As it roared to life with a loud bang, a horse tethered nearby reared in alarm. The boy grabbed its bridle and laughed. "Good luck to you, sir!"

"Let us hope I do not need it," Wolf said as he eased the car back onto the road.

The miles rolled by peacefully after that. The air smelled of damp earth and fallen leaves. Occasionally, he glimpsed another competitor in the distance, a small, moving shape against the horizon.

Near Crawley, Wolf passed a group of cyclists who waved enthusiastically, pedalling hard to keep pace for a few moments before dropping away. He saluted them with a lift of his hand. He decided that he loved the camaraderie he was experiencing.

The road began to rise again as he approached the northern edge of the Downs. The engine laboured but remained steady. Wolf leaned forward, as if doing so would influence the car's momentum. The countryside grew wilder, the hedgerows gave way to open chalk slopes, and the wind grew stronger and colder.

Wolf felt exhilarated, as if he were leaving behind not just London but all the constraints of his aristocratic life. Every stifling rule of etiquette, over-starched collar, interminable dinner party, and heavy responsibility seemed to be lifted, at least for the moment.

He briefly considered Tabitha and her scepticism about his new hobby. If only she could see him now, hair full of dust, eyes watering, but alive in a way he hadn't experienced since he left his thief-taking days behind in Whitechapel. As soon as this thought crossed his mind, Wolf was consumed by guilt; if he hadn't left that life, he never would've met Tabitha and wouldn't be happily looking forward to fatherhood. Still, even as he reflected on this, Wolf couldn't deny that driving the Daimler gave him a sense of freedom he hadn't experienced since moving to Mayfair.

Determined just to enjoy the sensation and not let his feelings of guilt overwhelm the pleasure, Wolf took a deep breath of the crisp autumn air and settled back into the Daimler's plush leather seats. The engine gave a reassuring thrum as the road levelled out at last. Ahead, the Downs stretched toward the sea, the horizon gleaming pale and endless.

Wolf adjusted the throttle and pressed on into the wind.

CHAPTER 6

E ventually, Wolf crested a rise and saw the sea sparkling ahead; he was nearly in Brighton. As much as he had enjoyed the drive, it had been long and physically exhausting. He looked forward to being met by Tabitha, then returning with her to the hotel for a cup of tea and perhaps a nice, hot bath.

Just as he was about to speed up slightly for what he hoped would be the final stretch, Wolf spotted another vehicle, awkwardly positioned just ahead, with one wheel half in the ditch. From his research before buying the Daimler, he recognised it as a De Dion-Bouton Vis-à-vis, the newest Paris model, painted in deep bottle-green with polished brass. Its driver, a man in a tan motoring coat, was bent over the bonnet. Steam hissed faintly from the radiator cap.

Wolf drew to a stop a few yards behind, switched off his engine, and climbed down. His boots sank into the chalky verge. "Everything all right?" he called, raising his voice over the wind.

The other man turned. He was stocky, red-faced, with a moustache streaked with dust. Wolf recognised him immediately; he was the man who had insulted Arlene.

It seemed the man recognised Wolf simultaneously. The nasty sneer from earlier returned to his face, and he snarled, "No need for help. Get back in your motor and mind your own business, you dastard."

Wolf removed a glove and wiped his goggles. "Suit yourself. I thought I would offer a hand before you scald yourself. But if you do not need help..."

"I do not!" the man snapped before returning to his vehicle.

As tempting as it was to do as the man commanded, Wolf felt obliged to try at least one more time. "There is no need to be stubborn, sir. If you need help, I am happy to provide it."

"I said I've no need of your interference." The man straightened, glaring. "Some of us know how to manage our own machines."

The tone was unpleasant, but Wolf had learned to choose his battles. "As you please," he said mildly. He tipped his cap and turned back towards his Daimler. Behind him, he could still hear the man muttering, metal clanging against metal.

He climbed into the Daimler, set the petrol tap and cracked the throttle, retarded the ignition, then stepped down to the starting handle. Two priming swings, compression in, a sharp pull. The engine coughed, caught, and settled. He advanced the spark, leaned the mixture a touch, and adjusted his goggles. As he guided the Daimler forward, Wolf cast another look at the unpleasant man, now hunched over his engine. He didn't look up as Wolf passed.

Determined to put the exchange out of his mind and enjoy the last few miles of the run, Wolf settled back and took in the view.

The road ahead narrowed, twisting between high banks before opening again onto the crest of another hill. Behind him, the De Dion disappeared from view, a small plume of steam marking its spot. He felt a faint prick of unease, though he couldn't say why. He told himself it was nothing, just a distasteful man, too proud to accept help.

Shifting into second gear, Wolf let the car roll down towards Brighton, the town and the sea spreading out before him in a shimmer of blue and white. This truly had been a wonderful day, he mused to himself. Already, he was wondering about where to drive next. There was no doubt that driving outside of London was much more enjoyable than dodging omnibuses and street urchins in the city.

Wolf wondered how feasible it might be to drive to Pembrokeshire someday. Certainly, having the motor-car while at Glanwyddan Hall would be wonderful. He imagined the lovely drives he might enjoy through the Welsh countryside. Perhaps he might even persuade Tabitha to join him one day. Of course, there were logistical issues with such a long journey, especially refuelling. Nonetheless, Wolf was sure these challenges could be overcome.

Now, the road began to dip steeply from the Downs. Wolf eased the Daimler into a lower gear, the engine protesting as the descent steepened. The wind met him full in the face, sharp and cold, yet with enough of a salt tang to be a pleasant reminder of the better aspects of their last visit to Brighton.

Finally, he saw signs of a town coming into view and saw a policeman on the roadside, waving Wolf toward the main approach. "Preston Park for the finish, sir! Keep to the left!" he shouted over the engine's noise.

Wolf nodded and pressed on. The outskirts were already crowded: cyclists, delivery carts, curious pedestrians craning to glimpse the arriving motor-cars. Children ran alongside for a few paces, shouting and laughing before dropping back. There was a celebratory air to it all that matched Wolf's elation at having made it all the way to Brighton. He honked the bulb horn in greeting. Although his arms ached from hours at the wheel and every joint in his body felt jarred from the rough road, Wolf was filled with fresh energy.

Through Patcham and Withdean, the route narrowed between hedgerows and villas. A horse shied violently as Wolf passed; its driver cursed, shaking a fist. Wolf grimaced, slowing only slightly.

Then, finally, the houses closed in, the hedges made way for rows of shopfronts and cheering spectators. A banner stretched across the road: **WELCOME TO BRIGHTON**.

A few hundred feet beyond the banner, he saw the cluster of flags marking the official finish at Preston Park. Wolf's pulse quickened. He shifted gears, the movement almost instinctive after all the hours driving, and guided the motor-car through the crowd as marshals waved him onward.

The noise was deafening. Steam vehicles hissed, horns blared, and motor-cars roared along the line to applause. Wolf slowed to a crawl as a uniformed official stepped forward with a clipboard in hand.

"Number twenty-three; Lord Pembroke, is it?"

Wolf removed his goggles, his face streaked with dust. "The same."

"Congratulations, sir. Time's been noted. You've made it in fine time." The man's grin was genuine.

Wolf tipped his cap and pulled the handbrake. The engine idled for a moment before sputtering to silence. For a heartbeat, he simply sat, listening to the ticking of cooling metal. The ache in his shoulders and the grime on his gloves all seemed insignificant compared to the satisfaction of a safe arrival.

Bear and Rat emerged from the crowd, smiling broadly. "You did it! I half expected to have to come and rescue you from a ditch somewhere," Bear said.

"I was concerned about that too, initially," Wolf admitted, climbing stiffly out of the Daimler. His legs trembled from the long ride. "But she ran true in the end."

"The ladies wanted to come out and meet you, but I pointed out that we had no idea when you'd be arriving, and I didn't think either of them should be standing in this chill for a long period," Bear explained. Wolf thanked him for his forethought.

As they talked, Rat jumped up and down with excitement. "Milord Wolf, can I get in her?" he asked eagerly.

Wolf smiled and nodded. He understood the boy's excitement; it mirrored his own. It had never crossed his mind to take Rat with him on this run, but perhaps he would next year.

Actually, Wolf thought, perhaps they wouldn't have to wait that long. "How would you like to drive back with me, lad?" he asked.

The offer was greeted with a wide smile. "Really? Can I steer?"

Wolf patted Rat on the shoulder. "Perhaps one day. However, I imagine her ladyship will be difficult enough to convince that you can sit next to me. Let us not ask for too much, just yet." Even as he said this, Wolf realised that this would almost certainly be a bone of contention with Tabitha. If she was reluctant to have him make the drive, Wolf knew how she'd feel about Rat accompanying him. However, having made the offer, he realised he would now have to find a way to persuade Tabitha.

The three of them stood watching the other entrants roll in for about twenty minutes. There were machines of every shape and sound. Some cruised into Preston Park triumphantly; others barely sputtered past the finish line.

When Arlene and Miss Hartwell still hadn't arrived, Wolf wondered whether he should be worried and how long he could justify waiting for them. Then, he caught himself in the thought; Arlene was not his responsibility, and he knew very well that Tabitha wouldn't appreciate him making her so, and so he put her out of his mind for now.

Wolf had considered whether he wanted to drive the Daimler from Preston Park to Brighton to store her, but he couldn't imagine getting back behind the wheel even for that short trip. He enjoyed his drive that day very much, but he was happy it was over.

Instead, he handed a few coins to the steward, who promised to have the Daimler fetched and garage it before nightfall. "Allen's yard off Lewes Road will take her, my lord," the man assured him. "They've seen to several already. They'll even drain the radiator and cover her for the frost."

"Good. Tell them not to spare the oil," Wolf said, patting the motorcar's bonnet once before turning away. The engine gave a final soft tick as it cooled.

Then, as an afterthought, Wolf said, "I passed a man broken down, about twenty minutes out on the Downs. He refused my help, but I thought you should know just in case he does not make it in. He was driving a bottle-green De Dion-Bouton." The steward nodded in acknowledgement of the warning.

Then, Wolf turned back to Bear and Rat, and the three of them began moving in the direction of The Grand Brighton. Bear and Rat had previously walked to Preston Park, but now, Bear asked if Wolf wanted him to hail a hackney cab.

"No. I would like to stretch my legs." Wolf turned his coat collar up against the brisk sea wind. The park behind them was still noisy: engines sputtering, men laughing, brass fittings clanging. Ahead, Brighton stretched down towards the Channel. They were close enough to hear the cries of gulls, if not to see the pier yet.

Wolf turned towards the gates, Bear falling in beside him with his usual silent tread. Rat lagged a few paces behind, looking all around at the mechanical marvels still entering the park.

"Never thought I'd see so many of them in one place," the boy said breathlessly. Now that he realised how enthusiastic Rat was about motor-cars, Wolf kicked himself for not bringing Rat to the send-off that morning.

The group crossed Preston Circus. Behind them, the park still echoed with engines cooling down and men cheering their own survival.

"I've earned a bath, a sandwich or two, and maybe a whisky," Wolf said, suddenly realising how hungry he was. Mrs Smith, their cook, had packed a hamper for Wolf to take with him, but he'd snacked on most of it before he was much out of London.

With that, Wolf drove his hands deep into his coat pockets, and the two men and the boy increased their pace for their walk to the Brighton seafront.

CHAPTER 7

W olf wasn't usually one to spend much time in the bath; he had too little patience to stay immersed in increasingly tepid water. However, the long soak after his drive to Brighton felt wonderful.

Tabitha came and sat beside him as he enthused about the trip. "She ran like a dream, no issues. Which is more than can be said for that awful man who insulted Arlene."

"Why, what happened?" Tabitha asked, trying not to bristle at the mention of Lady Archibald.

"I came across him with his head in the engine, trying to fix something. I stopped and offered him some help and was rudely rebuffed for my efforts."

"Well, at least you tried." Tabitha pointed out. "Another man might have kept driving and not even attempted to offer help after the earlier encounter."

"I was tempted to ignore his dilemma," Wolf admitted. "But there is a camaraderie amongst motor-car owners; there are so few of us and so it seemed only right to stop."

Tabitha smiled indulgently. She couldn't remember the last time she'd heard Wolf as excited about anything as he was about the Daimler. Despite all her misgivings, it was clear the motor-car was bringing her husband a joy that little else about the earldom had to date.

"I thought you might not want to go down to the dining room, so I have ordered food to be sent up," Tabitha explained as she heard a knock at the door.

"Thank you. I want nothing more than to put on my dressing gown and sit by the fire," Wolf admitted.

"Dry off and I will let the hall waiter in with the food," Tabitha said, rising and leaving the bathroom.

Tabitha was still smiling indulgently as she went to open the door. She had dispensed with protocol and had dismissed her maid, Ginny, and Wolf's valet, Thompson, for the evening. She knew Wolf preferred it when it was just the two of them, and the idea of curling up in the comfortable armchairs, in front of the fire, while Wolf continued to regale her with his adventures, sounded perfect to her.

She also suspected that the maid and valet would be delighted to have an evening off to enjoy a romantic stroll along the seafront. While Tabitha wasn't sure how far the courtship had progressed, Ginny smiled shyly every time Thompson entered a room, telling her all she needed to know about how her maid felt. She was reflecting on the sweet romance between the servants as she turned the doorknob and opened the door.

"Oh!" was all Tabitha said when confronted with the sight of quite a young man, with close-cropped black hair and startling blue eyes, standing on the other side of the door. Whoever he was, this man was not a hall waiter. In fact, if his clothes and general demeanour were anything to go by, Tabitha would have guessed he was a police detective.

"Can I help you?" She continued after collecting herself.

"Lady Pembroke?" the gentleman asked.

"I am she," Tabitha confirmed. "May I ask who is inquiring?"

"I am Detective Inspector Malcolm Maguire of the Brighton Constabulary. I don't believe we met the last time you visited Brighton, but I did have the pleasure of meeting your husband and the other Lady Pembroke." A slight shift in the inspector's expression indicated that meeting the dowager hadn't been such a pleasure.

"I am assuming there is a reason you are here at this hour on a Sunday evening and that this is not a social call," Tabitha said. She wasn't sure whether to invite the man in or carry on this conversation in the hotel hallway.

The question was answered for her when Maguire asked if he might enter. Tabitha stepped aside and allowed him in, closing the door behind him.

"My husband is just finishing his bath," Tabitha explained. "He did the motor-car run from London to Brighton today and was quite stiff at the end of it." As she spoke, Tabitha was trying to think of reasons for the unexpected call.

"Might you ask him to join us as soon as he's able?" the inspector asked politely, but firmly.

Tabitha had a good sense of how the dowager might handle such a visit and request. However, she realised there was little to be gained by antagonising this man unnecessarily. She excused herself and returned to the bathroom, relieved to see Wolf already out of the bathtub and drying off.

Even though they had been married for several months, Tabitha still felt a little shy about her husband's ease in walking around naked. When she entered the bathroom as he towelled himself dry, her first instinct was to apologise and leave the room. However, she fought the urge and even took a moment to admire what a fine figure of a man she had married.

Wolf looked up and smiled. He wasn't unaware of Tabitha's bashfulness and found it quite charming. Then, he noticed the serious look on her face. "Is something wrong, my love?"

"There is a Detective Inspector Maguire here to see you, Wolf."

As much as she wished otherwise, Tabitha noticed the alarm in Wolf's eyes and guessed what had sprung to his mind.

Confirming her fears, he asked anxiously, "Has something happened to Arlene?"

Tabitha did her best to control her tone as she answered, "He did not say. He would like to speak with you." Wolf assured her he would be out shortly, and Tabitha returned to the bedchamber.

It didn't take Wolf long to put on some clothes. While Thompson would have thought his attire completely inappropriate for greeting visitors, Wolf assumed Maguire wouldn't mind. And Wolf didn't care if he did. When someone came to a man's hotel room unannounced on a Sunday evening, they should expect to find the man in his shirt sleeves.

Wolf found Inspector Maguire standing awkwardly in front of the fireplace, shifting his bowler hat from hand to hand. Tabitha sat in one of the armchairs. Wolf wondered whether she hadn't offered the policeman a chair or if he had preferred to stand. Certainly, he appeared uncomfortable with whatever this conversation was to be about.

"Detective Inspector Maguire, to what do I owe the honour?" Wolf asked, sitting down and leaving Maguire standing. Wolf could have fetched the chair by the dressing table, but he wasn't keen to encourage the man to stay longer than necessary. Instead, he left him standing like a tradesman. If Maguire recognised the slight, he did not comment. He merely took a notebook and a pen from his pocket.

When they last met, Wolf had assessed the detective inspector as an ambitious man who had risen swiftly within the Brighton force by skilfully navigating the political landscape. He believed that Maguire had been all too eager to arrest an innocent, simple-minded man, because this provided a convenient narrative and was being encouraged by his superiors.

"I apologise for intruding, m'lord. I am sure you have had a long and tiring day. I hear you drove one of those motor-cars to Brighton." While Maguire's words were innocuous enough, he put enough emphasis on 'motor-cars' to make it very clear what he thought of rich men, playing with their toys.

Maguire continued, "I'm afraid I must trouble you with some unpleasant news. Mr Thomas Havers, the gentleman whose motorcar I heard from one of the stewards you stopped to assist on the Downs, was found dead not long after you departed."

Wolf said nothing. The fire popped in the grate.

"Dead?" he repeated finally.

"Very much so. Head wound. The local police were called to the scene by another driver a little behind you." Maguire flipped a page. "We have interviewed locals and it seems that a farm boy, standing just ahead reported seeing two cars stopped by the side of the road behind him, hearing raised voices, and then seeing a vehicle drive away,"

Wolf folded his arms. "I do not recall seeing any boy. And that witness must have excellent eyesight. There must have been at least half a dozen green motor-cars in the run. Why Havers's own car was bottle-green. How on earth is this witness so sure it was mine?"

"Yours is the only green Daimler. Certainly, I believe it is the only one with a family crest enamelled on each side of the bonnet." Maguire said as if this were damning evidence. "The witness made a point of mentioning a crest."

Wolf said, crossed his legs, and assumed his Earl of Pembroke pose and tone. "I do not deny that I stopped to ask Mr Havers, if that is his name, whether he needed help. He rebuffed my offer, and I drove off. If you wish to know what time that was, it was probably about twenty minutes before I arrived at Preston Park."

Maguire looked up from his notes. "The witness also said you appeared agitated. That you 'shot away like the devil himself was chasing you'."

Wolf gave a short laugh. "I did the decent thing and stopped to help, and in return, Mr Havers told me, in language not fit to repeat with a lady present, to drive on. I will admit that I was irritated, nothing more."

"Is that the only reason you were irritated, Lord Pembroke?" Maguire closed the notebook and looked at him directly. "Because I hear that this was not your only altercation with the deceased. In fact, I was told that you argued with the deceased in London."

Tabitha had to stop herself from gasping at these words; what was the detective inspector implying?

For his part, Wolf took a moment to consider the line of questioning. "Indeed. Mr Havers insulted a young woman at the start of the run in Whitehall. I insisted he apologise."

"And did he?"

"Eventually," Wolf admitted.

"More than one driver who witnessed the incident said that you almost came to blows." Then Maguire paused. "Would it be possible to speak to you alone, Lord Pembroke?" he asked.

"There is nothing you can ask of me or that I might say that my wife cannot be party to," Wolf informed him tersely.

Maguire nodded as if to suggest Wolf might regret that answer. "Very well then," the detective inspector continued, "I believe that you have a romantic history with the woman in question."

Wolf stiffened. There was no point in avoiding the question; it was clear Maguire already knew the answer. "Yes. Lady Archibald, as she is now, and I courted briefly more than a decade ago."

Tabitha felt she had to defend her husband. "Detective Inspector Maguire, I can assure you that, while my husband and Lady Archibald were once well-acquainted, what he said to Mr Havers in Whitehall was no more than he would have for any woman thus insulted."

The detective inspector offered no reply, but a slight raise of one eyebrow conveyed his scepticism about the truth of that statement. Maguire looked down at his notebook and continued, "Several witnesses recall you threatening him."

"I told him that if he spoke to her again in that manner, he would answer to me. A figure of speech, Inspector, nothing more."

"Figures of speech tend to sound literal after a man ends up dead."

Wolf gazed into the fire. "If you are implying that I killed Havers, say so plainly."

"I'm saying, m'lord, that the evidence requires explanation." Maguire opened his notebook once more. "Based on his first inspection, the police surgeon believes the victim was struck on the head with a blunt tool," Maguire said. "A Whitworth open-ended spanner was found nearby. It matches the Daimler pattern supplied with your car and is not commonly sold on its own."

Now, Tabitha was unable to control her gasp. "Surely you cannot imagine that my husband murdered a man in cold blood?" she exclaimed. "There were other Daimlers taking part today."

Wolf turned toward the window. "So that is it, then. A quarrel, a witness, and a misplaced spanner."

"For the moment, yes."

He gave a dry laugh. "Conveniently tidy." For the moment, he couldn't imagine how his spanner had ended up being used as the murder weapon and tried to cast his mind back to his interaction with Havers during the run.

Maguire allowed the silence to stretch out before speaking again. "You must understand, m'lord, I don't accuse you of anything yet. But until this matter is resolved, I am obliged to ask that you remain in Brighton. Preferably within the hotel. Your cooperation will spare us the indignity of formal proceedings. At least for now."

"You mean house arrest without the bother of paperwork."

Maguire spread his hands. "Let us call it an agreement of honour. I've been told your word is good."

"It is," Wolf said quietly. "But I've no intention of sitting here like a criminal while the real one walks free."

"That may be, but it's the safest course for everyone involved. The Brighton Argus evening paper today already has this on its front page."

Wolf's expression hardened. "They waste no time."

"They never do. If you were to leave town now, it would look like fleeing. Better to stay visible and cooperative while we complete our inquiries." Maguire paused, seeming uncertain whether to say more. Finally, he added, "As I am sure you are aware, Lord Pembroke, there is increasing pressure on those of us tasked with protecting the public to ensure our treatment of suspects is even handed, no matter their class. I have been informed from above that the best treatment you are to be given is the courtesy of remaining at this charming hotel rather than in our jail cell."

Wolf studied the inspector. "And when your inquiries prove I had nothing to do with it?"

"Then you'll have my apology and a clear name."

Maguire rose. "One other matter. The coroner's men will need another look at your motor-car. You'll permit it?"

"If I must."

"Thank you. I'll station a constable discreetly in the lobby. Don't mistake him for a guard; he's there to maintain order, not to keep you in. But if you require anything, you can send word through him. Oh, and the inquest is tomorrow afternoon. The constable will escort you there."

"How thoughtful," Wolf said without attempting to hide his sarcasm.

The detective inspector's face indicated he'd noticed Wolf's tone, but he said nothing. He merely gave a small bow, thanked them for their time, and left.

Once the door had closed behind Maguire, Tabitha and Wolf stared at each other in shock. Murder? How was that possible?

CHAPTER 8

T abitha and Wolf sat in stunned silence for a few moments before a polite rap on the door roused them from their contemplation of the situation Wolf found himself in.

Worried that the detective inspector had returned, Wolf stood and opened the door to find the hall waiter with a tray of food. He was tempted to send the meal away, but it occurred to him that Tabitha probably hadn't eaten either, so Wolf stepped back to let the boy in.

Once the food and wine had been laid out, and the boy had gone, Tabitha stood and said, "You begin to eat, I am going to find Bear and Mama to inform them of what has happened."

"Why are you leaving and I am staying?" Wolf asked.

"Because I am fully dressed and you are not. Also, I suspect you have not eaten for hours. You will need all your strength to face what seems to be ahead of us." Wolf was tempted to argue with her, but knew that this was not a battle worth winning; there was no good reason that even an expectant mother wasn't able to wander down the corridors of a luxury hotel and knock on a couple of doors.

Ten minutes later, just as Wolf had finished the soup that had been sent up and was making a start on the hearty, satisfying lamb stew, the door opened and Tabitha returned, the dowager and Bear in tow.

Bear carried a newspaper, and Wolf assumed it was the aforementioned Brighton Argus evening edition.

Under normal circumstances, the dowager might have commented on Wolf's casual attire, but even she had some compassion for his situation and said nothing. Wolf rose to offer her the armchair and went to fetch the dressing table chair while Bear retrieved the one by the little writing desk in the corner of the room.

Once everyone was seated, Wolf insisted that Tabitha take the tray on her lap and eat something while they talked. She was tempted to tell him she had no appetite but realised that her husband had more than enough to worry him and didn't need to add her wellbeing to that list.

"Let me see that newspaper," Wolf said to Bear, who handed over the periodical. Wolf scanned the headline. It didn't tell him anything that Maguire hadn't already said.

"Do not keep us in suspense, Jeremy. What does it say?" the dowager demanded.

Wolf read aloud.

Motor Run to Brighton Ends in Tragedy. Mr Thomas Havers Found Dead. Peer Under Suspicion.

Brighton society was thrown into turmoil yesterday after the shocking discovery of Mr Thomas Havers's body, a well-known investor in racing circles, found dead beside his motorcar on the London Road. The tragedy happened during Sunday's tribute to the 1896 "Emancipation Run," the first major procession of horseless carriages from London to Brighton.

According to police sources, the Earl of Pembroke, who was participating in the race, was the last person seen speaking with the deceased and was observed fleeing the scene. He is currently being held at The Grand Hotel while investigations continue.

A spanner belonging to the earl was discovered within a few feet of the body. According to medical testimony, the wound on the victim's head, was consistent with such an instrument.

While the authorities have been careful to speak of "assisting with inquiries," it is widely reported that the earl has been asked not to leave Brighton until the coroner's investigation is complete.

Witnesses describe a public quarrel earlier in the day between the two men, sparked by comments made to a titled lady. It is said that strong words were exchanged and that Lord Pembroke "would have satisfaction."

In every tavern and tearoom along the seafront, the question is being asked whether a man of humbler station would have been treated with the same leniency. Would an ordinary mechanic or clerk, found in such circumstances, have been permitted to remain in comfort at The Grand while the inquest proceeds?

"It's always the same," declared a man in the crowd gathered to watch the end of the run. "If a working man so much as lifts his hand, he's in gaol before sunset. But if a lord does it, they call it an unfortunate misunderstanding."

The Argus makes no accusations, but it cannot ignore the rising unease among decent working folk that justice must be fair for both rich and poor. The motoring craze has already been viewed with suspicion by many who see the machines as the playthings of the wealthy rather than a sign of progress. This tragedy will do little to reassure them.

Mr Havers, by contrast, was considered a self-made man, one of those dynamic entrepreneurs whose efforts have contributed to bringing industry to our shores. The story of how such a man should meet his end, whether by accident or otherwise, at the hands of someone born into wealth is one that will not sit easily with public.

The coroner's inquest continues tomorrow afternoon at the Brighton Town Hall. The Argus will report developments as they arise.

The article and the situation they faced were eerily similar to one they had dealt with only a few months earlier involving Viscount Tobias's father, Clarence, the Earl of Warwick, who had been accused of murder. One striking difference was that the Metropolitan Police had decided to make an example of Clarence and had detained him at Pentonville Prison.

As Tabitha reflected on the parallels between the two cases, she realised that the situation they faced could be worse; at least Wolf was being afforded the courtesy of remaining in his luxury hotel suite rather than being imprisoned in the basement of the Brighton Police Station. This was rather cold comfort, however, considering that, if they were unable to establish Wolf's innocence, there was little doubt about where he would end up.

Tabitha realised there was no point in dwelling on that possible outcome. Instead, they should dedicate all their energy and time to proving Wolf's innocence. She put the tray aside, rose, and went to the writing desk, returning with sheaves of notepaper and a pen. Carefully, she tore each sheet of paper in half in an attempt to approximate the note-cards she usually prepared for an investigation.

Taking three of these improvised notecards, she wrote a header on each: Motive, Opportunity, Evidence.

"There is little doubt that what Detective Inspector Maguire will argue is Wolf's motive. There were many witnesses to the altercation in Whitehall. While it is easy enough to claim that Wolf's threat to the victim was no more than what any man might say to prevent a repeat of the situation, that is unlikely to hold water at an inquest." As she said this, Tabitha jotted down a few points summarising what had transpired between Wolf and Havers in London.

Turning to the second notecard, she said, "However, when it comes to opportunity, I believe there is room to disprove Maguire's theory."

"It was terribly convenient that a witness just happened to be on the road to see Wolf leave," Bear said in agreement.

Tabitha addressed Wolf. "Did you see anyone as you drove away?"

Wolf shook his head. "No. But, there is no doubt I was incredibly irritated after my interaction with Havers. And why would I notice a boy by the side of the road?"

"I believe we should find this boy and question him," the dowager pronounced, evidently assuming her place front and centre in their new investigation.

It seemed Tabitha was not the only person to notice the dowager's use of the word we. "I want you to stay out of this, Tabitha," Wolf instructed. "I mean it. After what happened in Salisbury, I refuse to allow you to take any more risks." Turning to the dowager, Wolf said, "Lady Pembroke, I trust you will keep Tabitha company and ensure she rests and does not become involved in this investigation in any way."

"Wolf!" Tabitha exclaimed. "You cannot possibly imagine I will stand by and allow you to be falsely accused of murder and not lift a finger to prove otherwise."

"That is exactly what I expect. I will send a telegram to Langley and ask him to come to Brighton and he and Bear will conduct whatever inquiries we deem the police are investigating insufficiently. In fact, my preference would be for you to take the children and return to London."

Wolf was unaccustomed to asserting any sort of husbandly authority, and it didn't come naturally to him. Even as he said these words, he heard the uncertainty and hesitation behind them. He doubted that Tabitha or the dowager had missed this and was equally sure neither would agree to meekly taking the train out of Brighton. However, he hoped that, at the very least, he could persuade Tabitha not to involve herself in the investigation. He relied on Tabitha's memory of how distraught she'd had been in Salisbury when she thought she had put her unborn child at risk.

Tabitha tried to suppress her instinctive reaction to this sort of heavy-handed spousal behaviour; she understood why Wolf felt this way. Nevertheless, did he truly believe that the less stressful option for her was to return to London and leave his fate to the local police force?

After taking a deep breath and contemplating the most effective way to manage this deadlock, Tabitha said, "Wolf, you cannot imagine that I will do as you ask and leave you here to face who knows what. However, I agree that I need to be as cautious as possible. Asking Langley to come down, if he is able to take a break from his work, is a good idea. He and Bear can handle anything that is physically demanding or likely to be dangerous. Then..."

She saw Wolf about to interrupt and raised a hand. "Let me finish. Then, Mama and I will handle whatever remains. You know that we are capable of asserting ourselves in situations where Bear cannot." Tabitha realised she was on rather shaky ground here; while there was no doubt that if she and the dowager could exert their rank to persuade people's cooperation, so could Lord Langley.

Acknowledging this weakness in her argument, Tabitha pressed on. "We do not know that Langley will be able to drop everything immediately; there was a good reason he was unable to join us on this trip in the first place. Even if he can make some excuse to the Foreign Office, it is unlikely he will arrive much before the inquest. We cannot afford to waste time waiting for him. Mama and I will begin immediately and, if and when Langley can join us, I will reassess my involvement."

Wolf knew he wasn't going to win this argument, at least entirely. However, there was one point he could still insist on. "You cannot start immediately. It is already nearly eight o'clock. What can you possibly believe you can accomplish tonight? At least agree to wait until tomorrow."

Tabitha had anticipated this suggestion. "There is one thing we can and must do tonight; speak with Lady Archibald and Miss Hartwell. I imagine they are as weary as you are and will be resting at home for the evening. We need to know if they had any other encounters with Mr Havers on the run to Brighton."

With that, Tabitha rose and addressed the dowager. "Mama, I shall change my dress into something more suitable for a social visit, and we can meet in the lobby in thirty minutes. Bear, please request the hotel's carriage for us." And with that, she turned and left the sitting room.

Wolf sighed.

CHAPTER 9

The drive to Lady Archibald's grand townhouse in Sussex Square in the Kemptown neighbourhood of Brighton was brief. Certainly, it wasn't sufficient for Tabitha to decide how she wanted to approach Arlene. She sat for almost the entire journey, gazing out the window and contemplating the interview ahead.

Finally, as the carriage began to slow before one of the larger Georgian townhouses encircling the landscaped square, the dowager said in a matter-of-fact, but not unkindly tone, "Her wishes are irrelevant, Tabitha. He chose you. He will always choose you. And as much as she might try to pretend otherwise, Lady Archibald knows this."

Tabitha glanced at the old woman; she realised that the dowager was right. However, knowing her insecurities were irrational didn't ease them at all. She simply nodded in response, then prepared to descend and face her fears.

A tall, well-muscled, very dark-skinned butler answered the door. If he was surprised by two unaccompanied women making such a late social call, the butler was far too well-trained to let it show on his face.

The dowager and Tabitha handed him their calling cards and were immediately shown into an elegant, well-appointed drawing room. They each took a seat and only had to wait a few minutes before the drawing room door opened and Lady Archibald and Miss Hartwell entered.

Arlene entered first, gliding rather than walking, in a robe of violet velvet that shimmered in the firelight. The gown fell open at the throat, a single silk tasselled cord holding it together. Her hair, freshly washed and brushed to a high gloss, spilt in loose curls down her shoulders. The scent of roses trailed in her wake.

Miss Hartwell followed, dressed rather more practically in a soft grey silk wrapper belted at the waist. Her golden hair was pinned back loosely; her only adornment was a plain gold watch chain.

The dowager might have been tempted to comment on the women's casual attire. Still, she and Tabitha had visited unannounced and without invitation, and, like Wolf, the women must be exhausted.

"Lady Pembroke. Has something happened to Wolf?" Lady Archibald asked worriedly.

Tabitha suppressed her urge to respond jealously. She acknowledged, at least to herself, that she had no real reason to be upset that Lady Archibald thought the visit was because of Wolf; why else would Tabitha be there without him at that time of night?

Instead, Tabitha informed the women about the detective inspector's visit and that Wolf was being considered the prime suspect in Havers's murder.

"But that is madness!" Arlene exclaimed. She had been sitting, but now jumped up and started pacing in front of the fireplace. "Why on earth would they think that?"

After Lady Archibald had paced several times, Miss Hartwell spoke up. "Nene, calm yourself. Let Lady Pembroke explain everything." Then, addressing Tabitha, Isabella Hartwell asked, "What are their reasons for believing such a thing? I assume an earl wouldn't be accused of such a thing for no good reason."

Tabitha smiled at her, grateful for the calming words. Once Arlene had retaken her seat, Tabitha explained everything they'd been told. No one said anything immediately after she had finished.

Finally, after a few moments of contemplation, Arlene asked, "What are you planning to do about this? Because I am sure you do not intend to do nothing."

Unable to suppress a smile, Tabitha asked, "What would make you say that?"

"Lady Pembroke, may I call you Tabitha?" When she received a nod in reply, Arlene continued, "When you were last in Brighton it became obvious to me that you were no lily-livered society matron. And, of course, the other Lady Pembroke is a lioness. Just because Wolf cannot prove his innocence does not mean his family and friends cannot do so on his behalf."

The dowager spoke for both of them. "Of course, dear Lady Archibald, you are quite correct. And that is why Tabitha and I are here; to see what else, if anything, you know."

"I wish I could be more helpful. However, my only interaction with the man was what you witnessed in Whitehall. Isabella, on the other hand, does know something about this Havers. She was telling me some stories during our drive to Brighton."

All eyes turned to Miss Hartwell, who sat up a little straighter, ready for her moment to shine. "I met Thomas Havers, or Tommy as he's known in motoring circles in London, in the spring when I first arrived in Britain. I have a motor-car back home and had wanted to join The Automobile Club here. Of course, I should have guessed that The Automobile Club is much like every other gentlemen's institution in London and many back at home, filled with men quite certain that progress must remain their exclusive province. Still, I've attended a few of their luncheons as a guest of a member. They hold demonstrations and talks on engines and new designs at Whitehall Court, and one can learn a great deal if one listens between the boasts. Tommy had a reputation: clever, pushy, always boasting of his continental connections."

In a gossipy tone, she added, "From what I heard, he came from quite modest roots. We Americans don't have much of a problem with that, well, those of us who aren't Mrs Astor don't, but I've learned how much you British look down your noses at new money."

It took all of Tabitha's self-control not to snort with laughter at this comment, which was truer of the dowager than most people.

"Anyway," Isabella continued. "From what I've heard, Havers claimed to have made a fortune in bicycle parts and has been trying to move into automobile parts. He certainly liked giving the impression that he was independently wealthy, very showy clothes, a gaudy gold pocket watch. But there were rumours that while he dressed like Wall Street, his accounts were nearer State Street."

Looking around the room, Isabella realised that the allusion was entirely lost on her audience. "I think you British might say, he was all gilt and very little gold." She was rewarded with looks of comprehension. "I had also heard whispered rumours that this need for cash meant he was playing both sides."

"Both sides of what?" Tabitha asked.

"The Continent," Isabella said dryly. "From the rumours I'd heard, he was collaborating with a French syndicate, claiming he was able to secure German investors for their engines. Simultaneously, he hinted to certain German firms that he could obtain French designs for a fee. Essentially, playing both ends against the middle."

The dowager made a small sound of disgust. "Typical of that new breed of industrial parvenu."

"Still," Tabitha said slowly. "If this is all true, it makes his death... convenient for someone. If he was trafficking in secrets, there would be those who wanted him silenced."

"Exactly." Isabella leaned forward. "Most of the mechanics you saw helping with the motor-cars in Whitehall, then took the train down to Brighton to meet the drivers here. They bring spare tools, extra oil, and that kind of thing. Most of the drivers must return to London, so these mechanics will get the cars ready for the return trip. I know that is what I did. Given that, perhaps it would be useful to speak to the mechanic Havers used. I think the man is French."

Tabitha hadn't even considered this. She wasn't sure if Wolf's mechanic from Daimler had made the journey down; he certainly hadn't mentioned it.

"Where would we find these men?" asked Tabitha.

"The mechanics won't be difficult to find," Isabella replied. "Most of them came down on the morning train and gathered at Preston Park, the official finish. It's been turned into a sort of open-air workshop. Every car has its man, and they all wait there with their toolboxes and fuel tins, helping with repairs before the drive back to London. If Havers's French mechanic came to Brighton at all, he'd have gone there first. Someone will have noticed him; a foreign accent stands out. That's where we start looking."

"So, all the cars are being left there?" the dowager asked.

"No. Those who can afford it probably moved their cars at some point. But only a few yards in London are equipped to deal with them. I'm sure there are even fewer in Brighton. I assume the police have impounded Havers's car. I wonder if they've spoken to his mechanic."

Tabitha hadn't missed that Isabella had said we multiple times. "Are you offering to help, Miss Hartwell?"

"I believe," Isabella said, "that your husband's name is being used to hide something much larger. I also believe the motor-car may be one of the greatest innovations of our time." The dowager sniffed at this. Tabitha only hoped that Miss Hartwell didn't hear this. She continued, "I do not wish to see the industry tarnished, particularly in these early years when the general public remains so sceptical."

This had all been said quite seriously. Now, Isabella grinned. "And anyway, who wouldn't love the idea of helping to solve a real English murder inquiry!" Isabella said, her eyes alight. "I feel as though I've stepped straight into one of Mr Arthur Conan Doyle's stories, only without the pipe smoke and violin."

The dowager was herself a secret reader of the Sherlock Holmes stories and appreciated the allure of being involved with a case worthy of him. There was also something about Isabella Hartwell that attracted her. The woman was vivacious, independent, and adventurous. More importantly, she wasn't dull, and the dowager believed that to be true of few people she encountered.

Without waiting for Tabitha's response, the dowager said, "Then, welcome to the team, Miss Hartwell!"

Tabitha glared at her. It wasn't so much Miss Hartwell's assistance that she minded, but rather that it likely would involve Lady Archibald.

As if reading Tabitha's mind, Arlene clapped her hands as gleefully as if they'd been planning a picnic. "Yes! We must both help. After all, I know Brighton better than any of you, and I do have some connections here. I will do anything to save darling Wolf."

Did the woman not realise how inappropriate her words were? She was speaking of a newly married man! Tabitha did her best to suppress her growing irritation. After all, Lady Archibald had a point; she knew Brighton.

Trying to say it through anything other than clenched teeth, Tabitha accepted both women's offers of assistance.

During the carriage ride back to the hotel, Tabitha wondered how Miss Isabella Hartwell had become so involved with motor-cars. She was certainly an interesting woman, and so American. It was hard to imagine a young, unmarried woman embracing her independence as brashly as Isabella seemed able to. While there was little doubt that a wealthy father helped, Tabitha had come from money but certainly couldn't imagine a world where she would have been able to live this kind of life. She was both admiring and jealous of the beautiful American.

CHAPTER 10

Wolf had intended to wait up to hear about Tabitha's visit with Arlene, but by the time she returned, he was sprawled on the bed, a book by his side, snoring softly.

The following morning, he woke as soon as the first rays of sunlight peeked through the curtains. Usually, he wouldn't disturb Tabitha's sleep, but he knew she wanted to make the most of the morning before the inquest. He gently rubbed her arm until her eyelids fluttered open.

"Good morning, my love," Wolf whispered tenderly. "I am sorry to wake you, but I know you wanted to be up and about early."

Tabitha smiled, rubbed her eyes, and sat up. "Indeed. No need to apologise. This is not the day for enjoying a lazy lie-in."

"Did Arlene have anything useful to share?"

"Fetch me a cup of tea, and I will tell you everything," Tabitha offered, gesturing towards the tea tray Ginny had thoughtfully and stealthily brought to the room earlier.

A few minutes later, somewhat fortified, Tabitha relayed their conversation with Arlene and Isabella.

When she finished, Wolf let out a low whistle. "Industrial espionage? That is what Miss Hartwell believes this Havers was involved in?"

"Well, those are the rumours she had heard, at least. Of course, that neither means it is true, nor that it provides definitive motive for his murder."

They were still sitting in bed. Now, Wolf covered one of Tabitha's hands with his and gently stroked her thumb. "If you are uncomfortable with Arlene's help, you do not have to accept it. I have no doubts that you and Lady Pembroke, with Langley and Bear's assistance, will prove my innocence."

Tabitha had been holding her teacup in her other hand. Now, she placed it on her bedside table and then turned to face the love of her life full on. "Wolf, there is nothing I would not do for you. No, Lady Archibald is not my favourite person, and you understand why that is. Nevertheless, if she can be of any assistance at all, I will take that help."

Then, she leaned forward and brushed her lips against Wolf's. His senses were filled with the scent of her hair and the silkiness of her skin. Wolf wanted to deepen the kiss and to pretend, at least for a while, that all was right with the world. However, he knew that the sweetness of this moment had to be sacrificed so that he and Tabitha might enjoy many more years of such moments together.

Tabitha sensed his desire, but had the same thought; this was not the time, and anyway, there was the baby to consider. Instead, she pulled back from Wolf's embrace. "I will ring for Ginny and get ready. Lady Archibald and Miss Hartwell said they would meet us in the lobby at nine o'clock. I just hope Mama is up and ready."

Forty-five minutes later, Tabitha was dressed, had eaten some buttered toast, and was ready to do battle on her husband's behalf. While the detective inspector hadn't said that Wolf shouldn't leave his hotel room, he chose not to accompany his wife to the lobby. He wasn't ready to face the humiliation of having whoever constable Maguire had left guarding him watching his every move.

Given that Tabitha wasn't certain the dowager would even be awake in time to join the outing, she was shocked to see her sitting in the lobby waiting.

"Tsk, tsk, Tabitha," the dowager said with a triumphant look on her face. "One might have imagined you would be more prompt with your husband's freedom on the line."

Determined not to rise to the bait, Tabitha ignored her and asked, "Is Lady Archibald here yet? I assume we will use her carriage."

"She is not. Another slugabed it seems."

Now, Tabitha didn't even try to suppress the sigh that escaped her lips. "Mama, we agreed to meet at nine, and it is five to nine now. She is not late, and neither am I." She was tempted to comment on how surprised she was that the dowager was early. However, she knew better than to stir that hornet's nest.

Lady Archibald and Miss Hartwell sashayed into the hotel a few minutes later. Tabitha caught herself thinking a rather harsh judgement of their entrance. Then, she gave herself some grace for the perhaps uncharitable thought; in Lady Archibald's case, sashay really was the best way to describe how the woman entered the hotel, determined to be noticed and admired. Certainly, she was dressed to attract attention; her cerulean coat edged with silver fox, a matching hat perched at a jaunty angle atop her dark, glossy curls.

Miss Hartwell, by contrast, was dressed with the quiet confidence of a woman who could afford to wear only the finest of everything, but didn't feel the need to advertise it. Her coat was a lovely dove-grey wool trimmed with sable at the collar, tailored close to the waist and flaring neatly over her skirt. A soft felt hat of the same shade sat low over one brow. Everything she wore reflected Paris ateliers and top-quality craftsmanship; it was elegance without ostentation, designed for comfort rather than show. Tabitha approved. Of course, given Isabella's stunning beauty, she hardly needed to gild the lily to command attention.

"Dear Lady Archibald," the dowager exclaimed, approaching her and taking her hands. "How delightful you look." Of course, the dowager was never one to dress down if there was an opportunity to display her wealth and rank through her attire. It was hardly surprising she appreciated Arlene's similar ostentation.

For her part, Tabitha had dressed well but simply. She imagined they would have a morning of traipsing around Prescott Park and interacting with mechanics. It hardly seemed the right occasion to wear diamonds and mink.

"Shall we set off then?" Miss Hartwell asked. "I doubt that Preston

Park will be our last stop, and it would be wise to gather as much information as we can before the inquest. What time is it starting?"

"Two o'clock, I believe," Tabitha answered. "It seems there is another inquest before it."

"Then, we have five hours to find some evidence!"

Lady Archibald's carriage rattled along the Lewes Road as they headed towards Preston Park. Unlike the previous clear, sunny day, the sky was overcast, and a chilled dampness filled the air, which the dowager complained she could feel in her bones.

The road they were travelling along appeared especially full of ruts and ridges. Tabitha pressed a hand under her coat as the vehicle jolted, feeling the familiar flutter low in her abdomen. The baby had decided opinions about being jolted about so much. Tabitha would never complain; every kick and movement reassured her that her baby was healthy.

Lady Archibald, sitting opposite Tabitha, noticed the movement of her hand and gave a sly smile. Tabitha had unknowingly felt for the baby. Now, she wondered what she might have revealed. And did it really matter? She had been too cautious about the likely successful outcome of the pregnancy to announce it around London, but at this point, was it a secret?

After a few more minutes, Preston Park came into view ahead of them, its railings decorated with a few triangles of bunting left over from the previous day's celebrations. The carriage turned in through a side gate. Beyond, the park was dotted with motor-cars in various stages of repair: bonnets propped up on sticks, cushions lifted out and piled on rugs, rear wheels jacked up and spinning idly under a mechanic's hand. Men in dust coats and caps moved back and forth with spanners, preparing the vehicles for their return trip.

"Gracious," the dowager murmured, taking it all in with a mixture of relish and snobbish disdain. "It is a garden party for ironmongers."

The carriage came to a stop, and the four women descended. Their group drew some curious glances, but most of the men present were too preoccupied to bother with the well-dressed women strolling among them. One young man crouched beside a wheel, the tyre peeled back as he worked a blunt tool around the rim. In the distance, a pair of drivers argued in French at the top of their voices.

There were also a few men in bowler hats and long coats, carrying clip-boards or ledgers, who, Isabella informed them, were the stewards.

"They'll be tallying the finish logs, settling complaints, and making certain the cars left overnight are accounted for," she explained.

There were also what looked to be some journalists hanging around. Presumably, the murder had added to the general interest in the motor-car run, and the local newspapers, and perhaps even some national ones, were eager for any titbits they could pick up from the mechanics and drivers.

On one side, they spotted two constables standing next to a dark green motorcar under a tarpaulin. One was smoking a pipe, while the other kept a hand on his truncheon, glaring at anyone who lingered too close.

"I wonder where Havers's car is," Isabella mused.

"I am sure they will hold it till the coroner's done with it," Tabitha explained. "I wonder what will happen to it afterwards," she mused.

"Oh, he didn't own the motor-car," Isabella explained. "Very few automobile enthusiasts have the means that your husband and I do to buy these temperamental vehicles and then pay for the astronomical costs of their upkeep."

While Tabitha had realised that being able to buy a motor-car was a luxury few could afford, it hadn't occurred to her that the costs wouldn't end there.

Isabella continued, "Sometimes, the costs even give me pause, and I am never shy about spending my inheritance. These machines devour money. You need a trained mechanic, imported parts, special fuel, tyres that wear out like gloves, and a place to house the beast. It's not unlike maintaining a private locomotive."

Tabitha assumed Wolf had been aware of these ongoing costs before he purchased the Daimler. Certainly, he had sufficient money for such a hobby, and, as she had told herself when he first unveiled the motor-car, he spent very little money on himself otherwise. Some men had expensive gambling habits, maintained the high upkeep of a mistress's establishment, or had a taste for the finest foods and wines. Wolf was happy with a pie and a tankard of ale from The Cock and certainly did not indulge in either of the other vices.

Putting these thoughts aside, Tabitha focused on the relevant piece of information, Isabella: that Havers hadn't owned his motor-car. "So, if he did not own it, who did?"

"My understanding is that it belongs to De Dion-Bouton, the French company whose interests he represented. However, I don't think he liked to publicise the fact, preferring instead to maintain the illusion that he owned it."

Finally, Tabitha had to ask the question gnawing at her since the previous evening, "How do you know so much about motoring?"

Isabella laughed. "My father made his money in engines, first bicycles, then the small petrol-powered ones everyone's experimenting with now," she said, her tone matter-of-fact rather than boastful. "I grew up around workshops instead of parlours. He used to say a motorcar was just a bicycle with ambition. When he died, I inherited both his fortune and his curiosity. I suppose it never occurred to me that being a woman should make me less interested in how things work."

Again, Tabitha felt twinges of admiration and envy.

"Where should we start?" Isabella asked.

"The steward's tent," Tabitha said. "I am assuming there is a list of arrivals and repairs requested. It would be useful to see which other drivers clocked in not long after Wolf did." She pointed to a canvas shelter near the cricket pavilion.

Would they be able to persuade the stewards to show them the list? Even as Tabitha wondered that, Lady Archibald expressed the same question.

The dowager chuckled, "I have persuaded far more illustrious and self-confident men than these to comply with my demands. This will not be an issue." Tabitha knew that if anyone could impose her will on those around her, it was the dowager. It was one of the investigative tasks for which she was uniquely qualified. While Wolf had to force himself into his Earl of Pembroke persona, imperiousness came naturally to the old woman.

CHAPTER 11

B ased on the number of bowler hats, there were only a few stewards on site, but they seemed to defer to the one sitting under the tent, so the women began to move in that direction. The field was churned into mud by all the tyres and boots trampling through it. This wasn't helped by the slight drizzle that had started while they were making their way to Preston Park. The ladies had to pick their way carefully along the path, such as it was, skirts lifted clear of the growing puddles.

Ahead, the canvas tent was starting to sag under the damp. Beneath it, three men in overcoats stood consulting papers at a trestle table. One tall and silver-haired individual, with an impressive moustache, appeared to be directing the others. His boots were caked in mud, yet his bearing was unmistakably that of a military officer.

The dowager, who would have commanded great armies if she had been born a man, immediately recognised a fellow general and made her way towards the group. The men looked up as they approached, surprise flickering across their faces at the sight of four well-dressed ladies striding through the mud.

"Good morning," the dowager announced briskly. "I take it you are one of the stewards in charge?"

The man straightened. "Captain Lionel Forth, madam, Royal Engineers—retired. Yes, I'm overseeing the post-race accounts. May I..."

"Yes, you may," she interrupted. "I am the Dowager Countess of Pembroke, and this is my daughter-in-law, the Countess of Pembroke, along with our friends, Lady Arlene Archibald and Miss Isabella Hartwell. We require information."

Captain Forth blinked, recovering quickly. "Of course, your ladyships. How may I assist you?" Even as he posed the question, Captain Forth seemed to recognise the name and made the connection. "Wait, Pembroke, isn't that the name of the fella...?"

"Yes," Tabitha interjected. "My husband, the Earl of Pembroke, has been accused of murdering Mr Havers. That is why we are here."

The captain looked stupefied. "My apologies, but I still seem to be missing something."

Once the dowager was armed and ready for battle, she hated nothing more than her opening charge being thwarted in any way. Giving Tabitha a stern glance, which she hoped signalled that the younger woman should fall back, the dowager cleared her throat and stepped forward a little.

"Captain Forth, we are here to clear his lordship's good name; I would have thought that much would be obvious," the dowager said brusquely.

"Your ladyship, I am certain that the Brighton Constabulary has the matter under control and that, if his lordship is innocent, this will be proven in due course. You ladies should simply be patient and leave the investigation to the menfolk, who are both trained and more temperamentally suited for such matters." The captain said this in a condescending tone that he was likely going to come to regret very quickly.

The change in the dowager's posture and demeanour might have gone unnoticed by the untrained eye. Still, Tabitha recognised what was occurring and steeled herself for the inevitable fit of pique. She could have sworn that the already chilly, damp air dropped a few degrees in temperature as the dowager threw her already straight shoulders back a little more.

The dowager's reply was exactly what Tabitha had anticipated. "Captain Forth, need I remind you that our monarch is another lady. Would you advise her to leave the work of ruling over the nation to more temperamentally suited menfolk? I would happily pass along your advice the next time I am in her company." As far as Tabitha knew, the dowager was not a confidante of Queen Victoria; however, the captain didn't know this.

The captain's reaction was immediate and extreme. He turned quite pale, and his eyes widened in horror. He opened his mouth a few times, seemingly unable to form any words and looked like a moustached frog.

Finally, he appeared to compose himself sufficiently to answer. "Lady Pembroke, I apologise profusely if I offended you in any way. Certainly, it was never my intention to suggest..."

The man got no further. While no one relished a good grovel more than the dowager, she had limited patience for obsequiousness that went on for too long.

Putting up a hand to prevent any more toadying, at least around this issue, the dowager said, "I am glad we now understand each other regarding your full cooperation with my efforts."

If possible, the captain's eyes widened even further; it was clear he hadn't realised what his apology had implied. Tabitha almost felt sorry for the man as his eyes darted from side to side, trying to find a way out of his predicament.

Finally, she decided to offer him a helping hand, even if it might mean incurring the dowager's wrath for interfering. "Captain Forth, perhaps we might begin again," Tabitha said kindly. "I know my husband is innocent; of that there is no doubt. While you may harbour the appropriate scepticism for a stranger, I can assure you that anyone who has dealt with his lordship in any way will vouch for his decency. He is no killer. Therefore, mistakes, misunderstandings, and misinterpretations have been made by the Brighton Constabulary. All we are doing is trying to prevent a miscarriage of justice, and we need your help in doing so."

At that point, Captain Forth would likely have agreed to anything to escape the awkward situation he found himself in. He'd anticipated that morning would bring no more trouble than the more-than-usual number of journalists who were bothering the mechanics and stewards with their questions. If he had to answer a few questions put to him by this harridan and her minions to be free of them, then so be it.

"How can I be of assistance, milady?" he replied with a slight bow.

"The first thing we would like to see is the sheet on which you recorded the drivers' times. I understand this was done once in Croydon."

Captain Forth nodded. Tabitha continued, "And the process was then repeated when the drivers arrived here yesterday. We would like to see those sheets."

"Can I ask why?" the captain said before he thought better of it.

"You cannot!" the dowager informed him, raising her eyebrows at the mere temerity of the question. "You may continue, Tabitha."

Doing her best to control a smirk at the expression on the captain's face at this retort, Tabitha said, "We would then like to speak to Mr Havers's mechanic, assuming he took the train down here intending to meet with the deceased. Are you able to point him out to us?"

Happy to comply at least with this simple request, Captain Forth gestured towards a spot near the edge of the crowd of vehicles where a brown motor-car stood with a man bent over it.

"He hasn't been allowed to touch Havers's car, which was taken away, but he was also responsible for some other cars, including the one he's tinkering with. I believe the mechanic is a Frenchie. His name is Duval. Not sure how much English he speaks."

"And the lists?" Tabitha asked.

"What about if I make you a copy of the ten drivers before and after Lord Pembroke, both at the Croydon checkpoint and then again here?" At that point, all Captain Forth wished was to extricate himself from the conversation as quickly as possible and send the women on their way. "If you make your way over to the mechanic, I will begin working on it immediately and will bring it to you when I am finished."

With a smile of satisfaction that hovered somewhere between the cat that got the cream and the mother of a truculent child who had finally imposed her will, the dowager replied, "That will be acceptable."

As the women turned in the direction the captain had indicated, one thing quickly became clear: there was not even a hint of a path leading to the motor-car.

Looking at the churned-up mud, Lady Archibald said, "I believe I will return to the carriage and wait for you there.

As Arlene returned to the carriage, the three other women carefully picked their way through the mud to where a stocky man in oil-stained overalls crouched beside a chestnut-brown motor-car. His sleeves were rolled up to the elbows, revealing sinewy forearms streaked with grime.

Steam rose from the car's radiator. The man's head was bent over his work, but he looked up sharply when the dowager's cane struck the ground beside him.

"You there," she said. "Are you Duval?" She asked this in English, though Tabitha knew full well that the dowager spoke fluent French. Had she decided that speaking to a mechanic in his mother tongue was beneath her? Knowing how deep the woman's snobbery went, it was entirely possible.

The man wiped his hands on a rag, gaze shifting from her to Tabitha and Isabella. "Perhaps, madame. Who is asking?"

"I am the Dowager Countess of Pembroke," she declared, "and my companions are Lady Pembroke and Miss Hartwell. We have questions regarding the death of Mr Havers. We have been told you were his mechanic."

Duval's eyes flickered with surprise, then caution. "I have spoken with the police already."

"Yes, and now you will speak with us," the dowager said, stepping closer. "A man has been murdered, and my relative's name is being dragged through the mud."

Tabitha studied the mechanic. Adopting a lighter, friendlier tone than the one the dowager was employing, she asked, "We have been told that a spanner from my husband's car was found near your late employer's corpse. I know for a fact that my husband was not involved in Mr Havers's death, so do you have any thoughts on how it might have ended up in the wrong toolkit?"

Duval's mouth tightened. "How should I know? Perhaps Monsieur Havers borrowed it. Or someone placed it there."

"Someone?" Isabella asked. "Who?"

He spread his hands. "I cannot say. But many men stood close to the cars at the start: drivers, mechanics, onlookers. Tools change hands in such confusion."

"Convenient," murmured Tabitha.

Duval bent to his work again, voice muffled. "I know nothing of the English lord or his tools. I fix engines. That is all."

"Engines and alibis, it seems," the dowager said.

He looked up sharply, irritation flashing across his face. "You think I was involved in his death somehow and made sure the blame fell on your lord? For what? Monsieur's temper was his own undoing. He shouted at everyone, insulted me, and even the stewards. If I wished him harm, I would have left a week ago. He does not pay my wages; the company does."

Tabitha stepped forward, voice low. "You speak of Mr Havers fighting with everyone, and we witnessed some of that ourselves in London before the rally began. Can you suggest anyone in particular who might have wished him harm?"

"Non!" the man said, wiping his hands on a nearby towel.

"We understand that Mr Havers had to stop because there was a problem with his motor-car. I assume you looked everything over before he left London; after all, that was why you were there. I find it strange that Mr Havers had trouble given that," Isabella said. "These engines are very reliable when properly tended. What was the problem?"

Duval hesitated. "I do not know. They took the car from where he was killed, and I haven't been able to examine it. Probably a minor issue. Maybe the magneto. Maybe the fuel feed."

"Perhaps," she repeated. "Has this car had problems before?"

The mechanic shrugged. "When a man drives without patience, everything seems to fail."

Then he gave a curt nod, gathered his tools, and turned and stormed off

As he walked away, Isabella exhaled. "He knows more than he is saying."

"Obviously," the dowager said. "But the question is whether he knows something about the murder or merely has kind of bad manners one so often encounters amongst continentals."

Tabitha watched Duval vanish into the mist. Did this man hold the key to proving Wolf's innocence? She only hoped that the dowager's sharpness hadn't cost them the chance to speak to a vital witness.

CHAPTER 12

Their interaction with Duval had been so brief that Captain Forth hadn't had time to copy out the list of drivers. The three women returned to the tent, where Forth looked at them with concern; was he about to be berated again by that dreadful woman for his slow transcription?

Eager to defend himself pre-emptively, Forth said, "I am almost done. I apologise for the delay, your ladyships."

Tabitha saw the alarm in the man's eyes and sympathised with him. Jumping in before the dowager had a chance to make a cutting comment, she reassured the captain that they had finished their conversation sooner than expected and didn't mind waiting while he finished. The look on the dowager's face suggested that Tabitha wasn't speaking for her when she gave that reassurance, but, surprisingly, she kept her comments to herself.

Under the women's gaze, Captain Forth chose to sacrifice penmanship for speed, and within a few minutes, he had completed the duplication of the timing sheets. He handed them over with the look of a man who wished nothing more than to be rid of an obligation and then escape.

The dowager took the sheets from him. "Let us just hope we can actually read this scrawl," she said with a sniff.

Tabitha gave the man a warm smile. "Thank you very much for your cooperation, Captain Forth."

The socially appropriate response would have been for the captain to assure them that he was happy to answer any additional questions they might have in the future. However, he was unable to bring himself to make such an offer and instead, gave a quick bow and hurried out of the tent.

As the three women returned to Lady Archibald's carriage, Tabitha glanced at the delicate new bracelet watch Wolf had recently gifted her. It was already nearly eleven o'clock. Did they have time to investigate further before the inquest? Even as Tabitha wondered this, she realised they wouldn't know where to start even if there were time.

Once they were settled in the carriage, Tabitha said, "I think we need to take some time before two o'clock to review these lists and consider what we know. We will learn more information at the inquest, and it would be helpful to consider that in the fullest context possible."

Isabella tilted her head in surprise. "You have clearly been involved with such an investigation before, Lady Pembroke."

"Indeed," Tabitha acknowledged. "My husband and I, with Lady Pembroke's assistance," she hastened to add, "have been able to solve quite a few cases over the past year and a half. We have a certain methodology that works for us." She then told Arlene and Isabella about the notecards they always wrote up and the corkboard they usually used.

"So, you plan to return to your hotel and write up some of these note-cards now?" Isabella asked. When Tabitha nodded, she continued, "Would you mind if I joined you?"

Since the American heiress knew more about motor-cars and the motoring world than any of them, including Wolf, Tabitha was happy to have her assistance.

Arlene seemed less enthusiastic. "Why do I not drop you off at The Grand and then I can return later to drive you all to the Town Hall for two o'clock?" she said before Tabitha could accept Isabella's offer. If nothing else, the always stylish Lady Archibald imagined she looked rather windswept after their excursion and needed to return home to ensure she looked suitably impressive for the afternoon. She did not doubt that such a high-profile inquest, where the primary suspect was an earl, would draw a large crowd from a cross-section of Brighton's society.

As willing, almost eager, as Tabitha was for Miss Hartwell's input into the investigation, she had been prepared to forgo it if it meant tolerating Lady Archibald. Given this, she was pleased to accept the assistance of one lady while graciously excusing the other.

Just over thirty minutes later, Tabitha, the dowager, and Isabella Hartwell were dropped off at the Grand Brighton and proceeded up to Tabitha and Wolf's sumptuous suite. They found Wolf in the suite's sitting room with Langley and Bear.

The three men looked up as the women entered. Tabitha rushed to greet Langley. "Thank you for coming. I know that you were otherwise occupied."

Langley blushed at her thanks and replied, "Of course, I came. I am sorry I was unable to leave London until this morning. Still, nothing I was working on was more important than this."

Tabitha expressed her gratitude. Langley's connections in Whitehall and beyond had assisted them during multiple investigations, and she was certain Wolf's chances were better with the man at his side. She introduced Isabella Hartwell to Langley and Bear. The woman appeared somewhat intimidated by Bear's size and visage. Although this was common when people first saw him, it rarely took long before they realised what a kind and gentle man he truly was.

The men relinquished their seats to the ladies. Earlier, they had ordered a fresh tea tray and then, realising the time, asked for some sandwiches to be sent up as well. The tray was on the table between the chairs, and the ladies gratefully poured themselves cups of tea.

Tabitha held some more of the notepaper and had started jotting down the sparse details of their conversation with Duval. Meanwhile, Isabella was examining the sheets with the times of the checkpoints and endpoints.

"So, Havers hit the checkpoint about ten minutes before you did, Lord Pembroke," Isabella began to say.

"Please, call me Wolf. All my friends do, and if you are taking the time to help prove my innocence, you now count as a friend," he insisted.

Isabella smiled, before continuing. "Wolf. He arrived ten minutes before you, and no one arrived between the two of you."

"So, I was the first person to pass him when he had broken down," Wolf guessed.

"That would make sense," Isabella agreed. "And, by the same token, one would assume that the first person who found his body was the one who reported the death," she continued. Everyone nodded along.

Tabitha was the first to realise what Isabella was implying. "So, assuming it was someone taking part in the run who killed him, it must have been someone who was between Wolf and that person!"

"Indeed," Isabella agreed. "Unfortunately, this is not as simple to calculate as we might hope; after all, presumably, the driver who found the body spent quite a bit of time travelling to the police station and back to show where the body was. However, if we assume that most people were travelling at a steady pace, we should be able to narrow the field down somewhat with the checkpoint timings."

Now, Langley piped up. "We should find out who discovered the body at the inquest this afternoon. Of course, if there are other details that do not emerge then, for some reason, I am happy to exert any pressure I can through Whitehall to learn whatever information the police have."

Tabitha smiled gratefully; at moments like this, she often paused to marvel at how much she had disliked and distrusted Langley when they first met. She had found him cold, haughty, and almost reptilian in demeanour. Now that she knew him much better, she realised Langley was simply reserved, cautious, and genuinely quite shy. Now, she couldn't imagine him not being part of their lives and inner circle. Certainly, he had been nothing but a positive influence in the lives of Melody and Rat.

"One thing I hope we learn from the inquest is whether they believe the engine was tampered with." As Wolf said this, there was a knock at the door. Bear was the nearest and rose to open it. There, he found a floor waiter in the smart hotel livery, carrying a silver tray laden with sandwiches, sausage rolls, and what looked like slices of game pie.

Luckily, there was so much food that there was more than enough even to feed the extra people now gathered in the room. Once the hall waiter had set the tray down, accepted his tip, and left the room, the group returned to Wolf's last statement.

"If the engine was tampered with, then it is likely this was premeditated murder," Wolf continued. "If it was not, then we can assume it was manslaughter, and perhaps it was even an accident."

This made sense. However, it raised a question that only Isabella would likely know the answer to. Tabitha voiced it. "How obvious would it be if it had been tampered with?"

"Well, I am far from an expert on the De Dion-Bouton Vis-à-vis," Isabella explained. "But I did look into one before I bought my Panhard, and so I know a thing or two."

"You certainly know more than any of us, so any light you can shed on this will be helpful," Wolf conceded.

"Well, not to get too technical, but it's an air-cooled engine, which means there's no radiator to drain and fewer pipes one could tamper with. That does, however, leave plenty of small, delicate systems that might be interfered with. Someone might make a tiny hole in the fuel tap so the motor spirit would leak away. At first, the car would run perfectly well, then sputter and die eventually. I'd be surprised if it would have lasted to where Havers was killed, but it's possible."

"So that is the most likely method?" Tabitha asked. She was genuinely impressed by how much Miss Hartwell knew about motor-cars and saw that Wolf was even more so.

Isabella continued, "Well, there are other ways. A small wire to the ignition might be half-unscrewed, so it worked until the vibrations finally shook it free. I'd have expected it to take longer, unless it was only slightly loose. An oil feed left slightly open would bleed out slowly, and the bearings would overheat after some distance. Even a scrap of cloth in the cooling fan or air intake would let the engine warm until it gave up. The chain or sprocket, if eased, might jump once the metal wore a bit from the run."

The dowager, who disliked any discussion she couldn't dominate and was finding this one intolerably dull, finally interrupted impatiently. "And which of these do you believe it to be, Miss Hartwell?"

Either ignoring or not hearing the older woman's tone, Isabella considered, then said, "I'd put my money on the ignition wire or the loosened oil feed. Given how far he managed to drive before the trouble began, I think those are the most likely methods."

Tabitha had one more question: "Is it possible for any of those things to occur naturally or would they necessarily be evidence of tampering?"

"Any of these might have happened by accident," Isabella replied. "Nothing here shouts 'tampering' necessarily. Though, given that I am sure Duval went over every part of the motor-car thoroughly before the run, it seems less likely to have just happened."

Shockingly, it was left to the dowager to point out the obvious flaw in this case for premeditated murder. "I assume whoever tampered with the machine would have had no idea where and when it might break. What are we suggesting they did? Follow behind until he did?"

It was a valid question. Certainly, it didn't seem the most efficient way to kill someone.

CHAPTER 13

I sabella had returned to Arlene's house to change for the inquest, and everyone else tried to occupy themselves, though it wasn't easy, and the time dragged on. Eventually, everyone left the sitting room to change their clothes, leaving Tabitha and Wolf alone. He had already said he would walk to the Town Hall.

"Would you like me to walk with you?" Tabitha offered.

"Thank you," he said with a grateful smile. "However, it is still drizzling. Take the carriage with the other ladies. It will be good to have a few minutes to clear my head. I am assuming the constable will accompany me, but will remain at a respectful distance." This last was said rather sardonically.

Tabitha didn't argue and returned to the bedchamber to change her clothes. The rain had eased by the time the carriage pulled up outside Brighton Town Hall, but the pavements remained slick. Tabitha looked up at the clock tower; it was ten minutes until two o'clock. From the glances they received while descending, it appeared that every passerby seemed to know who they were and why they were there.

Inside, the vestibule hummed with a sense of anticipation. There were reporters with notebooks, clerks carrying ledgers, and the hum of conversation from the gathered members of Brighton society eager for scandal. The coroner's inquest had become an afternoon's entertainment.

Tabitha entered with the dowager on one side and Lady Arlene Archibald on the other. Miss Hartwell followed closely behind. Their arrival caused a commotion as women whispered behind their hands and gentlemen tried not to stare.

The women announced themselves to the usher. He was momentarily flustered, but quickly composed himself and led them to the front benches.

The dowager took the aisle seat with imperious calm. "Let them see us holding our heads up," she said under her breath. "Half the work of defending one's honour is appearing entirely," untroubled."

Lady Arlene's voice trembled. "Do you think they will make me speak?"

"They will," Isabella answered crisply. "And you will say what you saw, nothing more. No elaboration."

"I never elaborate," Arlene murmured, adjusting her gloves. "Merely highlight."

Tabitha sat quietly, her jaw clenched with tension. The day before, she had watched Wolf promise Detective Inspector Maguire not to leave the hotel; now she sat in the gallery where strangers would dissect and judge his character.

The twelve jurymen were already in their places: shopkeepers, tradesmen, a schoolmaster, and one respectable brewer. Finally, the coroner entered and took his seat at the head of the table. He was a neat little man with thinning hair and a serious manner.

At the far end of the room, Wolf sat beside his solicitor, Mr Anderson, who had insisted on attending as an observer. His expression was grave but steady. Tabitha was glad the man had insisted on taking the morning train to Brighton when Wolf had telephoned him the previous evening. Bear and Langley sat just behind them.

The coroner rapped for silence. "Gentlemen of the jury, we continue our inquiry into the death of Mr Thomas Havers, found deceased beside his motor-car on the sixth of November just past. The purpose of this inquest is to determine the cause of death and, if possible, the circumstances attending it."

A low murmur spread through the crowd. The coroner rapped his gavel again, and it subsided.

"To begin with, we will hear from the medical examiner, Dr Michael Frobisher, police surgeon for Brighton Borough."

Dr Frobisher was then called and sworn. He described the injuries to the deceased as consistent with a heavy blow to the temple, delivered with a blunt instrument. Death, he added, would have been instantaneous. The coroner inquired whether the injuries might have been caused by a fall. Dr Frobisher replied that the wound's shape was too regular and was more in keeping with a tool or spanner than with any natural surface.

"We will next hear expert testimony regarding the condition of the motor-car," the coroner said. "Mr Henry Pritchard, consulting engineer to the Brighton Corporation Gasworks, has been asked to examine the vehicle."

A tall man in a dark frock coat came forward, carrying his hat. He had a very competent air about him, which Tabitha hoped would translate into practical testimony that would help Wolf.

"Mr Pritchard," the coroner began, "you were asked by the Brighton Borough Police to examine the deceased's motor-car yesterday afternoon?"

"Yes, sir."

"Please tell the jury what you found."

"The vehicle, a French-built De Dion-Bouton Vis-à-vis, suffered a failure of lubrication," he said. "On examination I found the regulating screw of the drip-feed oiler had been turned down, so the supply to the crankshaft bearings was scant. After some miles, the bearings would over-heat and pick up, and the engine would seize."

"Not ordinary wear, then?" the coroner asked.

"No, sir. The regulating screw had been adjusted by hand. The marks around it show the use of a spanner not belonging to the driver's kit, which I examined. My professional opinion is that a Whitworth spanner was used."

A murmur rose from the benches. The coroner lifted a hand for silence.

"You are quite certain of this?"

"I am, sir," said Pritchard. "The screw shows fresh scoring inconsistent with the tools supplied by the manufacturer. It was turned recently, perhaps that very morning. In my professional judgment, the adjustment was deliberate, calculated to cause a stoppage after some distance."

Another rustle of surprise swept through the chamber. Tabitha felt Isabella's gaze meet hers. It was exactly what Isabella had suspected: a tampered oil feed, left slightly ajar so the engine would fail at some point.

The coroner leaned forward. "Is it possible that the driver himself might have made such an error inadvertently?"

Pritchard shook his head. "No experienced motorist would do so."

"And when the engine seized, what would the driver have done?"

"He would be obliged to stop at once, cool the bearings, and attempt adjustment. It would take several minutes, perhaps longer."

"Long enough for someone to overtake him?"

"Indeed, sir."

"One more question, Mr Pritchard. What kind of spanner does Lord Pembroke's Daimler come with?"

"To my knowledge, the British Daimler Company commonly supplies a toolkit with two fixed, open-ended Whitworth spanners." A murmur ran through the room, and the coroner called for quiet.

"One further point, if I may," Pritchard added. "Among motorists, it is common to mark tools with paint for quick recognition. A ring upon the shank or grip serves well in a crowded paddock. I examined Mr Havers's De Dion kit at the police yard and observed a consistent red mark upon his handles, oil can, and principal spanners. By contrast, the loose spanner found at the scene bore no colour. Its surfaces were plain steel, with ordinary wear but no band or daub. That absence suggests it did not belong to his set and may have come from another car's equipment altogether."

The crowd gasped again at this news. Once the audience noise had subsided, the coroner thanked the engineer. "You may stand down, Mr Pritchard," said the coroner. "Your testimony has been most valuable."

Isabella leaned over to Tabitha and whispered, "This is good news. Wolf had neither the time nor the knowledge to tamper with Havers's motor-car. If they believe this was premeditated, then that would seem to exonerate your husband." Tabitha gave her a wan smile in reply; she only hoped the American was correct.

"Next witness," the coroner called, "Monsieur Henri Duval, mechanic." The man they had spoken to that morning hesitantly stepped forward and nervously removed his cap. He appeared quite different from the cocksure, unpleasant man they had spoken to earlier.

"You are a mechanic by trade, Monsieur Duval?"

"Yes, monsieur, sir." Tabitha thought his accent seemed stronger than it had that morning; perhaps it was nerves.

"You were engaged by Mr Havers to oversee his motor-car during the event?"

"Non. By the De Dion-Bouton company. They own the motor-car. I work for them and was sent to assist Monsieur Havers for the run to Brighton. I prepare the machine, check the tyres, the oil."

"Did you find any fault with the engine's lubrication system before the race?"

Duval hesitated, glancing towards the jurors. "No, sir. Everything was in perfect condition when I left the car."

"None whatever?"

"None. I inspect every bolt myself."

Mr Pritchard, seated near the witness stand, raised an eyebrow but said nothing.

The coroner asked, "Did you remain with the car throughout the morning?"

"Nearly always," Duval said quickly. "But there were other De Dion-Bouton motor-cars and I was also to help them. I go once or twice to help another driver. Only a few minutes."

"How long, precisely?"

"Perhaps ten, fifteen minutes."

"Leaving the vehicle unattended?"

"Yes, but it was in the paddock with others with many eyes about."

The coroner continued. "Could someone have approached the car in your absence?"

Duval twisted his cap. "It is possible, yes. But who would do such a thing?"

"That," said the coroner, "is what we are trying to discover. Thank you, Monsieur Duval. You may step down."

The coroner turned back to the room. "We shall now hear testimony regarding the earlier encounter between the deceased and Lord Pembroke."

Tabitha felt Arlene tense beside her.

"Lady Archibald, if you would please approach."

Arlene rose, her veil trembling, and approached the stand. "Lady Arlene Archibald, wife of Sir John Archibald," she said softly.

"State what happened on the morning in question in London."

"Mr Havers addressed me improperly, suggesting I join him for a private dinner in Brighton. When I refused, he persisted. I struck him. Lord Pembroke intervened and demanded that he apologise. Mr Havers refused. There was no further altercation."

The coroner asked, "Was Lord Pembroke angry?"

"Yes, naturally. Any man would be."

"Did he threaten Mr Havers?"

"Lord Pembroke told him that if he ever approached me again, he would answer to him. A few other words were spoken. Her ladyship, the Dowager Countess of Pembroke intervened, and eventually, Havers apologised and left. That was all."

"Lord Pembroke said Mr Havers would answer to him? Those were his exact words?" the coroner pressed.

"If he ever approached me again. Which he did not," Arlene said very firmly.

The reporters scribbled; the dowager muttered darkly.

"Thank you, Lady Archibald."

Arlene returned to her seat, cheeks flushed, and immediately reached for Tabitha's hand.

The coroner called next. "Miss Isabella Hartwell."

Isabella stood, every inch the composed American heiress.

"Miss Hartwell, I believe that you were also present during this altercation?"

"Yes, sir. I witnessed the entire exchange. Mr Havers insulted Lady Archibald, and Lord Pembroke demanded an apology. No violence was offered."

"Did Lord Pembroke appear in a temper?"

"He appeared disgusted, not enraged. I have observed Mr Havers at The Automobile Club events I've been allowed to attend over the past few months and have noticed that he enjoyed provoking people; he treated offence as sport."

"Thank you, Miss Hartwell."

When she resumed her seat, the coroner's gaze moved to Tabitha. "The Countess of Pembroke, if she will oblige."

She rose, keeping her shoulders straight. The low murmur died away.

"You were present, Lady Pembroke?"

"I was."

"Describe what you saw."

"Mr Havers insulted Lady Archibald; my husband intervened. He raised his voice but did not raise his hand. The incident lasted less than a minute or two."

"Would you call your husband a man of temper?"

Tabitha chose her words carefully. "He has strong feelings, and the courage to express them. He is not violent."

The coroner inclined his head. "That is all, thank you."

Finally, the dowager was summoned. She swept forward like a frigate under full sail.

"You witnessed the quarrel, my lady?"

"I did. And I can tell you exactly what was said, though it hardly matters. A boor insulted a lady, and Lord Pembroke did what any gentleman would have done and told him to behave himself. Under the circumstances, I believe he showed enormous restraint."

When the witnesses had finished, the coroner called Detective Inspector Maguire to summarise his case. Maguire's tone was formal but not hostile. "We have heard that the deceased's motor-car was deliberately tampered with. We have heard that Lord Pembroke stopped to assist and then departed. We have a witness who saw his motor-car leaving the scene, and a spanner from his toolkit was found nearby. We have good reason to believe it was the murder weapon. Having searched Lord Pembroke's vehicle and its toolkit, the spanner was missing. Whether these facts point to guilt or coincidence remains for the jury."

At this, Mr Pritchard stepped forward once more. "If I may, sir, I do believe that the tampering alters the nature of this case. I had not heard the rest of the case against Lord Pembroke until now. Having now heard it, I feel compelled to point out that the damage could only have been caused before the car left London. That suggests preparation, not impulse."

The coroner nodded reluctantly. "Your remark is noted."

Maguire added, "We also have testimony from Monsieur Duval that the vehicle was unattended for a period that morning. That provides an opportunity."

The dowager whispered, "And if the jury cannot see where that leads, then I wonder why we entrust such matters to the general populace."

Finally, the coroner shuffled his notes, then looked up. "We shall now hear from Lord Pembroke himself."

Wolf rose, tall and composed, and stepped forward. The low murmur of the room subsided.

"You are Jeremy Wolfson Chesterton, Earl of Pembroke?"

"I am."

"You were taking part in the motoring event from London to Brighton?"

"Yes, sir."

"We have heard testimony about your altercation with Mr Havers. Is there anything you want to add?"

"No. That is exactly as it took place."

The coroner nodded, then continued, "Somewhere outside of Brighton, you stopped upon seeing Mr Havers's vehicle by the roadside?"

"I did. His engine had stalled, and he was working at it. I asked if he required help."

"What was his response?"

"He told me, somewhat sharply, that he did not. I then continued on my way."

The coroner peered at him over his spectacles. "Were there bad feelings between you?"

"None on my part. We had exchanged words earlier that morning when he insulted Lady Archibald. I considered the matter closed. He seemed to feel otherwise."

"Did you leave any tools with him?"

"No, I did not."

"And you have no knowledge of how the deceased came to be struck?"

"None whatever. When I left, he was standing upright, alive and cursing his engine."

The coroner gazed at Wolf sternly and said in a tone that suggested he was not overawed by rank, "You understand why your presence and the discovery of your tool are of concern to this court?"

"I do. However, someone tampered with that motor-car long before I saw it. Whoever did so is the murderer, not I." Wolf paused then added, "I would not have known how to do that damage to his engine even if I had wanted to, which I did not." He added, "If I had known what was to follow, I would never have driven on."

A rustle of excitement ran through the spectators at this statement. The coroner rapped for silence. "Thank you, my lord. You may stand down." He then adjusted his spectacles and continued. "The deposition of Mr Ernest Wilcox, the driver who discovered the body, has already been taken and read to the jury. His evidence concerns only the position of the deceased and adds nothing further to the cause of death."

After those words, the jury retired for deliberation. The chamber filled with subdued chatter as the spectators considered what they had heard and offered their guesses about the verdict.

Arlene dabbed her eyes. "Do you think they will accuse him outright?"

Tabitha looked ahead at the now-empty seats of the jurors, her thoughts racing through what they had heard. She was thankful for Pritchard's final comments; she hoped they were sufficient.

After twenty minutes, the jury returned. Their foreman, a florid grocer, read the verdict: "We find that Mr Arthur Havers met his death by violence at the hands of some person or persons unknown, and that there is insufficient evidence to commit Lord Pembroke for trial, though he should remain under restraint, pending further investigation." A murmur ran through the hall. Wolf inclined his head but said nothing.

The coroner banged his gavel. "This inquest is adjourned. Should further evidence arise, it will be reopened."

The group, including Wolf, left the inquest only to find it was raining harder than ever.

Arlene sighed. "At least they didn't declare you guilty, Wolf."

"Not yet," he said with more bitterness than he intended. "As I left,

Maguire stopped me and made clear that I am still his primary suspect and am still restricted to the hotel."

"Can he do that?" Tabitha demanded.

"He can, and quite properly," Langley said. "Until a magistrate directs otherwise, the police may require a suspect's cooperation. For a peer, that means remaining available under his own recognisance."

The dowager snapped open her umbrella. "Then we have work to do and no time to waste."

"Mr Anderson suggested that he request a copy of the full medical examiner's report. He will make the request today," Wolf told the group. Then he added, "Maguire did mention that he has requested that none of the drivers who checked in after me, including Wilcox, leave Brighton, and that includes their mechanics. That is something at least." He shrugged at this small compensation for the restriction of his freedom.

Tabitha tightened her grip on her cloak. "Well, then we need to make the most of that fact. We have Mr Pritchard's evidence to prove someone meddled with the motor-car. If we can trace that, perhaps we can clear your name."

Isabella smiled slightly. "Leave that to me. I will do everything I can to help."

The women walked together toward the waiting carriage as Wolf, Langley, and Bear, accompanied by the constable, started walking back to The Grand.

CHAPTER 14

On the drive from the inquest, Isabella asked if there were plans to regroup and discuss what they had learned. When Tabitha confirmed this was their intention, the American inquired whether she might join them, and Arlene once again apologised for dropping the women off rather than joining them. And again, Tabitha was happy to accept her apologies.

As they made their way through the lobby, Tabitha stopped at the porter's desk and requested that afternoon tea be sent to the room; they would all need some refreshments after the couple of hours they'd just endured.

Having completed that task, she turned to the dowager and said, "I would like to check on the children before we begin."

"You have children?" Isabella asked innocently.

"We have an adopted daughter, Melody. And my private secretary, Mrs O'Leary, has twin boys who share the nursery with her. Oh, and Melody's older brother, who lives with Lord Langley, is also with us." She paused for a moment, debating what else to say. Then, considering that she was sure Arlene had already guessed, Tabitha continued, "And I am with child and am expecting, perhaps in late January."

"Well, then, congratulations!" Isabella exclaimed with a warm, genuine smile. "What wonderful news." Then, slightly shyly, she asked, "Would you mind if I came to meet the children? While I am not sure whether marriage and motherhood are in my future, I do quite like the idea of tiny humans."

While Tabitha longed to ask why the beautiful, wealthy Miss Hartwell thought she might remain a spinster, she did not feel their relationship had advanced enough for such confidences. Instead, she replied that she would be happy to have company and that the children always loved meeting new people.

"Do you mind dogs?" Tabitha asked as an afterthought.

"I love dogs," Isabella assured her.

The dowager said she would return to her room and wash off the grime of close contact with the common people of Brighton, then meet them shortly in Tabitha's suite. The women took the lift to their respective floors and parted ways.

The nursery rooms occupied a quiet corner on the floor below Tabitha and Wolf's grand, sea-facing suite. It consisted of three modest chambers for the children, Mrs O'Leary, and their nursemaids.

Before Tabitha and Isabella had even reached the nursery rooms, they heard the children's giggles and delighted squeals, mixed with the occasional bark from Dodo.

Hearing the children enjoying themselves eased at least some of Tabitha's guilt. "This was supposed to be a fun few days at the seaside," she explained to Isabella. "A Punch and Judy show, playing on the beach, fish and chips, maybe even wrapped in newspaper. Melody had the chance to do those things the last time we were here, and I thought the twins would enjoy it."

"Well, they can still do all those things, can they not?" Isabella asked with the innocence of someone with little desire for motherhood.

Tabitha sighed. "Yes, of course they can, but I hoped to share in the fun, which now is unlikely to happen."

Inside the nursery suite, the chaos was exactly what the squeals and giggles had promised. Skittles clattered across the carpet, a nursemaid shrieked, "Not the wardrobe!" and one twin appeared to be pretending to be a lion tamer. Mrs O'Leary's steady voice rose above the din, promising the circus would be disbanded entirely if everyone didn't calm down somewhat.

As Tabitha and Isabella entered the room, Mrs O'Leary's eyes widened with concern. "Milady, I do apologise. Did the children's noise disturb you? We were hoping this would be a good way to pass a rainy day, but perhaps that was a poor decision."

Tabitha smiled at her private secretary. "Mrs O'Leary, all we heard were young children having a lovely time. Please, do not stop what you are doing."

At the sight of Tabitha, Melody hurried across the room and threw herself at her legs. "Tabby Cat, come and play," the little girl demanded. "I'm going to be the acrobat and do forward rolls. Then Rat is going to be a clown. I want Mary to paint his face, but he won't let her."

Tabitha and Wolf had taken all the children to Hengler's Grand Cirque a few weeks earlier, and the children had been reenacting their favourite acts ever since.

Laughing, Tabitha bent down to straighten the ribbon in Melody's hair, which seemed to have become askew during all the frolicking. "If Rat does not want that, then he can be a clown without a white face. You can still be an acrobat, though, Melody. I would like to see your act."

Melody pouted for a moment, then skipped back towards the rug, where Rat had arranged the nursery chairs into a wobbly circus ring. Tabitha and Isabella each took a seat, and the show began.

One nursemaid beat time with a wooden spoon while the twins clapped along in rhythm. Mrs O'Leary had been seated at a desk in the corner, writing, before Tabitha entered. Now, she retook her seat, periodically glancing up from her correspondence with the weary patience of someone who had long since surrendered to chaos.

Liam, the twin who had been the lion tamer, resumed that role with his brother, Willy, acting as the lion. The act quickly became silly and then descended into a sibling quarrel when the lion refused to do as he was told.

As promised, Melody performed some forward rolls and finished her act with dancing and twirling. Isabella watched the show with an amused expression on her face.

The final act was the clown. Bowing low, Rat announced he would tell some jokes. A little too late, Tabitha realised these must be jokes he remembered from his days as a street urchin in Whitehall.

The first story was harmless enough: a tale about a donkey who refused to move until promised oats. The second started innocently enough, but Tabitha's smile froze somewhere between the tavern and the bishop's hat. Too late, she realised what kind of punchline was coming. The nursemaids gasped, Mrs O'Leary dropped her pen, and Isabella gave a strangled cough that might have been laughter.

Rat blinked at them, puzzled. "What? It's just what the costermongers used to say."

"Perhaps we should move on from the jokes," Tabitha suggested quickly.

Rat was happy to comply. He then attempted a somersault and collided with a footstool. This probably wasn't helped by Dodo's insistence on being part of the act. The little dog had been happy enough to see Tabitha that she had sat still at first, content to be petted. However, eventually, she'd had enough of the affection and wanted to join in the game.

When the circus show was over, Tabitha and Isabella clapped enthusiastically.

"Is your nursery always this much fun?" Isabella asked.

"The twins have certainly livened things up," Tabitha admitted with a fond smile at the young boys.

Melody came over and climbed onto Tabitha's lap. "Tabby Cat, if it doesn't rain tomorrow, we're going to go and watch the Punch and Judy show again." On their previous visit to Brighton, Rat and Melody had seen the show performed in the Royal Pavilion Gardens.

As much as she enjoyed watching the children boisterously having fun, they were in a hotel, not at home. Given this, Tabitha decided that with the circus finished, it would be good to do something less energetic for a while. She suggested she read a story to the children. While Willy and Liam seemed less eager to sit quietly and listen, Melody was delighted. When Tabitha suggested reading *Treasure Island*, even Rat appeared interested in sitting on the rug and following along. Although the book wasn't Melody's favourite, Tabitha knew she enjoyed the swashbuckling adventure more than she'd admit.

Although Tabitha had been planning to read, at the last moment, she suggested that Rat read. After a moment's hesitation, the boy took the book and began.

He exhibited such worldliness most of the time that it was easy to forget that Rat was still only nine years old, or so they believed. When he first arrived at Chesterton House, he had been quite vague about his age and uncertain of his exact birthdate. Considering how malnourished he appeared, Tabitha wasn't sure if he was older than Wolf thought and merely undersized. Eventually, they decided to celebrate his birthday on Christmas Eve, and the most plausible age at that time was eight. Suddenly, Tabitha realised the boy would be ten years old before they knew it. The children were growing up so quickly!

Now, Rat sat cross-legged on the rug, the somewhat battered copy of *Treasure Island* open on his knees. The twins crouched on either side of him, wide-eyed, as he lowered his voice to a conspiratorial growl.

"'Fifteen men on the dead man's chest,'" he intoned, tapping his finger on the page. "'Yo-ho-ho, and a bottle of rum!'"

Melody gasped in delight; her brother tried to mimic a pirate's growl and nearly fell backwards with laughter. Mrs O'Leary looked up from her correspondence with a sigh.

Rat then launched into the following passage, adopting a sailor's limp and a wink that made the children shriek. "Old Long John, he's a clever one, never trust a man with a parrot, I say!"

Mary, the nursemaid, clucked in disapproval but didn't try to hide a smile.

Tabitha watched with amusement. While Rat's rendition of the story seemed to be veering somewhat from Robert Louis Stevenson's words, there was no doubt that everyone was enjoying themselves.

While Rat's speech had improved considerably since he had been living with Langley and being mentored by him, some of his original accent and enunciation surfaced as he read about pirates, mutiny, and buried gold. If anyone else noticed, they certainly didn't care. The twins idolised the older boy, and Melody adored her brother. The sense of adventure conjured by Rat's street-hardened voice charmed the other children, and even Tabitha had to admit she was drawn in by his storytelling.

Before Tabitha knew it, they had been with the children for over thirty minutes. She was sure the men must have returned by now and could only imagine the dowager's irritation if she were kept waiting any longer.

CHAPTER 15

B y the time she and Isabella had left the nursery rooms and returned to Tabitha's suite, everyone else had already gathered and were sipping tea and eating cucumber sandwiches.

"Nice of you to take the time to join us, Tabitha," the dowager remarked wryly.

Isabella answered for them both. "Apologies for keeping you waiting, Lady Pembroke. But the children were so delightful, it was hard to tear ourselves away." Tabitha flashed her a smile of gratitude.

"Well, now that you are here, shall we review what we have learned?" the dowager continued. "For my part, there did not seem much new information, merely a recitation of the known facts."

"That is not quite true, Mama," Tabitha interjected as she poured herself a cup of tea and took the chair Wolf had just vacated. "We learned the name of the driver who found the body."

Wolf retrieved Captain Forth's list from the drawer he had placed it in earlier. Returning to the group, he scanned it before saying, "At the checkpoint, this Ernest Wilcox was the sixth driver behind me." Thinking back to the previous day's driver, he said, "Not long after, I heard a sound from the engine, stopped the car, and a driver in a black car overtook me."

"Was that the only motor-car that passed you?" Isabella asked.

After considering the question, Wolf replied, "I think so." He returned to scanning the list. "According to the checkpoint, the driver behind me was a Major James Asher."

"I know who he is," Isabella said. "Well, I do not know him well, but he belongs to The Automobile Club. There aren't so many members, so after a couple of events, I began to recognise people and be recognised."

What Isabella didn't say, Tabitha thought, was that while any female motorist would have stood out, one as stunningly beautiful as Miss Hartwell, and an heiress to boot, likely made quite an impression. As she considered this, Tabitha wondered if the American beauty had any idea how beguiling she was. In Tabitha's experience, most beautiful women knew full well the effect their looks had on the men, and even women, around them. Certainly, Arlene was fully cognisant of her power. It was hard to imagine that Isabella wasn't, yet was it possible? Unlike Lady Archibald, she didn't walk into rooms expecting to be the centre of attention. Tabitha set this thought aside for now; it was irrelevant to helping Wolf.

Tabitha pulled herself out of her wool-gathering just in time to hear Isabella describe Major Asher's car. "I believe he also drives a Daimler."

"So, if our logic holds," the dowager mused, "then the killer is either this Major Asher or one of the other drivers before Ernest Wilcox."

"Can't we be even more specific than that?" Langley asked. "Surely, if Mr Wilcox found the body, then the killer must be the driver just before him."

This made a certain sense to the group, but Isabella quickly poured cold water on the theory. "Such a hypothesis assumes that none of the drivers stopped for any reason or overtook each other. I think we need to speak to all four before concluding that."

Langley sighed. "You are correct, of course, Miss Hartwell. It would have been a quicker, cleaner answer if you were not." Isabella grinned back at him. Addressing Wolf, he asked, "Who are the other three men?"

"Graham Smithers, Felix Dubois, and Gustaf Freund. Do any of those names ring a bell?" he asked Isabella.

"Smithers sounds familiar, but I don't recognise the rest. Given the second and third names, I'd guess one is French and one German. I wonder if they are representatives from the motor-car companies."

"Is that common practice?" Tabitha asked before nibbling on a perfect, crustless triangle of a sandwich.

"It is, from what I've seen. The companies often send their own men to these runs, agents or mechanics who know how to get the best out of a motor. It's good advertising when the motor-car performs well, and they report every fault back to the company, I'm sure. They want to make sure the motor-car finishes the course and that they gain as much good publicity from it as possible. Remember, I told you that Havers himself was one such representative."

Isabella's words made Tabitha think of something that had flickered through her mind the day before. "Why was Havers representing a French company and not a British one?"

The dowager seized on her words. "Indeed! Who in their right mind would choose anything made on the continent over the best that Britain has to offer?"

No one wanted to contradict her and point out all the wonderful things their European neighbours made so much better than the British, many of which the dowager herself enjoyed. After all, what was better than French champagne, Belgian lace, Italian opera, or Viennese chocolates?

If Isabella had any sense that she was on dangerous ground, it was impossible to tell from the breezy way she replied. "Oh, there's nothing unusual about it. The French have simply been at this longer, and their designs are rather more refined at present. De Dion-Bouton, Panhard, Peugeot, they've all set the pace for the rest of the world. Havers was hardly unpatriotic in representing them; he was being practical. Even Daimler, even with its workshop in Coventry, began with French engines and French ideas. Truthfully, very few of your so-called British motors are purely British yet. You're borrowing the best you can until your engineers catch up. It's progress, not betrayal."

The dowager's response was to raise her eyebrows and give one of her signature sniffs. However, Isabella's words had given Tabitha something else to ponder.

After a moment to consider how she wanted to phrase it, Tabitha said, "It is certainly interesting that two of the drivers who came after Wolf and before the person who found the body were foreign. If you are right,

Isabella, and Havers was playing fast and loose with his loyalties, might it have gone even further than you'd heard? Perhaps he was trying to wrangle money from even more foreign car companies. If he were, presumably they might bear a grudge."

"It is one thing to bear a grudge, another to strike a man over the head with a blunt instrument," the dowager said dismissively. Was it? Tabitha wondered. Perhaps it depended on how much money was at stake in the secrets Havers was selling to the highest bidder.

"We need to find a way to investigate all these men," Tabitha concluded. "I wonder how many are staying at this hotel?" It was a valid question; The Grand was probably Brighton's most exclusive, expensive hotel. If some drivers were merely paid lackeys for automobile companies, would they put them in such accommodations?

"Wolf, when you registered, did you have to tell The Automobile Club where you were staying while you were in Brighton?" Tabitha asked.

"Actually, I did. However, I cannot imagine this is information they would give out willy-nilly."

Tabitha realised this was something they should have asked Captain Forth for earlier. Now, she wondered whether it might be possible to use the man's clear desire to avoid the dowager to pressure him into giving it up.

Articulating this question, she suggested, "Let us have Bear return to Preston Park and make such a request. He can not-so-subtly suggest that Mama would be happy to return herself if necessary. I suspect that will have the desired effect."

From the look on Isabella's face, it seemed she was surprised Tabitha would so openly discuss the dowager's intimidation of the captain. However, if she'd been expecting the older woman to be offended by the implication that she had browbeaten someone, she must have been even more surprised by the obvious satisfaction the dowager took in being so characterised.

"Perhaps I should accompany Bear," the dowager added. "Between his brawn and my brains, I imagine we might persuade the good captain to hand over his mother at this point."

Fortunately, it was difficult to offend Bear, and certainly, if he had been inclined to take offence at the dowager's tendency to see him merely as a large, well-muscled henchman, he would have done so many moons ago.

Tabitha considered the dowager's suggestion. Certainly, there was some merit in giving her something to do that was so perfectly suited to her skills.

Finally, she decided that Bear and the dowager made the perfect team for any intimidation that might be required. However, given that, perhaps there was more that the two of them could achieve.

"Mama, if you return to Preston Park, perhaps you might also find out where we can find the mechanics for those men. Also, see if Captain Forth has any opinion on whether the foreigners are motor-car owners in their own right, or driving on behalf of a company."

The dowager's eyes lit up at the thought of the lethal combination she and Bear would make. During an investigation of her own the previous year, the dowager had borrowed a Goliath of her own, Little Ian, from the Whitehall gang leader, Mickey D. However, despite his size, the man had proved better suited for household chores than investigations.

The dowager leapt to her feet as swiftly as a woman her age was able and told Bear, "I will go and get my hat and coat and meet you in the lobby. Please arrange for transportation."

CHAPTER 16

With the dowager and Bear dispatched on their mission, the group considered their next move.

"I would like to examine Havers's De Dion," Isabella told them. "I would like to see the tampering for myself."

While there was no doubt the American heiress knew more about motor-cars than any of them, did she really know enough to second-guess what the expert witness, Mr Pritchard, had said at the inquest? Yet, no one felt comfortable voicing this question. It seemed there was no need for them to articulate their concerns; the expression on their faces was sufficient.

Isabella laughed. "I realise why you might question my authority, or at least my confidence in it. Certainly, it is quite outrageous for a young woman, or indeed any female, to consider herself more knowledgeable about such matters than a man."

Immediately, Tabitha felt ashamed of her reaction. She understood what it was like to be underestimated because of her gender.

Rather than pretending otherwise, she immediately acknowledged her behaviour. "I apologise, Miss Hartwell, Isabella. It is not outrageous at all, and I should not have reacted in a way as to imply otherwise."

With a kind and understanding smile, Isabella assured her there was no need to apologise. "My competence in this area is unusual, I realise that. However, I am the only child of a man who loved nothing more than tinkering with machines of all kinds. No matter how rich and successful he became, there was nothing that my father enjoyed half as much as taking something apart, understanding how it worked, and then reassembling it, perhaps even improving on the original," she added.

"And he shared this love with you?" Tabitha guessed.

"Indeed. My mother died when I was a baby, so there was no one to insist on piano lessons and hours spent embroidering. I had no aunts, not even a grandmother. Therefore, instead of learning the things that young girls are supposed to learn, I spent my time understanding the engineering of everything from the clocks in our drawing room to the water pump in the scullery."

"Really?" Tabitha couldn't help but exclaim, struggling to suppress even a hint of envy at the thought of a parent, let alone a father, opening up such possibilities for their daughter.

"Really. By the time I was twelve, I knew how to strip and reassemble the household sewing machine, and by fifteen I'd learnt to clean and tune the mechanism of my father's phonograph. Later came the camera, the typewriter, and one of those new calculating machines he'd brought back from New York. Engines were simply the next challenge. Once you've mastered how gears, levers, and valves cooperate, it hardly matters whether they belong to a watch or a motor-car; the principles are the same."

Her credentials confirmed, at least to Tabitha's satisfaction, the question was now how to gain access to examine the De Dion. After all, from what they understood, the vehicle had been taken into police custody.

"Let me see what I can do," Langley offered. He rose. "Does this hotel have a telephone?"

"I believe so," Tabitha replied. "Ask the porter." Langley nodded and left the room.

Ten minutes later, he returned. "I am assured that you will have access by tomorrow morning."

"Impressive," Isabella said. "Can I ask how you managed that?"

"I would prefer you did not," Langley answered before excusing himself for the evening.

Isabella stood. "Unless you believe otherwise, I am not sure there is much else we can do this evening. Assuming that Lord Langley is correct, shall I call for you at ten o'clock? It might be better to leave a little time for the wheels of bureaucracy to align in our favour."

Tabitha agreed. As Isabella turned to leave, Tabitha stopped her. "Thank you," she said simply. "You are under no obligation to help us as you are."

"Is Wolf innocent?" Isabella asked with a smile.

"Well, of course!"

"Then the obligation is self-evident. I will see you tomorrow." And with that, she left Tabitha and Wolf alone.

As they watched the door to the suite close behind her, Wolf observed, "She is a fascinating young woman. Just fascinating."

Tabitha agreed. Still, she made an observation that, once it left her lips, sounded rather waspish even to her ear. "How on earth did someone like Isabella end up friends with Lady Archibald?"

Wolf made no reply; he recognised there was no right answer to such a question. Instead, he moved over to where his wife was sitting, gently pulling her out of the armchair and into his arms. Bending his head to hers, he brushed Tabitha's lips gently.

Pushing gently away from the embrace, she asked, "Is that response supposed to assure me that I have nothing to worry about?"

His hand at the back of her head, Wolf gently pulled her back towards him. "Do you truly believe you have anything to worry about?"

Tabitha sighed. Of course she didn't. She knew that. More importantly, she knew how truly and deeply Wolf loved her. Dr Pauls had warned that expectant mothers sometimes become "overwrought", "melancholic", or "unusually sensitive", as he put it. Was that what this was?

Recently, she had begun to notice the physical changes happening to her body. While Wolf had assured her that she'd never looked more beautiful to him, there were moments when Tabitha felt anything but that.

There was no doubt that her stays no longer met neatly at the waist, her bodice required discreet adjustment, and her gloves fit too tightly across the fingers. When she looked at her reflection, she saw that the fine angles of her face had softened, and what had been a trim, confident figure now seemed rounder and unfamiliar. Ginny insisted she looked radiant, but Tabitha couldn't see it. There was a heaviness to her step and a faint flush to her cheeks that, in her view, suggested not radiancy but a body that almost appeared matronly.

Despite knowing she should, Tabitha felt unable to tell Wolf any of this, mainly because she despised herself for harbouring such feelings. All she had wanted for so many years was to have a child. Now she was, and yet she dared to be consumed with such ridiculous vanity.

The worst part was that, as much as such thoughts had crossed her mind before, it wasn't until she was faced with Arlene and her perfect, svelte beauty that Tabitha had truly felt these insecurities about her own appearance. She had been so lost in these thoughts that Tabitha hadn't realised how much time had passed since Wolf had posed the question to her.

Now, he pulled away from the embrace, held her at arm's length, and repeated, "Do you think you have anything to worry about, Tabitha?"

"No! Of course not!" she assured him, yet her tone suggested that Tabitha wasn't as certain as she wished her words to suggest. "I cannot explain why I feel this way," she admitted.

Apart from the physical changes to her body and her uncertainty about how Wolf might truly feel about them, there was the matter of their physical intimacy. Prior to her awareness of the child growing in her womb, she had delighted in Wolf's touch. When they were alone in their bedchamber, Tabitha had often been the one to seek her husband out in a way that had made her blush at first.

However, during Dr Pauls's first visit to the mother-to-be, he had warned that marital intimacy should be deferred for the duration of the pregnancy. He made it clear that, while this was usually his counsel, he was emphasising its importance now, given Tabitha's history of losing babies.

Whatever Tabitha's inclination might have been towards heeding this advice, Wolf had taken it very much to heart. Tabitha loved him for his desire to care for her and their unborn child, but she also felt a slight ache of loss. Their intimacy had always been as natural as breathing, but now there was an invisible line neither of them crossed. Wolf would kiss her gently, touch her cheek, and that was all. She couldn't deny that there were nights when she missed the quiet certainty of belonging wholly to him.

If Wolf had sensed any of this, he'd said nothing up to that point.

Now, he groped his way towards the words that would comfort her. "We will have a long lifetime together, Tabitha. These few months might have their challenges, but it will all be worth it when we hold our child. Even though I cannot express my love for you in every way I would like at the moment, you should not doubt that I have never loved you more. I need to know that you believe that."

The almost pain-stricken expression that crossed his face as he said this was all Tabitha needed to see.

Cupping his cheek in her hand, she said, "I do believe it, my love. And I am sorry if I caused you to doubt it for one moment."

CHAPTER 17

L angley, Tabitha, Wolf, and the dowager met in the hotel restaurant for breakfast the following morning.

"Were you able to get the information, Mama?" Tabitha asked as they sat down.

"What do you think, Tabitha? Do I strike you as someone who volunteers for a mission and then fails to complete it?"

"Well, you did not come by our suite last night, and so we wondered, that is all," Tabitha replied, wondering why she had to defend the question.

"After I had extracted all that I needed from Captain Forth, I felt quite peckish. Mr Bear kindly offered to escort me to a nearby public house for some refreshments."

Everyone stared at her. While it had long been evident that there were things about Bear the dowager appreciated, not the least of which was that he terrified people, the idea of just the two of them in a tavern, breaking bread together, was quite extraordinary.

It quickly became evident that the dowager had anticipated and relished their surprise.

Continuing as if nothing was out of the ordinary about the situation, the dowager said, "He found us a place with quite excellent pies and small beer."

Tabitha wanted to ask what the two of them had found to talk about during an entire meal. However, she knew such a question would only be used against her. From the look on the dowager's face, she seemed quite disappointed that no further challenge was forthcoming.

When it became clear that no one would take the bait, the dowager reached into her reticule and pulled out a folded piece of paper, which she unfolded with a theatrical flourish.

Still, no one said anything. Finally, after smoothing out the creases, the dowager asked petulantly, "Well, do you not want to know what I discovered?"

Doing his best to suppress a sigh, Wolf asked, "Lady Pembroke, what information do you have for us?"

"It appears that Graham Smithers is residing in this hotel. Felix Dubois and Gustaf Freund, as Miss Hartwell predicted, are representatives of the automobile companies and are staying in boarding houses. Dubois drives for Peugeot and Freund for Benz. Apparently, Mr Ernest Wilcox is also staying in a seafront boarding house. Major James Asher resides in Brighton. Given this, he is perhaps the least important to talk to immediately given that, presumably, he will not be in a rush to return home." The dowager relayed all this with a great air of self-satisfaction; she felt she had excelled in delivering the required information.

As almost an afterthought, she added, "The mechanics, meanwhile, are lodged in a couple of small inns near the station. It seems that the deceased's mechanic, the rude Duval fellow, is staying near Preston Park. I have the various addresses."

Wolf took the list and examined it. "Well, I will leave a note for Mr Smithers, requesting a meeting. That is at least one thing I can handle from captivity. For the rest, I think we should divide and conquer. Langley, would you mind accompanying Miss Hartwell?"

Of course, Langley had, as ever, been discreetly efficient. Before coming down to breakfast, he had spoken on the telephone with the Chief Constable of the Brighton Constabulary, who had already received an earlier call from Whitehall. Backed into a corner, the chief constable had granted permission, albeit reluctantly, for Miss Hartwell to inspect the De Dion. He'd sent a note to the hotel on letterhead explaining that Miss Hartwell was allowed to view the late Mr Havers's motor-car "for purposes of mechanical clarification."

Now, explaining this, Langley added, "While I received approval for Miss Hartwell to inspect the car this morning, you are right to suggest that I accompany her just in case she faces any stalling from the Brighton Constabulary." Langley had also sent a note to Mr Pritchard asking him to join them. He felt it was important that whatever Isabella discovered be verified by the police expert.

Nodding his thanks, Wolf suggested that Tabitha and the Dowager take Bear and visit the drivers who were not staying at The Grand.

He could see that the dowager was about to protest, probably claiming she did not need Bear's protection. Before she could speak, Wolf said, "One of these men is likely a killer. It can only be for the good if Bear accompanies you." Even the dowager had no retort to this, and so said nothing more.

With a plan in place, the group finished their breakfast quickly; this was not the time for a leisurely meal.

Isabella had arrived promptly. Langley climbed into the carriage and outlined the plan. He was already very impressed with the no-nonsense attitude of the American, and that admiration only grew as she explained what she intended to look for.

It wasn't long before they found themselves in the yard behind the police stables, where the De Dion-Bouton Vis-à-vis stood beneath a tarpaulin, its brass fittings already beginning to be dulled by the salt air. Mr Pritchard was waiting for them along with a police constable.

As Isabella and Langley greeted Pritchard, Detective Inspector Maguire hurried into the yard, looking rather flustered.

"It would have been nice if I'd been informed about this little circus and hadn't had to hear it from one of my constables as an aside at the last minute," he grumbled.

Langley muttered an apology, but Maguire didn't seem placated. "Smith," he barked at the constable, "uncover the motor-car so we can get this over with and I can get back to actual work."

The constable moved over to the De Dion, lifted the tarpaulin, and stepped back, clearly wary of the machine. The vehicle's wheels were covered in chalk and grit, and one lamp was cracked.

Mr Pritchard took a small tool from his pocket and carefully opened the bonnet catch. "The police have been careful not to disturb the mechanism," he said. "I have examined it briefly, though I confess this morning's light will make it easier to see than it was Sunday evening."

Isabella had already removed her gloves. "If you do not object, sir, I should like to have a closer look."

Whatever opinions Bernard Pritchard had about a woman, and a young American one at that, daring to second-guess his professional opinion, were entirely unknowable; the man's face was a mask of inscrutability worthy of the most professional of Mayfair butlers.

He hesitated only briefly before stepping aside with a gentle warning. "Be my guest, Miss Hartwell. However, nothing can be touched."

Isabella leaned in, examining the engine's narrow fittings and the brass oil-feed housing. "These are fine pieces of work," she murmured.

Pritchard bent beside her. "Hmm. See here, where the corners have been bruised. Someone's had at it with the wrong tool. As I said at the inquest, I believe it was a Whitworth spanner."

Isabella shook her head at once. "Not Whitworth, Mr Pritchard. Look again. Those jaws are too broad; they'd have slipped before biting. Look at these marks; the flats are pinched inward, not rounded out. Whoever turned this used a thinner key, the kind the Benz mechanics favour. See how clean the edges are, almost scored?"

He looked again, surprised, then let out a low whistle. "You may be right. That's no British tool mark."

"Nor a French one," Isabella said quietly. "The De Dion wrenches are broader still. Whoever adjusted this screw intended it to look fine, but it would fail over time. They left the oil feed too far open; it would run thin, starve the bearings, and seize the engine eventually."

Langley's brows drew together. "But there is no doubt it was deliberate?"

"Without question," Isabella replied. She pulled on her gloves again, her expression sharp. "As Mr Pritchard testified, there is no doubt that someone meddled with this machine knowing it would stop upon the road. Where he was incorrect was in his assumption that the tool used was a Whitworth spanner of the sort that Lord Pembroke has in his kit."

Pritchard slowly straightened himself. Addressing Detective Inspector Maguire, he explained, "I will be amending my report. It seems I was mistaken in my belief about the tool used to tamper with this motor-car. This young lady is entirely correct."

As he said this, Pritchard inclined his head in Isabella's direction in a show of respect. "I am always willing to admit an error or oversight, and that is very much the case here. I said at the inquest it was a Whitworth. But Miss Hartwell is correct; these marks are too sharp by half. They weren't caused by a British spanner. The spanner used was undoubtedly a narrow-jawed, hardened type that produced sharp, pinched scoring, and was likely German."

If Maguire had been grumpy before the inspection began, now he looked as if he had been forced to swallow something very unpleasant tasting.

He pursed his lips for a moment, considering his response. Finally, Maguire replied, "If you believe this will be absolution for Lord Pembroke, you are wrong. He still has motive and opportunity, and his spanner was found at the scene with blood on it. Perhaps Lord Pembroke did not tamper with the victim's car and instead came upon him, at which point they picked back up the argument from earlier in the day. Lord Pembroke took out his spanner, intending to offer help to Havers, but then, incensed at the man's words, he struck and killed him with it."

When he had finished, Maguire looked around at the gathered group, challenging anyone to dispute the tidy version of events he had laid out. No one did.

CHAPTER 18

While the day promised to be less rainy and dreary than the one before, it was definitely chillier. Tabitha snuggled into the fur collar of her thick, woollen coat and was grateful the hotel carriage had been available for their use, so they didn't have to walk along the seafront.

The wind off the Channel was bracing as it rattled the windowpanes of the buildings facing the water. The cries of gulls carried over the clipped rhythm of the horse's hooves as the carriage moved down Marine Parade

"Boarding houses," the Dowager observed, regarding the neat rows of stucco facades as though they were a personal affront. "The view may be identical to that from The Grand, but I daresay the aroma of fried kippers and the cheap curtains quite ruin the effect."

"Not everyone is as fortunate as we are and can stay in a luxury hotel," Tabitha replied mildly. Sometimes she wondered if the dowager said these things merely to provoke a reaction.

Bear, seated opposite them, kept his expression carefully neutral. As someone who had grown up without privilege or wealth, he likely harboured a view about the dowager's blatant snobbery. However, he had long ago learned that silence was the surest way to survive a journey in her company.

The carriage stopped in front of a narrow building with a peeling sign that read *The Sea View Boarding House*. Its bow windows jutted over the street, and lace curtains fluttered behind the glass. A young maid in a rather worn calico apron appeared in the doorway, wiping her hands on her skirt before sweeping the steps.

As the group descended from the carriage, the maid caught sight of Bear and her eyes widened in terror. That fear visibly increased when it became clear that the enormous man was approaching the steps she was sweeping.

During the journey to the house, Tabitha reflected on whether to suggest that Bear remain in the carriage; she knew the effect he usually had on strangers. However, she was mindful of Wolf's words; one of the people they would speak to that morning was a killer. And while Ernest Wilcox was simply the person who found the body, Tabitha was still sufficiently shaken from her ordeal in Salisbury to appreciate Bear's presence.

Tabitha asked the maid if they would find an Ernest Wilcox inside, and the young girl merely nodded, never taking her eyes off Bear. Tabitha wondered whether to walk into the house, but realised she didn't know where to start looking for Mr Wilcox. Instead, she asked the maid to show them where they might find the lodger. Again, the girl said nothing and nodded again.

Inside the house, the narrow hall, wallpapered in a rather garish floral print, was lined with framed seascapes. A barometer hung beside the hatstand, its needle trembling between "Change" and "Rain."

The dowager scanned the hallway with a look of distaste on her face. While she had certainly visited far scruffier establishments in the time she'd been forcing herself on Tabitha and Wolf's investigations, there was something more offensive to her sensibilities about pretension than poverty. Shabbiness, at least, was at least honest; this was contrived self-importance in cheap wallcoverings and imitation mahogany.

The maid led them upstairs to the first floor, where a door stood ajar. At the maid's timid knock, a man's voice within called, "Come in."

From the look of surprise on his face, it seemed that Ernest Wilcox, assuming this was him, was bemused as to why the elegant young woman, accompanied by a rather severe-looking older woman and a giant of a man, might be at his door.

Ernest Wilcox rose from beside a small writing desk and bowed slightly. He was an unassuming man, of below-average height and a compact build, with a hairline that had receded enough to make him look older than his years. His clothes were neat enough, but Tabitha noticed slight fraying on his cuffs. Nothing about the man or where he was staying suggested he had access to the money required to own a motor-car. Was he also a representative of one of the motor-car companies?

"Do excuse the interruption, Mr Wilcox," Tabitha said from the doorway. "I am the Countess of Pembroke, and this is the dowager countess."

Wilcox's look of confusion lifted. "Ah yes, of course, I thought I recognised you, but couldn't imagine why. Now I realise that I saw you both at the inquest."

"You were there?" Tabitha asked. Given that the man's response had been read at the inquest, she assumed he hadn't been in attendance.

"I was. The police said my written statement would suffice and, since I don't enjoy public speaking, I was happy to be spared that."

As he said this, Wilcox realised his visitors were still standing in his doorway. With many apologies, he invited them into the room. The room was neat but modest: a narrow bed, a washstand with a cracked jug, and a single window overlooking the grey expanse of sea. Besides the chair he'd been sitting in, there was also an armchair by the window, and then the bed.

Wilcox offered Tabitha his chair, moved the armchair slightly so the dowager could sit there, and then perched on the edge of his bed. Bear had remained standing, silently in the doorway. Now, he moved slightly into the room to close the door, and then stood as if guarding it. Every so often, Wilcox would throw him a nervous glance.

"How can I be of assistance?" Wilcox asked after the two women had taken their seats. "I was, of course, very sorry to hear that the inquest didn't entirely clear Lord Pembroke's name. Though I'm sure that he will be exonerated eventually." His manner was grave, unassuming, and entirely credible.

Tabitha watched him closely as he spoke: he had the deliberate enunciation of a man eager to be taken seriously. Yet, while he appeared to be trying to hide it, she was sure she detected a hint of a regional accent beneath the careful diction.

"Thank you for your kind words, Mr Wilcox. I must admit that this has all been a dreadful shock." Tabitha had decided to adopt the persona of the worried wife, at her wits' end about how to help her husband. Of course, she hadn't mentioned this on the drive over, and so it was highly likely that the dowager would put paid to this tactic soon enough. Even so, Tabitha decided there was no reason to reveal that they were conducting their own investigation; this wouldn't be a conclusion most men would jump to.

"Mr Wilcox, since you were the one to find poor Mr Havers's body, I thought there might be a minor detail you recall that could assist my husband's case. As you can imagine, I am utterly distraught." As she spoke, Tabitha wondered if Wilcox might question how she knew his whereabouts. Luckily, he did not.

Falling into the role of knight-errant to her damsel in distress as Tabitha had hoped, Wilcox replied, "It was a great shock, milady. I'd sooner mend a dozen broken axles than find one man lying dead upon the road. I came round the bend by Clayton Hill and saw the car standing half across the verge. I didn't realise it was Havers at first, and merely thought a driver had stopped to make an adjustment. I called out with an offer of assistance, but when there was no reply, I got out of my car and walked around to investigate. Then I saw..."

He paused, shaking his head. "Well, it was a sight I shall not forget in a hurry. Even though it seemed unlikely that he had survived such a blow, I checked for a pulse, which I could not find."

Something in his statement caught Tabitha's attention. "So, you knew Mr Havers?"

Wilcox started. "Did I say that?"

"Well, you said that you had not realised it was Havers at first, which implied you eventually recognised who it was. That suggests you knew him."

"I wouldn't say I knew the man. I recognised him. Motoring circles are quite small; eventually, we form a passing acquaintance. That's all."

Looking around the clean, but rather shabby room, the dowager asked in a sceptical tone, "Do you own the vehicle in which you drove down to Brighton?"

Wilcox smiled faintly. "I do not. I test and deliver cars for Humber, a firm in Coventry, and occasionally drive in events when the owner cannot.

Sunday's run was one such occasion. The driver became ill the evening before, and I was asked to take his place. It seems he'd promised the company that the motor-car would be involved, and they were keen that it still would be."

It was a reasonable enough explanation. Indeed, as Isabella had explained, these events were essential promotions in the highly competitive new motoring industry.

Tabitha asked, "You said you knew of Mr Havers before the run? Were you aware of any enemies he might have had?"

Wilcox chuckled. "From the little I knew of Havers, to speak with him was to be his enemy. Men in our trade are opinionated, Lady Pembroke. We each believe our make superior and so there is often debate. But Tommy Havers always seemed ready for battle."

Tabitha was tempted to point out that such an observation seemed to arise from more than the casual acquaintance Wilcox claimed. However, having seen firsthand how Havers could provoke people, perhaps that wasn't the case here.

Instead, she turned the topic back to the day of the race. "You came across the body and then reported the discovery at once?"

"I did, milady. I stopped a passing cart and asked the driver to go to Brighton for the police. Then I stayed until they arrived. Didn't seem right to leave him lying there alone."

"A very proper sentiment," the dowager said.

"Did you happen to touch the vehicle?" Tabitha asked.

"Only to check that the engine was off. The motor-car had stopped cleanly, as if seized. The poor fellow must have been trying to free the bearings when..." Wilcox let the sentence trail away, shaking his head again.

"I assume other drivers passed while you were waiting," Tabitha said.

"They did. However, given that the body couldn't be seen from the road, I just waved them on and said there wasn't an issue."

Tabitha considered this answer. "Why did you do that?"

"I knew enough to realise that the scene had to be as uncontaminated as possible for when the police arrived. Other drivers stomping all over, and perhaps even touching the body, would not have been helpful."

This was a sensible reply, and it was difficult to find anything to criticise in Wilcox's words.

It took the dowager to comment on what Tabitha had sensed but could not articulate clearly. "Mr Wilcox, you seem remarkably composed for one who has recently witnessed a violent death."

"I've seen accidents before, Lady Pembroke. When engines are untested, mishaps occur. One grows philosophical."

"I can imagine," the dowager said before continuing in a world-weary tone, "which begs the question why one would choose contraptions that explode or stop dead at whim to begin with."

Wilcox smiled politely. "Progress always begins with discomfort, your ladyship. Steam locomotion was once considered folly."

The dowager's eyebrows rose, but she kept her comments to herself; thankfully.

Tabitha hid a small smile. Wilcox's patience, she thought, was admirable. He met the dowager's provocations with the courtesy of a man used to being condescended to.

Suddenly, the dowager rose, seemingly bored by the lack of drama in the conversation. "Well, we have taken enough of this gentleman's time. Mr Wilcox, I trust you will convey any further recollections to the police."

"Of course, your ladyship. Anything that may help."

Bear opened the door for them. Wilcox bowed slightly, and Tabitha inclined her head in response.

Outside, the wind had picked up. The sea, pewter-coloured beneath the now greying sky, heaved against the pebbled beach. The dowager pulled her veil over her hat and said she longed for a cup of tea. Tabitha could only agree with her. Yet they had other calls to make before they returned to the hotel. She hoped that at least one man they called on might offer some refreshments.

CHAPTER 19

E ven though Detective Inspector Maguire had not stated that Wolf shouldn't move freely around the hotel, he still felt uncomfortable when he left the suite. The constable assigned to watch him never said a word, but Wolf sensed the man's eyes tracking him as he walked through the lobby to the restaurant for breakfast and then to the reception. Rationally, he knew this was a much better option than being confined in a jail cell. Still, something about the situation made him feel as if he must be guilty of something, even though he wasn't.

"I would like to leave a message for a guest, Mr Graham Smithers," Wolf informed the hotel clerk.

The clerk gestured across the elegant, marble lobby floor. "The gentleman in question is standing over there, by the hearth."

Wolf watched as the man's gaze shifted. A slender figure stood with his back slightly turned, speaking to another man seated in front of the fireplace. Smithers had the posture of a man of the world, entirely at ease with himself and his place in the world: one hand resting on a silver-topped cane, his head inclined as if listening intently to his companion and not missing a word.

Smithers's three-piece suit of grey-green tweed was tailored closely at the waist. A pale linen shirt, with a freshly starched collar, showed above the waistcoat, and a wine-coloured silk cravat shimmered beneath a pearl pin at his throat. The hand not resting on the cane held a cut-glass crystal tumbler repeatedly raised to his lips. Observing this, Wolf noted that it was not long after ten o'clock in the morning.

The firelight glinted on the polished toe of Smithers's boots and on the slim gold chain of his watch. He stood with effortless grace, smiling thinly now and then at some remark from the seated gentleman, but never fully engaging in laughter. An air of self-satisfaction hovered about the man.

Smithers appeared exactly as a successful man should: comfortable, urbane, and at ease, regardless of his surroundings. However, to Wolf's eye, something in his posture, too alert and rehearsed, hinted that beneath the calm exterior, he was waiting for someone to notice the illusion, as though aware he was the emperor in new clothes.

Wolf crossed to where Smithers was standing and stopped at a polite distance.

"Mr Smithers?" he asked politely.

Smithers turned at once, all cordial surprise. "Indeed. My apologies, sir. You have the advantage here." Wolf introduced himself.

"Lord Pembroke! May I offer my congratulations. Your Daimler behaved handsomely. I had the privilege of inspecting it at the finish."

"My thanks," Wolf said. "How was the drive for you?"

"Good enough, good enough," Smithers said with a rueful smile. "The Panhard dislikes the Downs. A Parisian sensibility. Give it a boulevard and it will sing. Hills, less so."

"You made excellent time in the end."

"So they told me. I confess I lost the clock somewhere near Pyecombe."

"Do you have a moment? I would be grateful for a word in private," Wolf asked.

"Of course," Smithers said at once. "Anything for a fellow driver. Where shall we go? I am lodged here, but my room is small and looks at a wall."

"My suite is a few floors up," Wolf said. "If that suits you."

"Lead the way."

The lift was in use, so Wolf took the stairs. Smithers followed him. On the second landing, a chambermaid curtsied and slipped past, carrying a folded tablecloth. Wolf caught the leer Smithers aimed at the young woman.

Reaching his suite, Wolf opened the door to the room and invited Smithers into the sitting room.

His guest looked appreciatively around. "Very nice! I was rather too late booking a room; otherwise, I would have been in one of these." Given that Wolf himself only entered the run relatively late, he wondered how true that statement was. He'd had no trouble securing appropriately lavish rooms for everyone in their party.

"Will you take something?" Wolf asked. "Tea, coffee?"

"I'll take a brandy," Smithers replied, "if you will not think me a barbarian at this hour." Since he'd already been drinking when Wolf approached him, this seemed a statement that didn't need a reply.

Wolf poured two glasses; he found it far too early for alcohol, but he wanted the other man to feel at ease. He handed Smithers a glass, and they took their seats.

Deciding to start off casually, Wolf asked how Smithers got interested in motor-cars.

"My father was Sir Alfred Smithers of Chislehurst," Smithers said easily, swirling the brandy in his glass. "You may know the place, a modest estate, though pleasant enough. I'm the younger son, so naturally the title went to my brother. I've had to make my own way, which is no bad thing. My mother was a Beauchamp, distant cousin to the baronet of Warwickshire."

It was unclear why Smithers threw this last sentence in unless it was merely to attempt to impress Wolf. It didn't, but he tried to keep his expression blank.

The man continued, "I've always been interested in the latest inventions, and motor-cars are one of the more interesting, and potentially revolutionary ones to come along in some time. It made sense for me to take the opportunity to invest in a British firm seeking to manufacture motor-car engines under French licence. Our consortium is negotiating to produce licensed Panhard-type engines domestically to avoid import costs. I've always had a knack for industry, I suppose; my father always said the age belonged to men who built rather than merely inherited.

Still, one cannot quite shake the habits of breeding, can one, Lord Pembroke?"

Wolf wasn't sure what answer to make to this, and so just nodded.

"How can I be of assistance, milord? Is this about the sad business on the road?" he asked. "I regret I can be of little help."

"Did you see Havers stopped by the side of the road?" Wolf asked.

"Well, I observed a motor-car pulled over with the bonnet up. I didn't see the driver. I called out, got no reply, and so drove on. One grows cautious in such situations."

"Cautious?" Wolf repeated.

Smithers offered a mild smile. "When a man is up to his elbows in a mechanical issue and in a bad temper because of it, he prefers not to be instructed by a stranger. Besides, three hands near an engine make a tangle. If a man wants assistance, he will say so. I assumed the driver heard me and chose not to call out for help."

Wolf asked, "Have you told this to the police?"

"No one has asked yet. However, I am very ready to give such a statement."

"Excellent," Wolf replied, while wondering why Smithers hadn't volunteered this information to the police unasked. "If you will indulge me, please describe how your day went. Begin at the start. I find I sort my own thoughts best by rehearsing the order of events, and another man's memory sometimes improves mine."

"By all means," Smithers said, pleasantly, as if the request was nothing more than a fellow driver wishing to reminisce. "We were mustered with brief ceremony. I was not far behind Havers, I believe."

Wolf said nothing to this. Smithers continued.

"The start was quite orderly. I kept to ten in town, both for appearances and because of the law. The first proper breath of fresh air on the road came after Streatham, as it always does. I kept to a steady pace. If you will forgive my pride, the Panhard runs smoothly at a dozen miles per hour and can be nudged to fifteen when the surface is good. Near Croydon, I saw a little gem of a De Dion dart past a couple of slower vehicles, its driver very proud. Havers, of course."

"Of course."

"Just outside Croydon, we had all that halfway nonsense: bunting, an officious steward, and the local boys shouting themselves hoarse. After that, the road emptied out and my goals simplified: I watched the road ahead, listened for changes in the engine, and hoped my legs would not cramp."

Smithers continued, "After Crawley, the road quieted further. Many had fallen behind. I kept my pace and my temper, which is the only way to arrive anywhere in one piece. Just north of Patcham came the episode I mentioned. The De Dion bonnet up, and no one in sight, so I drove on. I assumed Havers had gone to fetch water or was working beneath it. Thereafter, there was nothing but the sea, the wind, and the road. I reached the park in good time." This was said calmly, but somewhat tersely, as if Smithers were tired of the interrogation.

"Mr Smithers," Wolf said quietly, "I find myself under an obligation to know who was on that road and where they were. You were close behind. I must establish the order in which the vehicles approached Clayton Hill as well as possible."

"I understand," Smithers replied after taking another sip of brandy. "Prudence is only sensible. You have my word that I saw nothing of Mr Havers after Crawley."

"I have one last question, Mr Smithers; you recognised Mr Havers's car during the run. How well did you know him?"

In that moment, Wolf could tell that Graham Smithers was about to lie to him. Where his face had been quite open, even cheerful so far, an expression came over it that was quite different; his eyes narrowed a little and his mouth became tense.

Then, when he spoke, Smithers's voice sounded almost strangled. "Barely knew the man. Of course, motoring circles are small and so we all have a passing acquaintance with each other, but nothing more than that in this case."

Wolf stood. He saw no reason to call out the deceit, at least for now. "I will not take more of your morning. Thank you for the courtesy. If Detective Inspector Maguire requests it of you, you will oblige him with a statement."

"At once," Smithers said. He rose, took his cane, and placed the empty glass on the tray. "I hope, for all our sakes, that this sad affair proves simpler than it presently seems."

Wolf showed him to the door, and they shook hands.

When the door had closed, Wolf paused for a moment without moving. Everything about Smithers seemed just a little overly polished, from his boots to his answers. He wanted to learn more about the man before blindly accepting his version of events. In particular, he wanted to understand what Smithers's relationship was to Thomas Havers. He wondered how best to discover that. Isabella had said she recognised the man's name. Perhaps she would have some ideas about where best to start.

Just as he thought this, there was a knock at the door. Wolf assumed it was Smithers and that the man must have remembered something else. He was surprised to find Lady Archibald standing there, looking as beautiful and elegant as she ever had.

"Isabella mentioned that you would be here alone this morning, so I thought I would come and keep you company and attempt to lift your spirits," Arlene purred. Before Wolf had time to reply, she entered the suite and sat in one of the armchairs.

Glancing at Havers's empty glass and Wolf's untouched brandy, she smiled and said, "While it is rather early, I cannot possibly let you drown your sorrows alone."

CHAPTER 20

No sooner had the two women and Bear climbed back into the carriage than the dowager cast an experienced eye over Tabitha and said, "My dear, you looked quite spent."

Tabitha wanted to deny it. After all, they had made only one call so far that morning. Yet, she knew it would be pointless. While the utter exhaustion she had felt in the first months of expecting had mostly disappeared recently, she had to admit that she didn't have the energy she once did.

Perhaps the dowager noticed this conflict playing across Tabitha's face because she said with surprising gentleness, "Let us return to the hotel. Surely Miss Hartwell will finish her inspection shortly, and perhaps that will inform us of whom we should prioritise speaking with next."

Maybe it was a result of having such thoughtfulness and concern coming from such an unexpected source that made Tabitha accept the suggestion.

Fifteen minutes later, they were back at the hotel. The dowager and Bear had returned to their rooms to shed their outerwear. Given the time, meeting down in the restaurant for an early luncheon made sense.

When she approached the door to her suite, Tabitha realised how relieved she was that the dowager had pressed her to return and rest. She looked forward to a few minutes alone with Wolf before they went down to the restaurant. Those plans were shattered as she entered the room and found Wolf engaged in a cosy conversation with Lady Archibald.

It seemed that Tabitha was not the only one unpleasantly surprised. "Lady Pembroke, you are back so soon. I was led to believe you would be out all morning." Arlene didn't even attempt to mask her irritation.

Removing her hat and gloves, Tabitha noticed the glasses of brandy and found herself unable to reply with anything approaching politeness. "And so, knowing that, you felt it was appropriate to call on my husband?"

As soon as she said the words, Tabitha realised the mistake she'd made; the look that crossed Arlene's face spoke volumes about the trap Tabitha had stepped into.

Wolf had leapt up as soon as his wife entered. Now, noticing how tired she looked, he approached Tabitha and asked in a concerned voice, "Is everything alright, my love?"

While she appreciated the care and love in Wolf's tone, Tabitha didn't appreciate the situation she found him in. However, she realised that snapping at Wolf would further play into the scheming Lady Archibald's hands.

Trying to modulate her tone to avoid revealing her irritation, Tabitha replied, "Mama suggested it might be best to wait and hear what Miss Hartwell has discovered before questioning the other drivers." While that was not precisely what the dowager had said, Tabitha thought it was a reasonable approximation, given the circumstances. Indeed, if Wolf was inclined to doubt that he was being told the full story, he was sharp enough to realise that Tabitha wouldn't thank him for pressing the issue in front of Arlene.

Wolf knew there was only one way to salvage the situation; he turned to face Arlene. "Lady Archibald, would you excuse us? My wife and I need to discuss her findings."

If Wolf hoped that Arlene wouldn't need any further encouragement to leave, he was to be disappointed.

Instead, she took another sip of her brandy and replied, "Oh, don't mind me. I took a hackney cab here because Isabella has my carriage, so it just makes sense for me to wait for her. And anyway, I am curious to hear her findings."

Tabitha realised her husband was in a difficult predicament; there was no doubt that Lady Archibald had been, at least indirectly, helpful since he had been named the primary suspect in Havers's murder. Furthermore, he was a gentleman and, as such, could hardly order her from the room.

Wolf couldn't dismiss her, but Tabitha could. "Lady Archibald, I apologise, but I must echo my husband's request. I find that I am rather weary and need to rest in order to throw myself back into the fray of the investigation this afternoon. I am sure that the hotel porter will be able to call you another hackney cab."

The two women stared at each other; Tabitha refused to be the first to break eye contact.

Finally, Arlene set her glass on the small side table next to her chair, straightened up, and with a slight defiant shake of her head, declared, "Well, as it happens, I really should be going. I have a luncheon date with Lady Campbell and don't want to miss the chance to catch her up on *all* the latest gossip."

The manner in which she had emphasised that last statement gave Wolf enough pause that he felt compelled to say, "Arlene, I would ask that you keep to yourself anything you know about the attempts to clear my name. I do not want anything getting back to the police until we are sure of our facts."

Arlene approached him and took one of his hands in hers. "Do not fear, Wolf. I would never gossip about *you* and *your* situation." And with that, she flounced out of the room.

When the door was safely shut behind her, Wolf faced Tabitha with sincere contrition. "I am so sorry. I should never have let her in. But..." his words trailed off as he struggled to find a way to explain himself.

As irritated as Tabitha was, Wolf wasn't the one who had done anything wrong. "I know. While I do not claim to understand exactly what her aim is, there is no doubt that Lady Archibald enjoys being at the centre of melodrama. There is also no doubt that she enjoys riling me up, and I played into her hands just now. I should know better than that."

Wolf had no words, so he took his wife in his arms and kissed her hair. Finally, he found the words she needed to hear. "She means nothing to me and has not for many years. I know this stings Arlene, and so, she feels a childish need to try to prove she still has some power over me.

However, she does not, and I would choose you over her a thousand times over."

While she might have claimed there was no need to say these words, Tabitha couldn't deny that they made her feel better.

When she didn't answer immediately, Wolf said, "I will send her a note saying that all communication between us must cease immediately."

Tabitha pulled away from his embrace. "No. There is no need. More than that, it will complicate our efforts to prove your innocence. Isabella has been incredibly helpful and is staying with Lady Archibald and making use of her carriage. Assuaging my perhaps excessive sensitivity about the woman is not worth risking your freedom."

Despite her words, Tabitha could tell that Wolf wasn't entirely convinced. Moving back into his arms, she looked up into his kind, handsome face, and said with a sincerity he couldn't deny, "I may not trust Lady Archibald, but I do trust you. Completely."

They might have stayed there, entwined for longer, if there hadn't been a knock on the door. Wolf went to open it and discovered Isabella and Langley, returned from their inspection of the De Dion.

"We have news!" Isabella announced before she had even taken off her coat.

"Mama and Bear returned to their rooms, and we were planning to go downstairs for an early luncheon, but perhaps it is better and more discreet for us to order food up here again," Tabitha suggested. As she said this, she was reminded how parched she was for a cup of tea.

Wolf rang for the hall waiter, and they ordered food and pots of tea and coffee. He then went to inform Bear and the dowager of the change in plans.

Ten minutes later, they were all gathered in the suite, a promptly delivered tea tray on the table in front of them. When everyone was settled, Isabella shared her conclusion about the tampering done to Havers's car.

When she finished, Wolf leaned back in his chair and pondered the implications of her words. "Well, if nothing else, it is probably for the best that Tabitha and Lady Pembroke did not waste time interviewing Felix Dubois. If the spanner was German, then let us focus on Gustaf Freund for now," he said thoughtfully.

Isabella nodded in agreement. "Certainly, if we are trying to get to the bottom of who tampered with the De Dion, it makes far more sense that it was a German driver or mechanic, particularly if the rumours of Havers's double-dealing between the French and German car companies are true."

"Though," the dowager pointed out, "by the sound of it, the French would have a bone or two to pick with the man as well."

She had a point, but the group decided that, for the sake of simplicity, they would focus on the German driver and his mechanic.

After considering Isabella's news, Tabitha asked, "How precisely might the person who tampered with the car have managed to predict when the car would break down?"

"If anything, they might have expected it to happen earlier. If I had to guess, I'd say that whoever did this intended for the fuel to leak more quickly, but hadn't made the adjustment as severe as they'd intended."

"So," Tabitha continued, "they could not have predicted that the motor-car would fail in that particular spot. It might have happened anywhere. While it might make sense to drive behind Mr Havers until he was forced to stop and then kill him, it seems like a rather convoluted way to murder someone. And it is a plan quite prone to potential problems. What would have happened if the motor-car had broken down in the middle of a village or town? What if someone else was there helping when our would-be killer drove by?"

Wolf picked up the thread of her logic. "It does seem as if the killing and the tampering with the motor-car are two separate, probably unrelated events."

"The question is, will any of this matter to Detective Inspector Maguire?" Langley said. "Perhaps he can be persuaded that this was not premeditated murder by Wolf, but he is still the last person who saw him alive, as far as we know, and his spanner was the murder weapon."

The group considered Langley's words in silence. Unfortunately, his reasoning was impossible to refute. Finally, Tabitha gathered some of the blank, improvised notecards and noted down what Isabella had learned.

CHAPTER 21

Tabitha and the dowager relayed their conversation with Ernest Wilcox to the group. "My overall impression was of a man who is, what my mother would call, self-made, though she never means it as a compliment. I got the sense that Mr Wilcox does his best to disguise the fact. One almost feels he's ashamed of how far he had to come just to be where he is now," Tabitha observed.

Under normal circumstances, the dowager despised and mocked this kind of social striving and would have certainly made a snobbish comment. However, she despised Tabitha's mother, Lady Jameson, the Dowager Marchioness of Cambridgeshire, even more. Whether Tabitha had added in the comment about her mother to forestall the dowager's likely cutting remarks, it certainly had that effect.

"It's an odd industry, really," Isabella observed. "The world of the automobile feeds on privilege; only the wealthy can afford to play at it. Yet every advance comes from men with oil on their hands: mechanics, tinkers, inventors with grease beneath their nails. Half the manufacturers in Paris and Detroit began by mending bicycles or fashioning parts in borrowed workshops. The aristocrats may purchase the machines, but it is the industrialists who grow rich from them, rarely the inventors themselves."

Tabitha didn't say so aloud, but she wondered if it was any different from other inventions. Wasn't it always the case that those who laboured to create something new were seldom the ones to reap the greatest rewards?

The dowager's response was swift and perfectly in character: "Indeed, the lower orders invent the toys, and the upper ones make a spectacle of themselves playing with them." Just in case her point was ambiguous, she directed this statement at Wolf. It seemed as if she believed he had brought the accusations of being a murderer upon himself almost inevitably by his purchase of a motor-car.

Ignoring the dowager's mean-spirited comment, Tabitha reflected that the motor-car trade seemed an uneasy meeting of privilege and ambition. Could such tensions have played their part in Havers's death?

She caught sight of that morning's newspaper lying on the table in front of her, its headline proclaiming the run: *A triumph for British engineering*.

"It's extraordinary," Tabitha said, picking up the newspaper. "They speak of it as a triumph, yet a man was killed, and half the field seems not to have noticed his car by the side of the road and merely drove past. At least Wilcox stopped."

Langley leaned back. "Perhaps others merely thought he had stopped for adjustments. No one would imagine foul play on what was meant to be a parade of mechanical optimism and gentlemanly camaraderie."

Isabella shook her head. "A parade, yes, but how genuine the camaraderie is, well that's another matter, no matter what men may claim. Everyone called it a run, but it was a race in all but name. Every man who took part hoped to reach Brighton first, or at least not be last. These automobile companies have a lot at stake, and this run received a great deal of publicity. Sales and investments in companies may succeed or fail depending on how their representatives perform. When you have that kind of pride, and more importantly money, involved, men's willingness to lend helping hands tends to diminish."

Wolf had been gazing into the roaring fire as Isabella spoke. Now he looked up. "So, you are saying they simply drove past, choosing to ignore a fellow driver, potentially in distress?"

"I'm saying they saw what they wanted to see," Isabella replied.

"Engines fail; drivers tinker and curse and start again. I'm sure it happened a dozen times between London and Brighton. Unless someone was waving a white flag or bleeding in the road, no one would stop."

Tabitha frowned. "But surely a gentleman would at least slow down? After all, Wolf did."

"He did, and so did Mr Wilcox," Isabella said. "But remember, this run was a friendly motor down to Brighton in name, but for many, it would have felt far more adversarial; a motor-car halted by the roadside barely merits a glance unless it's blocking your way. In fact, such a motor-car is one less competitor to beat. A lot of money is at stake for whichever automobile companies come out on top."

The dowager gave a delicate sniff. "Well, if gentlemen insist on imitating tradesmen, they can hardly complain when they encounter tradesmen's misfortunes."

Wolf considered his conversation with Graham Smithers in the light of what Isabella had said. Did any of this explain the man's self-satisfied air?

He asked Isabella what she knew about the man. "I get the sense that he lied to me when he claimed to not know Havers beyond a vague acquaintance. I know that you had previously said the name sounded familiar, but nothing more. Has anything else come to you since then?"

Isabella shook her head. "However, I can send a telegram to someone who might know more. He's the friend who helped me attend the Automobile Club events."

"But he didn't take part in the run?" Bear asked.

"No. Colonel Markham is quite elderly, and his interest in automobiles is purely that of an observer. But he has been involved in the Club since its inception."

When it was clear she had piqued the group's interest, Isabella explained, "I first met Colonel Markham in New York three years ago. He was travelling through the States to study our engine patents and lecture on the progress of motoring in Europe. My father entertained him at dinner, mostly because the newspapers had described him as 'the apostle of mechanical locomotion,' which amused us all. He was terribly proper, of course, but once he began to speak about automobiles, he quite forgot his manners. We spent half the evening discussing ignition systems while everyone else fled to the drawing room. He's been kind enough to keep me informed ever since, and if anyone knows what's stirring within the Automobile Club, it will be him."

"Then send him a telegram right away," Tabitha requested.

"And see what he knows about all the drivers we are interested in."

Isabella agreed and immediately left to ask the hotel to send the telegram on her behalf.

As she closed the door to the suite behind her, Tabitha reflected on the immense help Isabella Hartwell was providing. While Lady Arlene Archibald continued to be a thorn in her side, never more so than that very afternoon, Tabitha couldn't be anything other than glad that she had taken part in the run. If she hadn't, it was unlikely they would have met Isabella, and she couldn't imagine how much harder it would be to prove Wolf's innocence without her.

"Even if we have, for now, dismissed the tampering as related to the murder, I believe it is worthwhile to interview the other drivers," Wolf told the group. "However, I also think the conversations will be more productive if Miss Hartwell is involved."

This was something that no one could dispute, nor did they try to. With her knowledge of the technology itself and her insights into the men who shaped the world of motoring, she had become an invaluable asset to the investigation.

"Then we should head out as soon as Isabella returns," Tabitha declared. "We do not know how much longer any of these drivers will agree to remain in Brighton, and cannot waste a moment."

Just then, there was a knock at the door. It was the hall waiter with their food.

"You are right, my love," Wolf said, addressing Tabitha. "However, waiting another thirty minutes so you can eat something will not make a difference."

"Indeed!" the dowager agreed. "I do not know about you, Tabitha, but I am ravenous. I refuse to set foot outside this suite until my hunger is assuaged."

Tabitha had been hoping to persuade the old woman that her presence was unnecessary for the afternoon's interviews. However, her comment left no doubt that she would not be excluded.

Wolf had reached the same conclusion, but added, "I insist that you allow Bear to accompany you once again." Tabitha saw no reason to object. It made sense to have a man with them, and although Langley commanded more respect in certain circles, there was no doubt that Bear was the more physically capable and intimidating.

However, this arrangement prompted a question from Langley: "Wolf, what would you have me do while they are gone? I feel useless just sitting around the hotel."

Wolf laughed bitterly. "I know exactly what you mean, my friend." Langley offered him a sympathetic smile. What else was there to do? Wolf thought about where Langley's talents lay. "While Isabella is hopeful that this Colonel Markham might be able to provide some motoring-related information about our suspects, it would be useful to have a clearer picture of who they are and their finances. You have more highly-placed government contacts than any of us, Langley. Can you see if you can find anything out?"

Langley stood, happy to be put to use. "I will start sending telegrams now."

Ten minutes later, Isabella returned, her task completed. Now, all that remained was for the group to eat a hurried meal, gather their outerwear, and depart. The carriage ride to the boarding house near the station, where Gustaf Freund was staying, wasn't far, and within five minutes, they pulled up outside.

CHAPTER 22

The boarding house was two streets away from the station, tucked behind the cab rank in a small terrace. The sounds of trains coming and going echoed beyond the brick arches. A bell-pull beside the door gave a jarringly loud clang when Bear tugged it. After a moment, a woman with reddened hands and a pinched mouth opened the door. It took her a moment to recover from the shock of seeing a group of toffs and a giant at her door, but then she steadied herself and bobbed a jerky curtsey.

"We are looking for one of your guests, a Gustaf Freund," Tabitha explained.

"You'll be wanting the Prussian sausage-eater then. He came in an hour ago, ma'am. Said not to bother him. Though, of course, I would for quality like yourselves," the woman added, anxious eyes flicking to Bear. Then, perhaps feeling she needed to explain her lack of patriotic discernment regarding her guests, she said, "He paid through the week. Keeps hisself to hisself, for all he's a foreigner."

The dowager drew herself up. "Spare us your chatter, woman. Take us to his room."

Following the landlady, the group climbed a narrow staircase carpeted with thin felt, the banister so tacky that the dowager chose to ascend unaided, even though she was wearing gloves. A kerosene lamp burned on the landing. The house's smells of boiled cabbage, rising damp, and an underlying lingering whiff of coal from the nearby trains were the building's capstone of unpleasantness.

Suddenly, from behind the door at the end of the landing came the scrape of a chair and a loud thump, then a short, strangled sound, abruptly cut off.

"Don't know what that can be. It's coming from Mr Freund's room," the landlady remarked in surprise.

Bear didn't hesitate. He covered the distance to the door in three quick strides and pounded with the side of his fist. "Freund! Open" up!"

There was no answer.

"Break the door down," the dowager commanded.

"You'll be paying for that if you do," the landlady complained. Bear ignored her and pressed his shoulder hard against the door. The latch tore free, and the cheap wood split easily. The door slammed inward against a washstand.

Bear had had the foresight to bring a revolver with him, and now he drew it and signalled that the women should stay well back on the landing as he entered the room. The first thing he noticed was that the window was open, with curtains flung wide and billowing in the wind. The next was that a man lay crumpled, half on the threadbare carpet, partly against the foot of the bed, his head at a terrible angle.

"Don't come any further," Bear called back, dropping to one knee by the body. He pressed his fingers to Freund's throat, then to the corner of the jaw, feeling for a pulse. "Warm," he muttered to himself. He eased the man's shoulder slightly, examining the neck. "But definitely dead." It was clear that the man's neck was broken.

Ignoring Bear's command, Tabitha stepped into the room, bracing herself against the doorframe at the sight of the body. The room was small: a single iron bed, a cheap chest with a warped mirror, and a table with an inkstand and a nearly burnt-out candle. Somewhere outside the window, a porter shouted, and a whistle blew for a departing train.

"Goodness," Isabella whispered. She had approached behind Tabitha and now stood beside her, a hand to her mouth, her eyes fixed on the body before them. "Did we just hear this man being killed?"

Bear nodded. "Whoever was here went out the window." He moved to the window and looked down without flinching. "There's a yard accessible via the drainpipe."

"Fetch a constable," Tabitha said. "The station is nearby."

Bear didn't answer. He rose immediately and left.

The dowager stepped into the room and surveyed the scene, with the landlady close behind her. The woman stopped, hovering in the doorway. "Oh, lawks," she said unhappily, looking at the body.

"Did Mr Freund have any visitors this afternoon?" asked Tabitha.

"Went out to get some coal, I did," the woman answered. "But when I comes back, I saw a man in a fine-looking coat going up the stairs. Never saw his face, though and don't know who let him in. Probably that Mrs Peeler. I keep telling her not to let the world and his brother in the house." The landlady seemed uncertain whether she should enter the room and enjoy the melodrama or faint at the thought of a dead body on her grimy floor.

The dowager resolved the issue for her when she said, "Shut the door, Miss Hartwell. We cannot have half Brighton blundering through and muddying the scene." She seemed to mean mainly the landlady, who was shut out of the room despite her grumbling.

Tabitha manoeuvred around the bed, keeping her skirts clear of the body. Gustaf Freud's hand lay open on the carpet, palm up, as if he had been about to bargain. The fingers were stained with oil beneath the nails. On top of the desk rested a small oilcan with German letters faintly stamped on the side. It had been placed over an envelope as a paperweight: the corner of foolscap showed beneath it, darkened where the oil had run.

"Here," Isabella said. "Don't touch the can; that oil is impossible to get out. Let me." She pinched the corner of the paper and slid it free. The oil made her fingertips gleam. "He was writing."

In a heavy, painstaking hand:

Sir, you will pay what we agreed, or I will tell what I saw on the road that day. I am not afraid; I will.

The sentence broke into a long blot and a scrawl, as if the writer had been interrupted.

The dowager's brows lifted. "A blackmailer. Charming."

"There's no name or address, only 'Sir'," Isabella murmured.

Tabitha looked around the room and spotted a glove on the floor, partly hidden by the bed's coverlet. It appeared to be made of high-quality leather with fine stitching. She lifted it by the fingertips and held it to the light. Given how grubby the boarding house was, it seemed likely that Gustaf Freund was not being well compensated by whichever motor-car company he worked for. That he was resorting to blackmail seemed to confirm this fact. Therefore, the very soft, supple, and clearly expensive fawn-coloured driving glove almost certainly didn't belong to him.

Footsteps thudded on the stairs; a constable's rattle of keys followed. Bear reappeared in the doorway with a short, square man in a policeman's uniform. The constable took in the scene, his mouth tightening; then, acknowledging the grand ladies, he had the presence of mind to pull off his helmet.

"Best keep back," he said. "No one touch anything." His eyes went to the glove in Tabitha's hand. The policeman addressed Tabitha. "Beggin' your pardon, is that there evidence?"

Tabitha placed the glove carefully on the table beside the blotched, unfinished letter.

Bear jerked his chin towards the window. "We believe the assailant went that way, down the pipe, into the yard." The constable moved to the window and looked out, nodding in agreement.

"What do we think happened?" Tabitha asked quietly, more to herself than to anyone else.

Isabella's eyes had gone to the floor again. She traced a line in the air from the chair to the letter, to the windowsill. "He must have been writing, and then the visitor came. There was an argument; Freund reached for the glove; perhaps it was proof of what he'd witnessed. The visitor tried to snatch it, and it fell to the floor. Then, there was a scuffle, which ended badly." She stopped, her face tightening as she looked at the unnatural twist of the neck.

"The visitor panicked and went out the window," Tabitha concluded. "Perhaps he heard us on the landing, which caused him to forget the glove in his haste."

The constable made a small, worried noise as he looked at the body again. "We'll need the detective inspector. And the coroner." He glanced at the dowager, Isabella, and then Tabitha, as if trying to gauge how much he could command the toffs. "Best if you step downstairs till we can take names and statements."

"I am not in the habit of being banished like a common busybody," the dowager said imperiously, but she gathered her skirts all the same. "Come, Tabitha. Isabella. Let us leave these men to clear up the mess." She paused and addressed the constable with a determined air of authority. "However, I will not deign to stay a moment longer than necessary in this hovel masquerading as a boarding house. You may inform Detective Inspector Maguire that he may call on us at The Grand at his convenience." And with that, she swept out of the room.

Tabitha closed the door softly behind them. "Whoever the killer was," she murmured, "he had a reason. Was it the man being blackmailed? I would imagine so." She hoped that this second murder would persuade Maguire of Wolf's innocence. After all, with a constable posted at the hotel, her husband appeared to have an airtight alibi this time.

There seemed to be nothing more to do than return to the hotel, inform Wolf and Langley, and then wait for Detective Inspector Maguire's visit.

CHAPTER 23

Bear decided to walk back to the hotel since the carriage was far too cramped when he rode in it. During the brief journey, the three women discussed the latest killing. Tabitha expressed her hope that this would persuade Detective Inspector Maguire of Wolf's innocence.

Isabella concurred. "How could it do otherwise?" she said brightly.

As much as she'd had a similar thought not minutes before, hearing the American express it caused Tabitha to reflect on the question more sceptically. "Of course, he might argue that there is no evidence that the two crimes are related," she mused.

"But of course they are," Isabella argued. "We saw the blackmail note he was in the middle of writing."

"Exactly! He was in the middle of writing it. Just to play devil's advocate for a moment, what if this was the first time he'd alerted Havers's killer to his supposed witnessing of the crime? One might argue that a man willing to blackmail once might have made it a regular habit. Perhaps the man who killed Mr Freund was another victim."

Tabitha sighed. As soon as these words left her mouth, she realised how likely they were to be the argument used by the detective inspector. Yes, one could claim a straight line could be drawn from Freund's apparent blackmail about one murder to his own killing. One might even say it was the simplest, and therefore the most likely explanation. However, it certainly wasn't the only explanation. There could be a host of other reasons

Continuing her train of thought, Tabitha said, "Perhaps Gustaf Freund owed money, and that was why he was stooping to blackmail. Maybe his creditor called on him to obtain his money, and a fight broke out." Again, the plausibility of this theory sounded depressingly likely.

Isabella appeared unpersuaded. "I cannot believe that theory will be sufficient to hold Lord Pembroke."

"But they are not holding him, are they?" Tabitha pointed out. "Perhaps if he were in a jail cell, this might be sufficient to persuade the police to release him. However, Wolf is being asked not to leave a luxurious hotel. It is hardly deprivation to insist he remain in our suite for a day or so more. And it does seem as if the detective inspector is under some pressure to appear even handed in his treatment of Wolf."

The dowager was similarly unconvinced. "Maxwell needs to demand of the Home Secretary that he intervene. To continue to deprive a peer of the realm of his freedom is unconscionable."

Tabitha didn't bother to point out how unlikely the Home Secretary was to throw his weight behind Wolf's exoneration without solid evidence of his innocence. While this may have been common practice a few years earlier, public opinion had become firmly and vocally opposed to those of rank and wealth receiving automatic leniency.

Luckily, before they knew it, they were pulling up outside of The Grand Brighton, and there was no need for Tabitha to continue to have the pointless debate.

The three women hurried to Tabitha's suite to alert Wolf to the shocking turn of events.

Wolf looked up as the three women burst into the room; something in their manner alerted him that something serious had happened.

"Was there a problem?" he cried, leaping to his feet in concern.

"We are all fine," Tabitha assured him. "Bear is walking back. However, there has been quite a dramatic turn of events."

After taking their seats, the three women described what they had discovered at Gustaf Freund's lodgings. They were partway through when

Langley entered the room, having just returned from sending his telegrams. This necessitated the story being retold from the beginning.

"Dead?" Langley exclaimed. "You found him dead?"

"More than that, we believe we heard him being murdered," the dowager said with rather macabre glee.

Langley wondered, "What does this mean?" Much more than Isabella and the dowager, he understood where public opinion stood concerning the idea of one set of laws for the common people and another for the upper classes. He was under no illusions that Maguire would feel compelled to absolve Wolf yet.

"Well, we will discover the answer to that soon enough. I am sure the detective inspector will be here shortly. Perhaps we should ring for tea before that. I am quite parched," the dowager informed them. Drinking tea and nibbling cake seemed as good an activity as any to pass the time while they waited for the policeman to visit, so Wolf rang for the hall waiter.

Detective Inspector Maguire arrived within the hour. The look on his face left no doubt about his irritation at having to follow them to the hotel. He came with the constable who had been the first on the scene at the boarding house.

As soon as he entered the suite, he said in a voice of barely contained anger, "Lady Pembrokes, Miss Hartwell, what precisely drew you to the late Mr Freund's lodging this afternoon? Sightseeing?"

The dowager pursed her lips. If the policeman had been more astute, he would have realised what he was about to unleash. "Detective Inspector, if I took up sightseeing, I should certainly not choose a dingy boarding house in Brighton! We came to speak to the deceased. We heard the sound of what appeared to be a fight. Our associate, Mr Caruthers, broke down the door. What we discovered was that someone had already spoken to Mr Freund, rather firmly it seemed."

Maguire gave a grunt that might have been amusement. "You forced entry?"

"What would you have had us do?" Tabitha asked quietly. "We heard a commotion. By the time we reached him, Mr Freund was dead. Should we have stood patiently outside the door?"

The detective inspector looked from one to the other. "And naturally, you examined the room before alerting the police."

"Of course," the dowager said. "Would you not expect us to see whether the killer was hiding in the room?"

Maguire's mouth twitched, but he took a small notebook from his pocket. "In a room that small? However, let us move on. Describe what you found."

Tabitha took over, recounting everything succinctly: the crash, the open window, the position of the body. She talked about seeing the letter and discovering the glove.

"Yes, it appears to be a blackmail note," Maguire agreed. "I assume you believe this pertains to Mr Havers's death. How very convenient."

Something in Maguire's tone didn't sit well with Tabitha. She debated whether to ignore it, then decided she could not. "Detective Inspector, are you suggesting in any way that we did not find the letter but rather planted it? Because if so, I suggest you speak to the landlady."

"Was she in the room at all times?"

Of course, as Tabitha realised when he asked this, the landlady hadn't been. They had shut the door to the room and left the landlady outside just before discovering the letter.

Isabella took the opportunity afforded by Tabitha's pause to respond for her. "Detective Inspector, I only met Lord and Lady Pembroke a few days ago. I would have no reason either to aid them in such a deception nor lie about it."

They would never know whether Maguire was inclined to be swayed by these words. Before he could reply, the dowager interjected. "Let me inform you, young man, that the last person to accuse me of any kind of duplicity was the Prince of Wales. And he realised the error of his ways quite quickly and apologised. While you might deem him to be worthy company to find yourself in, I would suggest otherwise. I am the Dowager Countess of Pembroke, and I do not lower myself to the kind of subterfuge and machinations you are suggesting."

There was much to be pondered about this statement, not least of which was the question of what precisely had happened with the Prince of Wales? While Tabitha and Wolf learned during an investigation that the dowager had once blackmailed Bertie, the Prince of Wales, this statement hinted at other, less-than-pleasant interactions.

Perhaps the details didn't matter so much as her mention of royalty and her tone, because Maguire raised his hands in a gesture of surrender. "Of course not, your ladyship. Please excuse me if anything I said suggested anything other than that the letter was found on the desk."

The harrumph he received in reply told Detective Inspector Maguire what the dowager thought of his statement.

"Returning to the subject of the letter," Tabitha said. "Mr Freund wrote of 'what I saw on the road that day.' He must have known something. And someone wanted to stop him from telling it."

"That appears to be what it indicates. And are you about to tell me that if that person killed him, then it cannot be Lord Pembroke because he was at the hotel this afternoon?"

Refusing to fall into the man's trap, Tabitha said nothing. Maguire pressed on. "Firstly, I cannot be certain that Lord Pembroke never left the hotel. My man is stationed downstairs, but he still might have slipped out somehow."

This comment was met with stony silence. Maguire then outlined the other possibilities that Tabitha had already anticipated. "And so, in conclusion, nothing about this second murder leads me to conclude that Lord Pembroke is innocent."

"And what of the glove?" Tabitha asked.

"What of it? What does it prove? We don't even know when it was dropped. There is nothing about that boarding house that suggests it is cleaned regularly. Perhaps the item was dropped by a prior guest."

He closed his notebook with a snap. "Your ladyships, your timing is either remarkably unfortunate or remarkably convenient. Two dead men connected by motoring, and both last seen by Lord Pembroke or his acquaintances. You see my difficulty."

"I see your limitations," the dowager said sharply. "You persist in seeking the nearest aristocrat to blame."

The detective inspector offered her a thin smile. "I merely go where the evidence leads, m'lady. It tends to save time."

"Then allow me to save you more," she said. "Mr Freund's death was neither an accident nor an accidental quarrel. Mark my words, you will discover your murderer among those with the most to lose if the truth about Mr Havers comes to light."

"And who would that be?"

She met his gaze steadily. "I am an old woman, and each extra day I get to spend on this earth is a gift. If I knew the answer to that question, Inspector, I would not be wasting my limited breath on you."

Maguire turned away, muttering something that, luckily, the dowager didn't catch. He signalled to the constable. "Return to the boarding house and bring the body down when the coroner's cart arrives, if it hasn't already."

Tabitha rose as he prepared to leave. "Detective Inspector," she said quietly, "whatever your opinion of us, we have no interest in misleading you. If you learn anything, anything at all about Mr Freund's visitor, please tell us."

He hesitated and then nodded. "I'll not keep secrets from you, m'lady. Heaven knows, it appears that you will only find them out anyway."

When the door closed behind him, the dowager exhaled. "Well," she said. "That is another corpse the police will make a muddle of and another murder we will have to solve ourselves." Again, her apparent glee was rather disturbing.

CHAPTER 24

As the late afternoon wore on and afternoon tea gave way to dinner, the group still hadn't coalesced around a solid primary suspect. Though now that one of them had been murdered, it had limited the list.

They agreed that speaking with Felix Dubois and James Asher was crucial. Langley had sent a note to Major Asher when he dispatched his telegrams, asking if he could call on him. After he received an answer, he would also plan to talk with Felix Dubois. They realised that anyone even glancing at a local newspaper that morning would know why the Earl of Pembroke was contacting them, but the Earl of Langley might have the advantage of surprise. He didn't receive a reply until just before they went to dinner, so he planned to visit Major Asher the following morning.

"Alone?" the dowager wondered.

"I am more than capable of questioning a suspect," Langley replied. He had known the dowager for too many years to allow himself to be baited by her.

"Are you, Maxwell? Are you? After all, you do not have the deep and broad investigative experience that I have," the dowager replied, before adding, almost reluctantly, "or even that Tabitha possesses, to some extent."

"There really is no need for you to join me, Lady Pembroke," Langley assured her. Then, he quickly added, "Though of course you are more than welcome to if you so choose."

"Well, it depends on what else needs my unique set of skills and oversight," she told him. Turning to the others, she asked, "What other activities will be taking place tomorrow?"

It was a valid question that Tabitha had been considering since Maguire had left. Moving to the desk where Wolf had stored the lists they received from Captain Forth, she examined the checkpoint and endpoint timings.

Then, she voiced the question that had been nagging her all afternoon. "How did Gustaf Freund observe anything of the murder? He was just behind Havers at the checkpoint and ahead of all the other suspects at the endpoint. But if our assumption is that his blackmail and subsequent murder rule out his guilt, at least as Havers's killer, then the murderer must have been driving in front of him."

Tabitha considered what she'd just said, and continued before anyone could comment, "Though, he did lose some time, almost ten minutes it seemed based on the Preston Park timings. So, perhaps he stopped and witnessed the murder, somehow found the gloves, then immediately left the scene without the murderer noticing him. I cannot imagine precisely how he did that, but it is the only scenario that makes sense, is it not?"

Addressing the dowager's earlier question, Tabitha made a decision: "I think we need to view the scene of the murder to understand how the timings would have worked."

"While I agree in principle," Wolf replied. "I cannot leave this hotel, so how will you ensure you are looking at the right spot?"

Tabitha had an idea: "Perhaps we could ask Mr Wilcox to join us. He was very helpful earlier and has expressed a willingness to assist if needed in the future. After all, not only does he know where Havers's car stopped, but he also found the body. I will send him a note asking if he will join us tomorrow morning."

His fears for Tabitha's well-being compounded Wolf's frustration at being unable to participate in the investigation. "Again, I would ask you to let Bear accompany you. We have no idea if the killer is watching our movements."

"I agree, that makes perfect sense," Tabitha agreed. "However, I would also like Isabella to join us. She is the only one of us, besides Wolf, who knows anything about cars and can ask Mr Wilcox relevant questions." Isabella had left an hour earlier, but no one doubted that she'd be happy to join them, so a note was written, and Bear went to ask the porter to see to sending it and Tabitha's note to Ernest Wilcox.

There was no doubt that Tabitha, Isabella, Bear, and Mr Wilcox would be more than enough people for a carriage ride longer than a few minutes. While everyone was reluctant to be the one to say it, what hung in the air was that there really wasn't room for the dowager.

Perhaps the dowager realised this, or merely decided that questioning James Asher would be more fun than driving in a cramped carriage for an hour in each direction, only to stand on a hill in the middle of the countryside on a dreary, cold November day to do nothing more than discuss the placement of a motor-car.

Whatever the reason, the dowager surprised everyone by saying, "I will accompany Maxwell. Let us be honest, none of us trusts him to do this alone." While neither Tabitha nor Wolf agreed with her statement, they wisely decided to keep those thoughts to themselves. A brief glance at Langley's face made it clear that he understood their silence and harboured no ill will towards them for obliging him to tell the dowager how happy he would be for her company.

And so, the group's plans were made for the following day.

Before the evening ended, they received positive replies from Isabella and Ernest Wilcox; the latter agreed to meet them at the hotel at nine o'clock the following day. Langley also received a response from James Asher, saying they were welcome to call on him at his home, just outside of Preston, at half past ten the next morning.

The following day, Tabitha and Bear met in the lobby at nine o'clock, where they found Ernest Wilcox waiting for them.

"Mr Wilcox, thank you so much for agreeing to accompany us today," Tabitha said.

"I made the offer that I was happy to help in any way I could, and I meant it," the man replied with a genuine smile. "Though, I am still not sure what it is you are hoping to learn."

Tabitha and Wolf had discussed at length over breakfast how much to reveal to Ernest Wilcox. Gustaf Freund's murder was splashed across the headlines of the local newspapers. Still, nothing had been stated to connect his death to Thomas Havers's directly. Instead, the newspapers, or at least the more populist ones among them, ran headlines suggesting that perhaps the link between the deaths was that motoring was a cursed pastime. They failed to explain what it was about having a passion for motor-cars that might lead men to be murdered.

Even with the news of his murder being made public, Tabitha agreed with Wolf that the blackmail note and the glove were not necessarily items they needed to share with a wider audience.

Now, Tabitha gave the excuse they had concocted: "Mr Wilcox, with all the confusion printed in the newspapers, we hoped to trace the route ourselves, to understand better how Mr Havers's body was not found until you stopped. How did the other drivers fail to notice him lying there? Since we hope to persuade the police that it was one of the drivers between you and my husband who must have been the murderer, this seems like an important point to understand. As you were the one who found him, your recollection is invaluable. And..."

Tabitha hesitated just briefly and looked up at Ernest Wilcox with what she hoped was the doe-eyed expression of a devoted young wife, and nothing more. "I suppose it matters to me, after all that has been said of my husband, to see the place with my own eyes."

She was rewarded with a gentle, sympathetic smile. "I understand completely, Lady Pembroke. I am happy to help in any way in which I can."

Five minutes later, Isabella arrived in Arlene's carriage. Tabitha had forgotten that Mr Wilcox hadn't met Isabella the previous day. Now, his eyes lit up at the sight of the loveliness before him.

Tabitha introduced the two. Wilcox took Isabella's hand and bowed deeply over it. "Miss Hartwell, I must confess that I noticed you at the start of the run in Whitehall and was immediately taken by your beauty. While the circumstances under which we are meeting are most unfortunate, I cannot pretend to be upset at the opportunity for a formal introduction to such a beautiful woman."

From the expression on Isabella's face, she was not looking forward to spending the morning listening to such effusions. However, as Tabitha reflected, it must have been something she was accustomed to, given her extraordinary looks.

Tabitha had never considered herself beautiful; she believed she was quite pretty and had always appreciated her hair colour. Certainly, men had flirted with her during her season, but she usually attributed it to her being the daughter of a wealthy marquis and assumed that was the main reason for their interest. Of course, Wolf constantly told her he thought she was the most beautiful woman in the world, and she didn't doubt that was true as far as he was concerned. However, Isabella Hartwell's beauty was so glorious, so utterly beyond compare, and Tabitha could only imagine how the constant mention of it irritated the no-nonsense, very practical young American woman.

If Isabella was worried that Ernest Wilcox would cling to her side like a limpet, then her concerns were confirmed when he insisted she take his arm, let him escort her out to the carriage, and then made sure to sit next to her.

CHAPTER 25

Langley wasn't sure what to expect from Major Asher; motor-cars were not cheap, and it was hard to imagine that a major's pension, assuming he was retired, would stretch to such an extravagance. He made the mistake of voicing this question to the dowager during the journey to Preston. Then he had to endure her commentary on those who had the temerity to seek to elevate themselves beyond their natural sphere.

Major Asher's villa stood in a neat row of similar residences along London Road. It was simple and sturdy, and while lacking ornament, everything looked shipshape and Bristol fashion. It was just the sort of house one might expect a no-nonsense, retired military man to favour. Its brickwork was scrubbed, its brass numbers polished, and its gravel path lined with geraniums arranged in precise military formation. The front door opened the instant Langley rang the bell, as if the man inside had been standing to attention behind it.

The major was the very image of a military man: tall but slightly stooped, with iron-grey hair cropped close, a moustache trimmed to regulation neatness, and blue, slightly watery eyes. His tweed suit was pressed to a sharp edge, and his boots polished to a high shine.

"Major James Asher," he said, bowing slightly. "You honour my house, my lord, my lady."

Langley returned the bow with easy civility. "We hope we are not intruding, Major, but we have a few questions, if you might indulge us."

"Always a pleasure to be of use, Lord Langley. Please follow me, I hope my study will suffice; it is where I seem to spend most of my time these days."

The study was, in fact, larger than expected; every inch filled with evidence of an ordered, inquisitive mind. Maps were tacked squarely to the walls, each framed by string and brass pins. A table stood at the centre, its surface crowded with neatly arranged volumes of *The Engineer*, a microscope, and several small brass models of bridge trusses. Some blueprints were also laid out.

Asher indicated the chairs by the hearth. "Please, sit. I regret that my man has stepped out, but the kettle will still be hot if you will take tea."

The dowager removed her gloves and looked around her as if inspecting quarters for dust. "Thank you, Major, that will not be necessary. We shall try not to distract you from your blueprints any longer than necessary."

"They are merely references, madam." He remained standing, hands clasped behind his back. "How may I be of service?"

Deciding to ease into the more awkward questions he needed to ask, Langley started in a conversational tone. "I assume you are retired from the military now, Major Asher. What was your role?"

"Royal Engineers, twenty-five years' service. I built bridges in Egypt, mapped coastlines in Malta, that sort of thing." The major's response was succinct, but not rude. Nevertheless, he gave the impression of a man who didn't beat about the bush and didn't appreciate it when others did.

Langley took the hint and continued to the point of their visit. "Major Asher, we understand you took part in the London to Brighton run. My friend, and her ladyship's relative, Lord Pembroke, is much involved in that unfortunate affair concerning Mr Havers's death."

Asher's expression tightened slightly. "A tragic business, my lord. This kind of press is not what the motoring world needs." Then he paused. "Though it is perhaps not surprising that such an incident should befall Mr Havers."

"Really?" Langley asked mildly. "You knew him?"

"As a fellow driver only. I have interacted with him at the Automobile

Club. Loud, self-assured, in it for the wrong reasons, in my opinion. I remarked to his mechanic, Duval, before the run began, that the man treated a motor-car as he might a racehorse, with far too much whip and not enough sense."

The dowager folded her hands in her lap. "You are acquainted with Monsieur Duval?"

"Professionally. I'm a practical man, Lady Pembroke. I have more time for mechanics than for those who see motor-cars as the latest shiny toy."

If this was the man's opinion, perhaps it was all for the best that Wolf was unable to come, Langley reflected.

Changing the subject, Langley asked, "Have you been long retired from the service, Major?"

"Four years this January. I keep myself occupied with some small inventions of my own and the occasional article for *The Engineer*."

"I see. And you took to motoring as... a new field of experiment?"

Asher's face brightened slightly; this was familiar ground. "Exactly so. The motor-car signifies a revolution in applied mechanics. The average Englishman has yet to understand that the engine is a discipline, not a mere amusement. I keep a Daimler myself, Coventry-built, none of your French frivolity."

"Quite," Langley said, concealing a smile. "And you found it reliable on the run?"

"Perfectly. I adjusted the mixture at Crawley and had no further trouble. A fine piece of work, so long as one treats it properly."

The dowager examined the small brass model nearest her. "I daresay Mr Havers's French machine offended you on principle, then."

"It offended me in execution," Asher said crisply. "Those De Dions are over-lubricated and under-tested. I told Duval at the start that his oil feed was set too freely. He said it was by design. I told him, design or not, it would seize before Brighton."

Langley raised his brows. "You predicted failure?"

"I did, my lord. Ask anyone around me that morning."

The dowager tapped her walking stick against the rug. "And did you see Mr Havers after that prophetic remark?"

"Only at the start line. I overtook his car once on the road near Clayton Hill; he must have stopped to adjust something. I didn't see the man but assumed he was under the vehicle. After that, there was nothing until I heard of his death." Before they could ask the obvious question, Asher added, "No, I did not stop to offer my assistance. Perhaps I should have, but there you have it, I didn't."

Langley exchanged a glance with the dowager before asking, "Did you speak with Mr Wilcox at any point?"

"Wilcox?" Asher frowned. "The fellow who discovered the body? We were introduced at the Club last year. A sound man, I should think. At least, motor-cars are his profession and not the hobby of a wealthy dilettante."

The dowager smiled thinly. "He will be gratified to know that you consider him sound."

Asher seemed to want to say something, but was unsure how to begin. "Brighton is a small town, Lady Pembroke. One cannot prevent gossip. I heard talk after the inquest that someone tampered with the machine, but I cannot believe it."

"You cannot believe it?" she repeated. "Because such wickedness is improbable, or because the machine itself was above reproach?"

His colour rose slightly. "Because no Englishman of breeding would stoop to such a thing. I might suspect a foreigner, but not one of us. Of course, the French are ingenious to a fault; they'll sacrifice reliability for cleverness. Their bolts are too fine, their oil too light. English engineering may lack elegance, but it endures."

The dowager gave a slight smile. "Like the British Empire itself."

"You say no Englishman would stoop to such a thing," Langley observed, "but there were men of other nationalities present, mechanics among them."

Major Asher inclined his head, conceding the point but still looking unconvinced. "Perhaps. Yet I find it difficult to believe that anyone dedicated to motoring would behave so dishonourably. There is ingenuity, and then there are dirty tricks."

Given his insistence on the subject, there seemed to be no point in pressing him. Instead, the dowager asked, "Can you think of any reason why Thomas Havers might have been murdered?"

The major's gaze shifted to the dowager. He shook his head before asking, "Do you mean to investigate the case yourselves? Shouldn't that be best left to the Brighton Constabulary?"

"Good heavens, no," the dowager replied in a horrified voice. "We mean to do it rather more effectively."

Asher inclined his head stiffly. "If I may ask, have you reached any conclusion as to who might have interfered with the car? And, perhaps more importantly, whether this was connected to Mr Havers's death."

Langley answered as vaguely as possible. "We are exploring possibilities. You mentioned foreign mechanics. Might you recall anyone near Havers's motor that morning, apart from Duval?"

"Let me think. There was the German fellow, Freund, tall fellow with spectacles. Seemed very interested in everyone else's engines. And a Frenchman, whose name escapes me, poking about under the excuse of offering advice."

"Freund is dead," the dowager said.

Asher looked sharply at her. "Dead?"

"Murdered in his lodgings yesterday. Did you not read about it in the newspaper this morning?" Langley asked

Rather than answering that question, Asher absorbed the news in silence, hands clasped in front of him, with fingers tightening visibly. "Then you believe the two deaths are connected?"

"We are considering it," Langley said. "Did you know Freund well?"

"Barely. He spoke poor English and had worse manners."

Langley smiled. "Your recollections are extremely useful Major Asher. Have the police interviewed you yet?" The major indicated they had not. Langley continued, "May I ask whether you noticed anything unusual among the other competitors, an argument, perhaps, or any display of bad feeling?"

"Bad feeling? Just the usual between classes. Half the men there were tradesmen pretending to be gentlemen. Havers was one of them, if you ask me. And as for the Americans, I'm not sure why they don't stick to their side of the Atlantic. Wasn't that why they fought their War of Independence, after all?"

"Ah," the dowager said. "Then you noticed Miss Hartwell?"

"The American heiress? Impossible not to. I don't attend many club meetings in London these days, but she was at the last one I did. A pretty girl, but far too sure of herself."

"I find her very agreeable," Langley replied mildly.

"Many are easily impressed," Asher replied. Then, realising who he was speaking with, he added, "Apologies, my lord. But I speak plainly. It's a habit of soldiers."

There was a question Langley wanted to ask, but he was unsure how to phrase it delicately. Finally, deciding there was no way to do so, he simply asked: "Major Asher, I apologise if this is a rather crass thing to ask, but how do you afford motoring? What we have come to learn is that the owners of motor-cars are usually aristocrats or wealthy industrialists, yet you are neither."

Major Asher chuckled, "No offence taken; it is a reasonable question. Yes, it is not a cheap hobby. However, along with my pension, my father left me some solid investments in Birmingham Gas and Midland Rail. I have no wife, no children. If I choose to spend my time and money on these machines, there is no one to argue. Let me show you my Daimler, if you will indulge me."

He led them out of the house and through a narrow garden to a shed. Inside stood a Daimler, not unlike Wolf's, but painted black, every brass fitting gleaming. A workbench on one side held tools arranged with parade-ground precision.

"I'm no sporting man," the major explained. "The motor-car, to my mind, is not a toy but an experiment in applied mechanics. During my years in the Engineers, we built and tested everything from pontoons to steam engines. This," he gestured toward the Daimler, "is simply the next step in that progression. Mark my words, before we are too far into the next century, the roads will be full of these vehicles."

The dowager gave a snort of disbelief. "I can assure you that I will never consent to travel in one; of that you can be quite certain."

"Lady Pembroke, they are the transport device of the future, I can assure you." The dowager's expression was all the answer needed to what she thought of that statement.

There appeared to be nothing further to discuss. Langley thanked the major for his time and asked him to leave word at The Grand if he recalled anything else, and they took their leave at the gate.

Once they were seated in the carriage, the dowager looked out of the window for a moment before turning back to address Langley. "A tidy man," she said. "I distrust tidy men."

Langley smiled. "You think he is hiding something?"

"I am unsure," she acknowledged.

They rode on in companionable silence, each lost in their thoughts of the conversation with Major Asher. Their next stop was to be the boarding house where Felix Dubois was staying. He was the only suspect who hadn't been interviewed yet, and both the dowager and Langley reflected on all that had been learned so far and what their line of questioning should be.

CHAPTER 26

I t was a chilly but clear and sunny day, and the carriage ride should have been pleasant; there were hot bricks to keep their feet warm, thick blankets on their laps, and the view over the Downs was delightful. Despite this, it was one of the more uncomfortable trips Tabitha had experienced for some time. Well, she reflected, perhaps being tied up and shoved in a sack at the back of a cart during her kidnapping in Salisbury was literally more uncomfortable, but this ride was certainly unpleasant.

The problem was Ernest Wilcox. The man appeared to be trying to achieve several goals at once: perhaps foremost, he was trying to flirt with Isabella in the most awkward way imaginable. Although Tabitha was sure Isabella was immune to compliments about her beauty at the best of times, she visibly recoiled every time Mr Wilcox attempted to praise her. The fact that the man seemed completely unaware of how unwelcome his gestures were made them even more clumsy.

When he wasn't attempting to woo Isabella, Mr Wilcox was prodding Tabitha for updates on the investigation. While it was understandable that he was curious, and indeed, their current trip was related to the case, his failure or reluctance to pick up on the hint that she didn't want to disclose more than necessary tested Tabitha's patience to the limit.

It was rare for Tabitha to regret that the dowager wasn't present, but this was one of those times. The sharp-tongued, impatient old woman would have had no qualms about putting the inquisitive man in his place. Tabitha felt herself unequal to the task of doing so in a way that wouldn't antagonise him and jeopardise the purpose of their expedition.

Every so often, Wilcox would ask a question that Tabitha was unable even to attempt to answer in a suitably vague fashion, and Isabella would catch her eye and smile in solidarity.

Finally, Mr Wilcox knocked on the roof of the carriage to signal that they should stop. He informed the group that they were now near the spot where Havers's car had been found.

When he raised his hand to knock, Tabitha's eye fell, almost idly, to his hands. His driving gloves were neat and fine, the stitching small and regular. They were far finer than she might have expected, given the frayed cuffs he tried to hide. They were of a quality far beyond a hired driver's means: soft French kid, stitched by hand, the sort sold at Gieve's or Swan & Edgar's.

Wilcox followed her glance and smiled. "A gift from a satisfied client. One must look respectable when one represents a firm," he said lightly.

"Of course," Tabitha replied

The drive to Clayton Hill had taken nearly an hour, but felt twice as long to Tabitha. She sighed at the thought that even after they finished inspecting the site, they would still have to endure the journey back to the hotel. Trying to push this unpleasant thought from her mind, Tabitha suggested the group leave the carriage and that Mr Wilcox walk them through his movements on the afternoon of the murder.

They stepped out of the carriage onto a quiet lane. Tabitha surveyed her surroundings, taking in the view of the English Channel in one direction and, in the other, the spot where a man had recently been murdered. To her right, the verge dropped into a shallow ditch and then rose again onto a grassy bank. Ahead, if she turned her back to the channel, the road curved and disappeared from sight.

"Where was the motor-car?" Isabella asked.

Wilcox stepped forward, all business now that his testimony put him at the centre of attention. "Havers had halted here," he said, pointing to a spot ahead. "Across the verge at an angle, nose just off the road. The bonnet faced Brighton; he'd been coming from London, of course."

Isabella had a notebook out, and now she marked a small cross on her page. "And you?"

"I came round the bend," Wilcox said. "Slowed down. When I saw the vehicle, I called out. When there was no answer, I pulled up just beyond there." He indicated a patch of verge where the grass had been flattened a few days ago and had only now regained its spring. "I left the engine running and went towards the motor-car. It was then that I saw..." He paused dramatically. "He was on the far side, on the ground, which is why no one just continuing to drive by had seen the body."

"Under the motor-car?" Tabitha asked. The words came out sharper than she had intended.

"Not entirely. His head was slumped to the left." Wilcox's face assumed a distressed expression. He set his jaw, as if mastering distaste at the memory. "I assumed he had fallen and been hit by something when I saw the bloody wound on his head."

"Where?" Isabella asked immediately, still not looking up from her page. "Where was he hurt?"

Wilcox gestured absent-mindedly; his gloved hand moved to his own left temple and touched it lightly. "Here. I assumed that he'd slipped and that when he fell, he struck the motor-car." He turned and pointed, almost with relief, at the very edge of the imaginary De Dion's bonnet. "That hinge there," he said, pointing. "The edge of the bonnet where it meets the radiator is sharp as a chisel, as you know, Miss Hartwell." Even now, as he relived what must have been a horrific moment of discovering a dead body, Ernest Wilcox couldn't help but say this last sentence in a coy, almost playful tone to Isabella. He was rewarded with a scowl that he seemed not to notice.

Isabella's pencil stilled, then moved again. "Forgive me," she said, not attempting to hide the scepticism in her voice, "but how could you tell? About the temple, I mean. If he lay with that side of his head on the ground."

"While he lay with his face turned," Wilcox said. "I could still see the edge of the wound and there was a lot of blood, including some on the ground. His cap was lying away from the body." His gaze flicked away from hers to the hedge. He drew a breath and released it. "I had never seen a dead man before." He offered a strained, foolish little smile. "It unsettles one."

"Yes," Tabitha said quietly. "It does."

Isabella nodded and resumed. "What did you do then?"

"I hailed a cart. Over there." He pointed to the rise where the road straightened. "A small dray came down with a boy. I told him to fetch the constable from the station. I thought it would be quicker than sending it back to Patcham or waiting for another motorist to arrive. The boy went at once. I remained."

"Did you touch the body at all?" Tabitha asked.

"No," Wilcox said. "I..." He made a small motion with his hand, as if the words were too difficult to express. "I could not bear the thought of touching a corpse. But..." He looked at Tabitha, and something like dignity overtook him; he straightened his shoulders. "Lady Pembroke, I realise that my impulse was not brave. However, in my defence, there seemed little doubt the man was dead, and so I felt no need to try to save him."

Tabitha thought there was little point in questioning the man's certainty and instead inclined her head. "How long before the cart returned with the constable?"

"Thirty minutes. Perhaps a little more. I was in no state to count."

"So, you were alone here?" Isabella's voice remained very neutral.

"Yes." Then, after a brief pause: "No. Not entirely. A cyclist passed by, and I waved him on, and one or two motorcars also went past. They called out asking if I needed help, but I said I did not."

Ernest Wilcox had not mentioned Gustaf Freund's death, and Tabitha had spent much of the carriage ride debating whether to bring it up. She did not want to taint Wilcox's recollections by suggesting something he then felt he obliged to include in his narrative.

However, even without referencing the dead man, she felt she could ask a question. "Mr Wilcox, aside from the motorists who passed you, did you notice anyone possibly stopped nearby? Perhaps a little further ahead or maybe behind? Perhaps around that corner, hidden by the hedge?"

They all shifted slightly towards the hedge. Isabella went to it and bent down to look through. "One can see everything from here," she said after a moment. "Without being seen from the road."

Wilcox did not turn to look at her. Instead, he kept his gaze fixed on the spot where he claimed the De Dion had stood, as if it was still visible to him. Then, he turned back and said in a strained voice, "I was so horrified by seeing Havers's corpse that, if there had been someone by that hedge, I would not have noticed. All my attention was concentrated on the dead body."

Tabitha considered it a reasonable answer.

"What did you notice about the motor-car?" Tabitha asked. "Anything unusual?"

Wilcox glanced at her and then back to the spot where the De Dion had been. "Hard to say. There was... my attention was not on the machine. I believe there was a smell." He frowned. "Not burning. Old oil." He made a small, helpless gesture with his hand again. "Now that I think of it, perhaps it looked as if he had been trying to free something. His arm was extended, as if he had just..." He stopped.

"As if he had just reached for the oil feed, perhaps?" Isabella asked.

Wilcox's face closed. "I am not a mechanic, Miss Hartwell."

Then, Tabitha asked a question that seemed to stupefy Ernest Wilcox momentarily: "Did you see a spanner next to the body?"

The man seemed unsure how to answer, so Tabitha tried again. "Did you see a spanner lying on the ground anywhere? The police said they found it, so presumably it was here somewhere."

Finally, Wilcox answered. "I did not. But then, I was so shocked by seeing Havers's dead body, that I could barely notice anything else." He paused and seemed conflicted about what to say next. He chewed on his lip for a moment before continuing, "Your ladyship, I have no doubt about your husband's innocence. Even if Lord Pembroke's spanner was the murder weapon, I'm sure there is a perfectly good explanation that does not involve him being the killer."

Given that Tabitha knew there was, she merely nodded.

They all stood in silence for a few minutes, observing the scene. Isabella's pencil scratched again, then paused, and she turned a page. Tapping her pen against the notepad absentmindedly, she said, "You mentioned a cap. "Where did it fall?"

Wilcox blinked. "What?"

"Mr Havers's cap. You said it had fallen."

"Oh." Wilcox looked down at the verge, then across to the ditch. "There," he said. "By the wheel. It seemed to have been thrown a little." He accounted for the distance his memory required and paused, placing his boot precisely on a darker rise of grass. "Here."

Tabitha stared at the spot. She could imagine that if Havers had tripped and fallen, perhaps his cap might have been dislodged from his head. However, they knew that wasn't what had happened. The medical examiner was sure that Havers had died from an intentional blow to the head with a blunt instrument. Given that, how did the cap end up so far from his body? It occurred to her that perhaps it had been deliberately removed and thrown from the body to make it appear as if Havers had fallen and hit his head.

She looked down the road in the direction Wolf would have come, her eyes tracing the bend and the rising line until it disappeared. She imagined him stopping to offer help, only to be brushed off. Then, she visualised others not even bothering to stop until Ernest Wilcox stumbled upon Thomas Havers's body. As aggravating as this man was, at least he had attempted to try to help a driver in distress.

She pulled herself back from such thoughts. "Mr Wilcox," Tabitha said, still gazing at the bend, "when you waved down the cart, where did you stand?"

"Here." He moved to the centre of the road without thinking.

"And you remained after the cart left," Tabitha stated. "Why did you not go with it to be sure it brought the constable, or to point the way?"

Without hesitation, Wilcox said, "I would not leave the body. It didn't seem right. The boy assured me he knew where the nearest police station was and understood the importance of speed. He seemed trustworthy, and so I had no cause for concern."

"Of course," Tabitha said, although she secretly wondered at his willingness to put his faith so firmly in a random young farm boy.

Isabella slipped her pencil into the spine of the notebook and closed it with a firm clap. "Thank you," she said. "This was very helpful."

"Do you think so?" A hint of genuine fatigue crept into Wilcox's voice.

"Yes," Tabitha replied. "It helps to see what your eyes saw." Was there anything else to ask, she wondered. Then she considered the glove found at Gustaf Freund's lodgings and asked Wilcox if he'd noticed a glove on the ground when he'd found Havers's body.

"Not that I remember," he said after considering the question. "May I ask why you believe a glove was found here? I don't recall that being mentioned at the inquest."

Given the earlier decision not to reveal that she and Isabella had been the ones to discover Freund's body and the glove nearby, Tabitha had to consider carefully how to respond to this. She silently scolded herself for not thinking of a suitable reply before mentioning the glove. Still, what was done was done, and she now needed to cover up that mistake.

Finally, adopting as casual an attitude as she could, Tabitha said nonchalantly, "I thought Detective Inspector Maguire had mentioned it, but perhaps I was mistaken."

Wilcox cast her a somewhat suspicious look, but she met it with what she hoped was an open, guileless smile, and he seemed placated.

They rode back to Brighton mostly in silence, for which Isabella and Tabitha could only be grateful. Everyone was lost in their thoughts. Wilcox sat forward, hands resting on his knees, staring out of the carriage window.

When they entered Brighton, Wilcox cleared his throat. "I am sorry if our visit distressed you ladies in any way."

"There is nothing for you to apologise for," Isabella said. "We chose to go."

"It was not a memory I wish to relive again," he said, almost to himself.

"I can imagine," Tabitha said sympathetically. This was the first time that day that Ernest Wilcox had appeared truly distressed. Earlier, his reactions had seemed almost calculating, which Tabitha believed was due to his desire to present himself in a certain way in front of Isabella.

At The Grand, Wilcox helped the two women down and then took each of their hands in turn, bowing deeply over them. "Good afternoon, Lady Pembroke. Miss Hartwell." He hesitated. "If your husband, if Lord Pembroke, requires my testimony again, I am at your disposal."

"You are very kind," Tabitha said.

Bear excused himself to return to his room, while Tabitha and Isabella took the lift to the suite.

CHAPTER 27

W hen Tabitha and Isabella entered the suite, the last thing they expected was to find Detective Inspector Maguire already there. He had evidently only just arrived, but the atmosphere was tense. The two men were standing facing each other with Maguire's back to the door. Wolf's expression was tightly controlled.

"Ah, you are all returned," Wolf said evenly. "Detective Inspector Maguire has brought the medical examiner's report for our perusal. Apparently, we may read it only under supervision, so your timing is excellent."

Maguire turned, his face composed into a mask of official stubbornness. "As I have explained to his lordship," he said, "you may read it here, but the report remains in the coroner's custody until the inquiry is concluded. I cannot permit its copying or removal without his consent. It is not standard practice to provide such documents to interested parties. You will forgive me if I adhere to regulations."

It appeared that Wolf's solicitor, Mr Anderson, had exerted just enough pressure on the Brighton police to ensure this visit took place.

"That will suffice," Wolf replied stiffly.

Tabitha and Isabella removed their gloves and coats. Wolf took the papers Maguire had removed from his case and scanned them. After a moment, he gestured for Maguire to sit as well. Despite there being sufficient armchairs, Tabitha chose to stand at Wolf's shoulder, her hand lightly on the back of his chair. Isabella moved to the other side, quite deliberately excluding the detective from their circle as they read the report.

The heading was written in a neat, deliberate hand: *Post-Mortem Examination of Thomas Havers, conducted at the Brighton Mortuary on the sixth of November, eighteen ninety-eight, by Michael Frobisher, M.R.C.S., Police Surgeon for Brighton Borough.*

Wolf perused the report silently at first, his mouth a firm line and his expression unreadable. *External examination: male, approximately fifty years old; robust build; a bruise on the left temple; abrasion on the right palm; contusion on the left shoulder. Internal examination: depressed fracture of the left temporal bone; subdural haemorrhage; lungs and heart otherwise healthy; no odour of alcohol detected in the stomach.*

He paused.

"Will you read it out?" Tabitha asked.

"There is a scalp wound on the left temporal region measuring two and a quarter inch long, running slightly upward and backward. Beneath this, the bone is depressed and fractured; the surrounding margins show irregular contusion. There is a matching bruise on the skin with slight tearing of the scalp tissues." He turned the page. "The injury might have been caused by a blow from a blunt instrument, possibly cylindrical or oval in section, such as a hammer, starting handle, or bar. I cannot exclude a fall against the corner of a fixed object. The depression does not correspond precisely to the width of the iron spanner jaw produced by the police, being of greater breadth and showing curvature."

Wolf stopped for a moment. "Go on," Tabitha said, very softly.

"There are superficial abrasions on the right palm and left forearm consistent with a fall onto rough ground. There are no signs of strangulation or severe struggle. Death would have occurred within minutes of the injury, not instantly; the man might have spoken or moved briefly afterwards. In my opinion, the most likely cause of death was a skull fracture with haemorrhage resulting from a blow with a blunt instrument." He set the sheet down.

Tabitha looked up at Maguire. "The depression does not correspond precisely to the width of the iron spanner jaw produced by the police," she repeated. "Those are the medical examiner's words."

Maguire's jaw worked. "You will find, my lady, that surgeons phrase things to give themselves room. He says a blunt instrument. A spanner is a blunt instrument, and it was the only such item found at the scene."

Isabella leaned over and tapped the relevant line with one finger. "He also mentions cylindrical or oval in section and of greater breadth. Did your men show Lord Pembroke's spanner to the doctor?"

"We did," Maguire admitted, visibly uncomfortable. "As an illustrative implement. The doctor saw it. He did not exclude it."

"Yet his report plainly does exclude it," Isabella said. "He wrote what a conscientious man writes when pressed to name a thing that does not fit. The wound shows curvature, but a Whitworth spanner's edge is perfectly straight."

Maguire's mouth set stubbornly. "It is possible the bruising spread wider than the edge. Skin swells. Heads bleed. I have seen it often enough."

"Yet you have built your case on little more than that my husband's spanner must have been the weapon," Tabitha said. "You told the coroner's jury you had a spanner from my husband's car found near the scene, a witness who saw his motor-car, and a quarrel that morning. Your statement allowed no hint of doubt."

Wolf's tone was measured. "My recollection from the inquest is that Dr Frobisher said only that the wound's shape was regular and more in keeping with a tool or spanner than with any natural surface. You turned that into an assertion that my spanner was the only possibility."

Maguire's colour deepened. "Because it was the only such tool recovered," he said sharply. "What else was I to deduce? A jury will likely do the same."

While they spoke, Isabella continued rereading the report. "Dr Frobisher says curvature and greater breadth," she murmured. "What of the starting handle? Or the jack-handle? Either would match such a description."

"And where is it if it was one of those?" Maguire countered. "There was nothing else lying about."

"Have you considered the possibility that the killer took it with him?"

Tabitha asked. "Did you check if all of Mr Havers's tools were accounted for?"

He hesitated. "We did not," he acknowledged finally. "Your point is noted. I will have my men look into it."

"I would suggest Mr Pritchard assist them," Isabella added. "Your constables may not be familiar with the standard De Dion toolkit."

Maguire's response was a sound halfway between a grunt and a sigh.

"There was a small spanner clutched in the victim's hand," Maguire admitted, rather reluctantly. "However, it was too small to have been the murder weapon, and of course, in his own hand. And so, we discounted that."

It was a reasonable conclusion, and so Tabitha changed tack slightly. "Where exactly was my husband's spanner found?"

Maguire hesitated. "Near the scene."

"How near?" Isabella pressed.

"Forty yards or so beyond where the De Dion stood," he said finally. "On the right-hand side of the road as you face Brighton. In the water-table by the ditch."

Both women glanced at each other, picturing the bend and hedge they had seen that morning.

"That is downhill," Isabella observed. "On the Brighton side."

"What of it?" Maguire asked, though his tone betrayed less certainty.

"So," Isabella said, patient and precise, "if the killer struck Havers at his car, he must then have carried the bloody tool forty yards downhill and thrown it towards the town. Why would he do that?"

Maguire gave a thin smile. "What would you have him do? Leave it beside the body? He meant to dispose of it, and one of my constables happened to spot it."

"Or," Isabella said evenly, "the spanner fell out of Lord Pembroke's motor-car when he drove away after offering help. Which explanation better fits its position, Inspector?"

He did not answer. His finger traced the brim of his hat nervously.

"I remember now," Wolf exclaimed in relief. "I used my spanner when I stopped earlier to check a noise in the Daimler. I threw it into the tool tray rather than stowing it properly. The road beyond Clayton Hill was rough, with deep ruts and holes. Just after I left Havers, the car lurched.

The tool must have bounced clear into the ditch. Forty yards sounds about right."

Maguire drew a slow breath. "What a very convenient memory to surface now," he observed caustically.

Wolf's nostrils flared. "Are you calling me a liar?"

Maguire did not answer.

Tabitha stepped in. "Inspector, perhaps we could pause this discussion until you have examined Mr Havers's tool tray. If anything is missing, that might settle the question."

Maguire nodded once. "Very well, my lady."

Wolf's tone was cool. "I assume I still remain confined to the hotel."

"Nothing discussed here makes you less my primary suspect," Maguire said. He placed the report in his case. Then looked at Wolf and said pointedly, "My men and I are investigating this crime and should be the only people doing so." Then, he bowed curtly and left.

When the door closed, no one spoke for some minutes.

At last, Tabitha said, "If Wolf's spanner was not the weapon, and it seems increasingly clear it was not, then another tool was, and the killer likely took it with him."

"Wouldn't he have disposed of it immediately?" Isabella asked.

"Perhaps," Wolf said. "Or perhaps he decided it was safer to keep it. After all, a starting handle or jack-handle is not easily hidden or explained."

Tabitha considered the report they'd just read. The words "greater breadth" and "curvature" stood out in her memory. Whatever the truth, it was not what Maguire wanted it to be, and she intended to uncover it.

"We need to search everyone's rooms," she announced. "We need to find the murder weapon."

"Firstly, you are not doing anything that dangerous," Wolf said immediately. "Beyond that, we do not even know if the killer still has it."

"We do not." Tabitha agreed. "However, as you just said to Isabella, it would not be the easiest thing to get rid of. The only question is how we go about it. I assume we can cross Gustaf Freund off the list." Everyone agreed there was little point in returning to Freund's boarding house.

. . .

Isabella looked pensive. "The more I think about it, the more certain I am that Havers would have had his starting handle to hand. His engine had seized," she explained for Tabitha's benefit. "He would have tried the starting handle to see if it would turn again. Any driver would. You test the resistance by hand first, then with the handle. If the bearings had locked, he'd have known it immediately. Moreover, it must be missing. If it had been there, surely it would have been considered a possible murder weapon." Her words made sense.

"The starting handle makes far more sense than my spanner," Wolf agreed. "The handle is solid iron, rounded, heavy enough to kill with one blow if swung in anger. My spanner's flat and narrow; it would have left a clean edge. Frobisher's report mentions curvature and breadth, not a straight impression. Whoever struck him likely took the handle afterwards. It would explain both the missing tool and the wound."

CHAPTER 28

"Well," Wolf said, "searching Smithers's room seems the obvious place to start. I can at least be the one to do this part. We only need to know the room number and when he goes out."

Isabella smiled, a mischievous glint in her eyes. "Leave that to me," she said, and she swept out before either Tabitha or Wolf could stop her.

Tabitha watched her go. "What on earth is she going to do?"

"I must confess, I have no idea," Wolf replied.

Then, with a wry smile, Tabitha added, "I cannot imagine how we would have managed without Isabella."

He nodded. "Nor I. I feel an absolute dolt about motor-cars beside her. Her knowledge has been invaluable. And..." He hesitated, unsure how his wife might react to his next thought.

Wolf needn't have worried. She laughed softly. "You can say it. I will admit that I had an initial prejudice against her because... well, you know why. However, I like her very much. She is someone I could imagine being friends with."

Even as Tabitha said these words, she realised how true they were. If Tabitha were honest, she didn't have any real friends. There was Ginny and Mrs O'Leary, but they were her employees, and so there could never be the kind of genuine candour and ease that she had always envied Wolf in his friendship with Bear.

With Isabella gone, Tabitha suddenly realised how hungry she was and rang the bell to order food. The hall waiter was just leaving with the order when Isabella returned with a triumphant look on her face.

"Success!" she announced. "His room number is 149, and it seems he has requested the hotel carriage to take him to Rottingdean this afternoon at one o'clock. Apparently, he has a sister who lives there."

Tabitha and Wolf gazed at her in amazement. "How on earth did you find all that out and so quickly?" Tabitha stammered.

With a slight roll of her eyes, Isabella explained, "I am not oblivious to the fact that my looks are considered, well, they are considered rather striking." While striking was probably an understatement, Tabitha said nothing and let the young woman continue. "To be honest, normally, I find the attention they attract to be annoying. So few men bother to even try to see beyond my superficial beauty. And women, well, it may sound conceited to say it, but there it is, most women seem to take an immediate dislike to me."

If anyone else had said this, it might have sounded quite boastful. However, since Tabitha had seen no sign of vanity in Isabella, in fact, the opposite, she was prepared to take the words as merely a statement of the obvious. It was one she could readily believe.

"In fact," Isabella explained, "that was one of the first things that drew me to Nene; she does not doubt her own beauty and does not find another woman's any threat." Bizarrely, Tabitha could believe this. Lady Archibald was nothing if not vain; one might almost call her narcissistic. It was plausible that she didn't believe any woman could outshine her own beauty, even the luminous Miss Hartwell.

"Anyway, to get back to the point, as I said, I find this beauty of mine to be a millstone around my neck almost all the time. Except when I need to do something like, for example, persuade a young, infatuated desk clerk to share some information with me." As she said this, Isabella gave them a smile that was both playfully innocent and genuine.

"Well, however you managed it, Isabella, I am grateful," Wolf said to her. "Then, we have time to eat something before breaking into his hotel room sometime after one o'clock."

A knock at the door interrupted them. The porter entered with a silver tray. "Telegram for Miss Hartwell, ma'am."

"Thank you," Isabella said. She broke the seal, scanned the message, and her expression grew intent. "Not bad news," she said slowly, "but interesting." She read aloud:

FROM: COLONEL MARKHAM, LONDON AUTOMOBILE CLUB

TO: MISS HARTWELL, GRAND BRIGHTON

SMITHERS ASSOCIATED IN FAILED MOTOR ENTERPRISE LAST YEAR STOP ALLEGED FRENCH LICENCE FRAUD STOP MARKHAM

She handed Wolf the telegram. He read it twice, his expression tightening. "This is worse than I imagined," he said. "If these two were once partners, that links them directly. Perhaps Havers uncovered something in their dealings."

"Which would explain why Smithers was so uneasy when Havers's name was mentioned," Tabitha observed.

"Blackmail?" Wolf suggested.

"It would fit," she said. "Ambitious, reckless men often try to turn knowledge into advantage. Havers was both."

"And Markham's wording, 'alleged fraud,' suggests it was never proven," Wolf said. "If Smithers persuaded investors that he had rights to build French engines he never actually licensed, and Havers learned of it, he would have had leverage."

Isabella nodded, pacing as she considered. "Precisely. A scheme like that would ruin reputations if uncovered. Havers may have threatened to disclose it, perhaps seeking money or partnership. Instead, someone silenced him."

Wolf folded the telegram. "This certainly increases our need to see what Smithers is hiding."

He stood. "We shall wait until he is safely on his way to Rottingdean. Then we shall see what secrets room 149 contains." Pausing for a moment, he addressed Isabella. "I would understand if you said no, however, would you consider...?"

He made no further attempt before Isabella slipped the telegram into her reticule. "I do enjoy a bit of light burglary after luncheon," she said, entirely too cheerfully. "I would be delighted to join you."

Tabitha sighed, though she couldn't help but smile. "Let us hope we do not end up explaining it to the Brighton constabulary."

The threesome ate a light lunch and kept a close eye on the clock. Just before one o'clock, Wolf sauntered down to the lobby under the pretence of looking for the afternoon edition of a newspaper. He lingered at the desk, where copies of every local and national periodical were displayed, until he saw Graham Smithers meandering out of the lift.

Smithers caught sight of Wolf and tipped his hat. "How are you this morning, Lord Pembroke? Any relief in sight from that dreadful business?"

"Not yet, Mr Smithers, but I remain hopeful."

"Jolly good show. Stiff upper lip and all that. What ho!" The string of well-bred platitudes was almost comical, and it made Wolf wonder what Smithers's background really was. Everything about the man, from his dress to his speech, seemed like a caricature of an English gentleman.

Wolf watched Smithers approach the porter and be directed outside to where the carriage was waiting. He made sure to watch until Smithers had got in, and the carriage had driven off. He then stood watching for a few more minutes to ensure they didn't turn back for any reason.

When he was finally sure that the man had left the hotel, Wolf went back upstairs to fetch Isabella and his lockpicks. Tabitha suggested that she stay in the hallway to watch for any maids who might come to clean the room, or even Smithers returning sooner than expected. Wolf refused to let her put herself in any possible danger. Reluctantly, she accepted his decision.

CHAPTER 29

They waited until half-past one before leaving their suite and descending to the first floor, where Smithers's room was situated. The hotel corridor was quiet, except for the muffled clatter of dishes from the dining room below. Wolf hoped that most hotel guests would be at luncheon and that the staff would be otherwise occupied as a result.

"Do you do this sort of thing often?" Isabella asked under her breath as she walked down the corridor, attempting to look as natural as possible.

"Only when absolutely necessary," Wolf replied. "You will find I am remarkably law-abiding except in the pursuit of justice."

"An admirable loophole," Isabella murmured with amusement evident in her voice.

Room 149 was located near the end of the corridor, overlooking the narrow lane behind The Grand. There was no doubt that this was one of the least desirable rooms in the hotel, at least according to its position. The lock was easy to pick, and within a minute, the door was open, allowing them to enter silently. Wolf closed the door behind them and relocked it. If a maid, or even Smithers, tried to enter, it would slow them down, hopefully.

The room was as small, as Smithers had suggested. It appeared that the maid had not arrived yet. The bed was unmade, and a folded morning paper lay beside a breakfast tray that hadn't been removed. A single suit-case stood open on the stand, its contents neatly arranged.

"Where should we start?" Isabella asked quietly. Wolf thought about the question. They were searching for evidence of the potential murder weapon, as well as any papers that might establish a link between Havers and Smithers.

Wolf crossed to the desk and examined the tidy stack of papers there. Receipts, a few envelopes, and a letter written on fine cream paper with a London address. He opened it and read the first lines, then frowned. "It appears to be correspondence from an investor, or perhaps a supplier. Look here, 'Regarding your inquiry into the manufacture of ignition components under your licence agreement with Monsieur Lefèvre.'"

"The French," Isabella said thoughtfully. "That confirms Colonel Markham's report. Lefèvre is a legitimate engineer in Puteaux. If they claimed his licence, it would have seemed perfectly respectable. However, how do we prove that Smithers and whoever he was working with don't have the licences they must have claimed to possess?"

"I am not sure that matters. All we need is evidence of Havers's black-mail, assuming that is what happened."

Wolf checked the drawers. In the bottom one, he found a small tin of pipe tobacco, what looked like some contracts written in French, and a leather-bound notebook. He lifted it carefully onto the desk.

"Do you mind looking through it?" Wolf asked. "You are far more likely than I am to spot something amiss."

Isabella opened the notebook. The first page held lists of figures, with margins filled with initials and symbols. She turned to another page and paused for a moment. A heading, written in a confident hand, read: *De Dion design comparisons. Below were sketches of a motor-car's gear mecha-nism, traced in pencil with meticulous precision.* At the bottom, a note read: *Adapt for British casing, omit French patent marks.*

Wolf let out a low whistle. "That looks incriminating."

"It looks like theft," Isabella corrected. "These are De Dion compo-nents. If he was copying French patents, then he was no mere enthusiast. He was a thief of ideas."

She turned the next page. "Here! There are lists of costs, names of suppliers, even one in Coventry. Smithers must be preparing to build engines himself."

Wolf examined the contracts. "And look at these. Some of these are signed with two sets of initials: G.S. and E.W."

"Could the E.W be Ernest Wilcox?" Isabella mused. It certainly seemed probable, though, of course, this was hardly conclusive proof of anything. Under the notebook, they'd discovered an envelope addressed to Smithers. The flap was unsealed. Wolf removed it and unfolded the single sheet inside.

The handwriting was bold and angular, the words hastily scrawled: You would not want your investors or partner to discover how you acquired the French drawings. Ten pounds in ready notes, delivered to me by Thursday, or the truth will reach Coventry.

Wolf read it twice, then passed it to Isabella without saying a word. She frowned, reading the line aloud. "That sounds rather like blackmail to me."

Wolf turned the letter in his hands, thinking aloud. "It also suggests that Smithers may have acted alone. I assume the partner refers to Wilcox. Could it be that he was unaware of what Smithers was doing?"

"It seems possible, at least," Isabella replied.

Wolf exhaled slowly. "If Havers were the one making demands, that would give Smithers at least a clear motive for wanting him silenced."

"Quite," Isabella replied. "And yet, given that the note is unsigned, this seems impossible to tie to Havers."

She folded the letter again and put it back in its envelope. "Whatever the truth is, it seems Mr Smithers's affairs are more complicated than we thought. Blackmail is a nasty business, and it never ends well."

Wolf nodded grimly. "No, it does not."

They continued their search. Beneath a pile of spare shirts in the wardrobe, Wolf found a long parcel wrapped in brown paper. He untied the string and unrolled it. Inside, there was a set of French technical journals, with covers stamped *Revue de l'Automobile*. The pages were marked and underlined in blue pencil.

Isabella stepped closer. "I believe that the annotations show which elements he intended to duplicate."

"Then these," Wolf said, holding up the parcel, "are our proof that Smithers is involved in some sort of industrial espionage."

"Perhaps," Isabella said. "Or perhaps they prove he was merely studying his competition."

Wolf frowned. "You sound unconvinced."

"I am cautious. Motives in business are never as simple as theft or honesty. And men like Smithers often blur the line."

A sudden knock on the door froze them both. Isabella's eyes widened. Wolf gestured for silence. The knock came again, louder this time.

"Housekeeping," called a voice through the door.

Wolf stepped forward. "One moment," he called, lowering his tone. He crossed to the window.

Isabella was already acting. She took one of the contracts and tucked it, along with the notebook, into her reticule, then swept the rest back into place.

"I am so sorry, sir," the maid said through the door. "I was told this room was empty."

"It is," Wolf called out. "I am just leaving. Can you perhaps return in fifteen minutes?"

He waited until she had gone, then turned back to Isabella. "That was close."

She nodded, exhaling slowly. "But we have what we came for."

Wolf gestured toward the desk. "You took the notebook and papers?"

Isabella nodded. Then asked, "If he notices they are gone, would he have any cause to suspect us of taking it?"

"No reason whatsoever, and definitely no reason to suspect us of taking them," Wolf insisted. He locked the door behind them, then they headed back to their suite with no trouble.

Tabitha was sitting by the window when they entered, a book unopened in her lap. She looked up sharply. "Well?"

Isabella placed the notebook and papers on the table. "We found sketches of French engines copied by hand, costings, and supplier names. And more importantly, repeated use of the initials G.S and E.W. It seems certain that Smithers and Wilcox are business partners and that, at least Smithers, is involved in fraud of some kind."

Tabitha leaned forward, scrutinising the pages. "If these are genuine De Dion designs, then have you uncovered the fraud?"

"Indeed," Wolf said. "But what troubles me is how perfectly it all fits. Too perfectly. A man with a guilty conscience seldom keeps such records in plain sight."

"Unless," Isabella said thoughtfully, "he wanted to hide them where no one would think to look, because he assumed no one would dare enter his room."

"Or because he no longer feared discovery," Tabitha suggested. "If Havers, who may have known about the fraud, is now dead, then Smithers may have thought himself safe."

Wolf then showed her the unsigned blackmail note. Tabitha sighed, realising it was helpful, but not as much as it would be with Havers's signature on it.

Wolf poured a small measure of brandy and contemplated what they had discovered. What they hadn't found was anything that could serve as the murder weapon. Did that mean that Smithers hadn't killed Havers, or simply that he had already disposed of it somewhere?

Wolf expressed this concern. "There was always the problem of how he might have smuggled it into the hotel unnoticed. So, perhaps it was never here to begin with."

There was a moment of silence as the meaning sank in. Then Tabitha spoke. "Certainly, without it, I do not believe we have sufficient evidence to go to Detective Inspector Maguire with." The silence that followed was an acknowledgement of the truth of her statement.

"I believe we should show what we have to Langley. Regardless of whether Smithers is a murderer, there appears to be evidence of fraud, and Langley will know the right person to whom we should take this," Tabitha continued when it was clear no one was going to contradict her.

Wolf closed the notebook and put it aside. "Then it is time to stop chasing speculation and begin looking for evidence that Maguire cannot ignore."

"I am interested to hear what her ladyship and Langley have learned about the other two drivers," Tabitha said, suddenly aware that the two had been gone for a long time. "I wonder where they have got to."

It was clear from the look that had come over her face that Tabitha had begun to worry. Wolf placed his hand on her arm. "I am sure they are alright."

CHAPTER 30

While their next destination was supposed to be Felix Dubois's boarding house, suddenly, the dowager declared herself peckish. Langley knew her well enough to realise that this was not a mere statement but a command to take her somewhere she could eat immediately. He also knew of her somewhat surprising predilection for working-class fare, usually enjoyed at a public house. They found one that seemed a bit more respectable than others and shared a delicious meal of pie and chips.

As she sipped her small beer, the dowager asked, "So, Maxwell, what did you make of Major Asher?"

Was this a trap? he wondered. Was the dowager asking for his opinion just to tear it to shreds as she forcefully voiced hers?

Cautiously, he replied, "The man seemed quite open and guileless from what I could see. There was nothing about him that suggested deceit, let alone that he was guilty of murder." There was a brief pause, and Langley assumed the dowager was gathering her forces before eviscerating him.

Given this, he was utterly shocked when she said, "Yes, I agree. The man is as dull as ditchwater, of course. All that talk of engineering. Who, pray, is expected to care about bridges? Still, I believe that is the worst he can be accused of."

Langley understood there was no use in suggesting that everyone cared about bridges, especially their safety, when they had to cross them. Instead, he kept quiet, knowing that in any conversation with the dowager, reason rarely overpowered her opinion.

After their meal, the two headed to the address they had been given for Felix Dubois. The landlady who answered the door at 16 Western Road looked wary when Langley and the dowager announced themselves. She was a woman of middle years with reddened hands and a nervous manner. The dowager, in her plumed hat and sable collar, made an impression that seemed to overawe her entirely.

"We have come to call upon Monsieur Dubois," the dowager said. "Is he at home?"

The landlady twisted her apron. "He went out some time ago, ma'am. Down to his place in the mews. He's been there nearly every day since the run, working on his motor. I told him he'll blow himself up one of these days."

"He keeps a workshop nearby?" Langley asked.

"Yes, sir. Hanover Mews, just off Upper North Street."

The dowager thanked the landlady in a brisk tone that suggested dismissal, and she and Langley got back into the hotel carriage.

They travelled in silence for most of the brief journey. Langley was still contemplating their earlier conversation with Major Asher. As much as he found the dowager as challenging as most others did, Langley held great respect for her intelligence. More importantly, once one managed to see past her snobbery, her judgements of people were usually quite astute. If she also regarded Asher as credible, then it was likely they could dismiss him from their list of suspects. With Gustaf Freund dead, the field narrowed considerably to Smithers and the man they were about to speak with.

As they turned onto Upper North Street, Langley gazed out of the carriage window, lost in thought. Suddenly, he spotted a column of grey smoke rising not far ahead.

They stopped at the entrance of a narrow lane flanked by low carriage houses. Several people stood in the road, pointing and shouting. Langley caught the words "explosion" and "fumes." His stomach sank.

"Stay here, Lady Pembroke," he said, already opening the door. "It looks as if there has been an accident."

"Nonsense," she replied, gathering her skirts. "If one of our suspects has blown himself up, I intend to see the matter firsthand."

Ignoring his protest, she climbed down and marched towards the commotion. The workshop stood near the end of the mews, its wide doors flung open. A cloud of dark smoke hung just below the rafters. Two men were attempting to haul debris away from the threshold, shouting for water.

Langley pushed forward. "Is anyone hurt?"

"One man inside," came the reply. "French fellow, works on those motor-car contraptions. We heard a bang and the roof came down."

It appeared that whatever had happened had caused more smoke than anything else and there didn't seem to be a fire still ablaze.

Langley took a handkerchief from his pocket, tied it loosely over his mouth, and ducked into the doorway. The air shimmered with heat and ash. He could see the twisted front of a motor-car, its bonnet buckled, a wheel splintered against the wall. Near it lay a figure in a dark coat.

He crouched beside the man he assumed was Dubois, whose face was smeared with soot; one sleeve was torn, and the other was scorched. Langley could just feel a pulse at his throat. He shouted that the man was alive, and they needed to get him out of there and to a doctor. The two men from outside entered with a makeshift stretcher, a shutter pulled from its hinges, and together they carefully lifted Dubois clear of the smoke.

The dowager waited just beyond the doorway. "Good heavens," she said. "Is he dead?"

"No, but he needs a doctor at once." Langley nodded towards a bystander. "You, run to the nearest chemist's or doctor's surgery and fetch one. Quickly."

The man obeyed. Dubois began to stir, muttering in French. Langley leaned in closer, catching a few broken words. He thought he heard "the Englishman" before the man's eyes rolled back.

The dowager straightened. "Did he say what I think he said?"

Langley hesitated. "He said something about an Englishman, yes. It could have meant anything."

She drew herself up, satisfied. "Obviously, he was referring to our killer. It is plain as day that he came here and tried to set fire to this place."

"There is no evidence of that," Langley replied. "We do not even know what caused the explosion."

Langley turned towards the doorway once more. A small crowd had gathered, including a constable, who had finally arrived and was trying to assert his authority.

The dowager, of course, pushed through the crowd and exclaimed, "Constable, this man has been injured in what seems a deliberate act. You had better ensure containment before the whole mews goes up."

The constable looked unsure whether to salute or object, but Langley spared him the decision. "Contact Detective Inspector Maguire immediately. There is good reason to believe this explosion is linked to the recent murder of Thomas Havers. Ensure that no one touches anything inside until the detective inspector arrives," he said. "There may have been tampering with the fuel tins."

That caught the constable's attention. He peered inside, frowning. "Looks like one of them tins burst, sir. Might've been the heat."

Langley entered again, now less cautious since most of the smoke had cleared. He looked around the area near the vehicle. One of the petrol tins was split open, with warped and blackened metal. Another was dented, showing deep gouges near the cap, as if someone had tried to prise it open. A small oil lamp was overturned nearby, its glass chimney shattered.

He turned and saw the dowager standing in the doorway, hands on her hips. "You should not be in here," he told her.

"I have no intention of fainting," she said. "What have you found?"

He gestured towards the tin. "It might have been prised open with a spanner or screwdriver. If vapours were present, the lamp could have ignited them."

The dowager looked pensive for a moment. "Do you think that Dubois could have done this himself?"

"It is possible."

"Possible, yes, but not probable. Is it not more likely that someone aimed to silence him, and it was only by Providence that we arrived when we did?"

Langley did not answer. He had noticed a tool tray in the corner of the workshop nearest the door. He went over to it and lifted the canvas covering it. A starting handle lay among spanners and rags, its iron shank dull with use, the wooden roller scarred. What caught his eye was a small band of paint at the drive end, a neat stripe of red. He glanced at the other implements. Dubois had marked his tools in blue. Even the oil can bore a blue ring around its neck. He turned the handle in his hands, frowning. It was heavier than the others and a little longer. Why would a red-marked piece be here at all, and whose colour was red?

Something was nagging at the edge of Langley's memory. He picked up the starting handle and took it outside to show the dowager. He noticed the colour difference and recalled hearing someone mention something about colours on tools, but he couldn't remember who or the context.

Rather smugly, the dowager told him, "You know, Langley, you are considerably younger than I am, yet I remember very clearly what you are talking about. It is quite remarkable how often my advanced age is used as a weapon against me, even though this is merely another example of how I am the most mentally astute of you all."

Langley took a moment to compose himself before replying with admirable patience, "Indeed, Lady Pembroke, you are an inspiration to us all. Now, would you mind sharing the memory you have regarding these colours?"

No less smugly, she told him that Pritchard, the engineer who spoke at the inquest, had said that motorists often paint their tools with a dab of colour for quick identification, and that Havers's tools were painted with red stripes.

As soon as she said this, Langley recalled Pritchard having made the remark. Of course, he and the dowager had been eating pies and drinking beer when the detective inspector visited Wolf's suite earlier and reluctantly handed over the medical examiner's report. Because of this, he hadn't been part of the conversation about the likely murder weapon. Even without this information, Langley considered how strange it was to find what was probably Havers's starting handle among Dubois's tools.

"We need to show this to the detective inspector when he arrives," Langley told the dowager, who agreed. He placed it in the hotel carriage for the time being, just to keep it safely out of the way.

Just then, a horse-drawn ambulance arrived from the infirmary closely followed by a fire truck. The ambulance attendants lifted Dubois onto a proper stretcher and carried him away, his face pale against the grey blanket. The dowager announced that she would accompany them.

Langley blinked. "Are you sure that is wise, Lady Pembroke?"

"It is necessary. The man may recover his senses at any moment, and I intend to be present when he does. You will stay here and speak to the constable. Ensure that nothing is removed before Detective Inspector Maguire's men have inspected the scene."

Langley knew better than to argue. She climbed into the ambulance with surprising agility and was gone before he could protest.

He spent the next quarter-hour overseeing the constable's efforts to cordon off the workshop. Several curious onlookers proved to be mechanics from nearby stables, who offered opinions in abundance. One insisted he had seen "a well-dressed gentleman" leaving the mews not long before the explosion, though he could give no proper description beyond "looked respectable, had a hat." Another swore there had been two men in the lane, one carrying a walking stick. It amounted to nothing concrete, but Langley noted it all carefully.

Eventually, Detective Inspector Maguire arrived. He made no effort to hide his irritation at finding a member of Wolf's entourage at yet another crime scene. "Am I to believe that it is merely a coincidence that, once again, someone in Lord Pembroke's close circle is the first to discover a crime committed against one of the other drivers?"

"It may be a surprising, even improbable coincidence," Langley conceded. "However, that is exactly what it is." He then explained that he and the dowager had been hoping to question Dubois, but the workshop explosion intervened.

"And why were you hoping to question Mr Dubois? This is a matter for the police, and we have it well in hand." Maguire was barely controlling his temper. "I have only recently come from having a similar conversation with Lord Pembroke."

"The purpose of our conversation was unrelated to your investigation," Langley lied smoothly. "Lord Pembroke wished to make use of his motoring expertise."

"Really?" Maguire's tone was laced with heavy sarcasm.

Langley had genuinely intended to bring the starting handle to the detective inspector's attention, but he now questioned whether there was any point. Instead, he bade the policeman farewell, got back into the carriage where the starting handle was securely stowed, and returned to the hotel.

By the time he returned to The Grand, the dowager had already arrived ahead of him. She was seated in the hotel lounge, drinking a cup of tea, clearly waiting for him.

"Have you been to report to the others yet?" he asked.

"I have not. I wanted to hear what that detective inspector had to say first. And I found I was too parched to wait for that hall waiter to deliver a tea tray. However, my thirst is quenched if you want to go up there together now."

"How is Dubois?" Langley inquired.

"Alive, though half singed. They believe that he will recover, though he is unconscious for now. I have instructed the doctor and nurses to send word as soon as he wakes."

Langley went to pull the dowager's chair out, saying, "Then let us go and tell Tabitha and Wolf of what we have discovered today."

At that moment, the dowager realised he was holding something wrapped in a blanket from the carriage. "You did not leave that handle with the police?"

Langley didn't bother giving her the full explanation and merely indicated that a starting handle was what was wrapped. "I will hand it over once I have shown it to Miss Hartwell."

CHAPTER 31

B y the time the two groups gathered in Tabitha and Wolf's suite, there was so much to share that Tabitha worried they might overlook important details if some order wasn't established.

It quickly became clear that the dowager would not be satisfied until she had given all her news. Tabitha said, "Mama, why do you not go first? Let me get some blank notecards and then you can tell us all that you and Langley have been up to."

Before Tabitha and Wolf started using their trusty corkboard to pin their notecards, Ginny had helped create an improvised board by sewing some material tightly over a painting. They had used some of her steel dressmaker's pins to attach the notecards.

That morning, before leaving for the drive to Clayton Hill, Tabitha mentioned to her maid that it was rather pointless writing up the note-cards as they had been doing without being able to view and move them around. She had returned to an excellent imitation of the original board, with fabric sewn over what she could only assume was a painting taken off the hotel room's wall. Now, she fetched the new board, and Wolf pinned the existing notecards onto it while she wrote up the new ones.

The dowager started her recitation with her opinion of Major Asher.

Langley sat quietly nearby, only interrupting when he believed she had grossly misrepresented something.

"I would say that the man is rather serious and continues to take a keen interest in engineering of all kinds," was one such comment, after the dowager had declared the major to be dry as dust. He was rewarded for this correction with a glare.

"May I continue, Maxwell? Or do you have any further edits to make to my account of our interview?" she asked acerbically.

"I do not," he answered with a sigh.

"Then, let me proceed. It is my belief, and Maxwell concurs, that Major Asher had nothing to do with Mr Havers's death. Besides being the worst kind of snob, he had little to add to what we already know."

Tabitha wondered what the dowager considered the 'worst kind of snob to be', given her own propensity for looking down her nose at others, but she knew there was little point in making such an observation.

The dowager appeared to have concluded her recount of the visit to Major Asher's and was eager to share what she deemed the more dramatic part of her day.

Before she moved on, she reluctantly asked, "Do you have anything to add, Maxwell?"

While her tone left Langley in no doubt that his answer was supposed to be in the negative, he felt obliged to add in a few details that the dowager had glossed over. "Major Asher was behind Mr Havers, saw his vehicle stopped on Clayton Hill, but did not stop himself. His assumption was that Havers was under it or had walked away. There was nothing in his account that seemed disingenuous."

The dowager sniffed. "How was that statement different from what I have already relayed? Really, Maxwell, I did not realise that you were one of those people who speak merely to hear the sound of their own voice. Do you have anything else to add before I move on?" Langley shook his head.

"Very well." She then described the explosion at Dubois's workshop and the discovery of the starting handle, which was accurate mostly, but somewhat overly melodramatic in its pauses. As she said this, Langley took the starting handle from the blanket it had been wrapped in and placed it on the table between them.

As soon he saw the handle, Wolf jumped to his feet. "You found it? Are you sure it is Havers's?"

"Well, as I had to remind Maxwell, that Pritchard fellow had mentioned that Mr Havers's toolkit was daubed with red paint, which this one is, yet this French fellow's tools were otherwise daubed with blue. Of course, I still do not understand why there is paint on them in the first place."

Isabella could answer this query. "If you remember, your ladyship, Mr Pritchard mentioned this point at the inquest. He explained that many teams mark their tools for identification. De Dion uses red; Peugeot tend to favour blue."

The dowager didn't appreciate the suggestion that her recollection of events was anything other than perfect, and Isabella was rewarded for her explanation with a long, hard stare. "That is all very well, Miss Hartwell, but I am still not sure why this matters."

Wolf then described Detective Inspector Maguire's visit and what they had deduced from reading the complete medical examiner's report.

"So, you believe this might be the murder weapon?" Langley asked in amazement. When Wolf indicated yes, Langley continued, "Does this mean that Dubois is our killer?"

"Then why would he mutter something about an Englishman, Maxwell?" the dowager asked dismissively. Langley resumed describing the explosion at the workshop.

"Do you believe it was an accident?" Wolf asked.

"Well, I am hardly qualified to make that assessment," Langley pointed out. "However, that the only thing Dubois said was 'Englishman', did seem telling. Of course, that could mean other things as well. Certainly, it seems suspicious that what appears to be Havers's starting handle turned up in Dubois's tool tray."

Tabitha often found pacing to be conducive to grappling with knotty problems. Now, she put her notecards aside, stood, and began walking up and down the room.

"You will wear out the carpet if you are not careful, Tabitha," the dowager said. "Is there any point to such perambulation?"

Ignoring her, Tabitha tapped her pen against her lips, a habitual gesture when she was deep in thought.

Finally, she verbalised what she had been struggling with. "I believe there are several possible scenarios before us. Perhaps the most obvious is that Dubois killed Thomas Havers using Havers's own starting handle as the murder weapon, which he then took with him."

"As you say, that is rather obvious, Tabitha. Do you have anything else?"

Tabitha was tempted to point out to the dowager that she had not finished speaking, but there seemed little point in doing so. Instead, she carried on as if she had not been interrupted. "The second possibility is that someone else killed Havers and slipped the murder weapon into Dubois's tool tray, perhaps at the finish line at Preston Park. Under both those scenarios, we face the question of whether the explosion at the workshop was an accident."

"If Dubois was the killer, why would someone else have sabotaged his workshop?" Langley asked. At this point, Wolf realised that he and Isabella hadn't informed the others about their search of Smithers's room and the evidence indicating that he was involved in fraudulent activities related to French motor-car designs.

Wolf quickly filled the others in. "This was initially suggested by Colonel Markham's telegram, but Isabella and I found what seemed to be clear proof in Smithers's room." Wolf then retrieved the notebook and papers they had taken earlier.

As he suspected, Langley was convinced that various government bodies would be interested in discovering what Smithers was doing. "I shall take the papers to the Patent Office of the Board of Trade to begin with," Langley said. "If the licence claims prove false, their Comptroller can verify it quietly and inform the Registrar. Should they find clear evidence of the deception, the matter can be referred to the Director of Public Prosecutions without any publicity in the press. If Smithers has been trading on stolen designs, they will uncover it."

"I think we should hold onto this a little longer," Tabitha replied. "If it is related to Havers's death, then Maguire needs to see it. If it turns out to be unrelated, then you can take it back with you to London." This made perfect sense, and Langley concurred.

Tabitha resumed her pacing. "We seem to have two separate, but perhaps related crimes: the fraud and the murder. There is no doubt that

Gustaf Freund was blackmailing our killer; the glove we found in Freund's room and the note he was writing seem to indicate as much. Additionally, someone was blackmailing Smithers." She paused for a moment. "And finally, Felix Dubois's workshop explodes, which may or may not be sabotage. However, whether knowingly or not, it appears Dubois was in possession of the murder weapon. Have I missed anything?"

Isabella spoke up. "I am not sure you've left anything out, but we haven't told her ladyship and Lord Langley about our trip to Clayton Hill. Perhaps we should do that."

Tabitha agreed, and Isabella succinctly recounted their morning trip to the murder scene. When she had finished, the dowager said rather snidely, "Well, that was a long way to go to learn so little, Tabitha."

Langley, however, had perceived something much more significant in Tabitha's account of their trip. "So, from Wilcox's description of the scene he had discovered, you believe it possible that the killer attempted to stage the murder to resemble an accident!"

"Yes, that was our assumption. And, of course, why wouldn't he? After all, if the person came after Wolf and the spanner had indeed fallen out of his Daimler into the ditch, there would be no reason to think blame would fall on him. In fact, the killer probably had no idea Wolf had even stopped and offered Havers any help."

Wolf, who had the benefit of some hours since hearing this news to reflect on it, vocalised what he'd been worrying over. "Of course, even if we could get Maguire to accept that the scene had been staged, I cannot imagine why he would be inclined to believe that vindicates me. He would just claim that I was the one who had moved the hat and the body." Tabitha sighed; she suspected he was right.

For a few moments, the group was silent; it felt as if they had reached an impasse. Then, Wolf had an idea. "A driver wants gloves for grip on the starting handle and tiller, to spare his knuckles if the engine kicks back, to keep oil and heat off the skin, and for warmth in the wind," he said. "If our man spoiled or lost one, he would seek a quick replacement, given that he will have to drive back to London." Of course, this assumed that the dowager and Langley's assessment of the Brighton-based Major Asher was correct.

Turning to Isabella, Wolf asked, "I am not sure how often you have stayed with Arlene, but do you have any idea where a good quality pair of gloves might be purchased?"

Isabella smiled. "One does not need to have been staying with Lady Archibald long to experience many of Brighton's finest purveyors of luxury goods. We should start with the best. Hanningtons on North Street will have a glove counter. Vokins on North Street is nearly as good. If those fail, we can try Sharman's on Western Road."

Tabitha smiled at Isabella's inclusion of herself in this excursion. Then, looking at the clock on the mantel, she noted that it was far too late in the day to do so that afternoon; this would have to be postponed until the following morning.

~

Coming Soon: An Impertinent Heiress, book 1 in The Isabella Hartwell Society Mysteries. Preorder now and meet your new favorite sleuth

London, 1899. American heiress Isabella Hartwell came for adventure, not a coronet. But when a young lord dies at a country house party moments after quarrelling with her, suspicion turns her way.

Refusing to be sent home in disgrace, Isabella begins an investigation of her own. With the indomitable Dowager Countess of Pembroke at her side, she soon learns that beneath silk gowns and polished manners lie secrets worth killing for.

CHAPTER 32

The following morning, a debate over breakfast centred on who would join the excursion to the shops where replacement gloves might have been bought. There was also the question of what story they would tell to persuade the shop girls to cooperate.

"Well, I need to do some shopping anyway," the dowager announced. "I only expected to stay for three days and have now worn the same hat multiple days in a row. If I do not visit a milliner's immediately, people will start to talk."

Tabitha was too distracted by the waiter bringing a fresh pot of tea to question who exactly in Brighton society the old woman thought would be judging her for a lack of diversity in her headwear. Instead, she responded, "Then, by all means, Mama, join us."

"Us? Why is it a given that you will be one of the party, Tabitha?" the dowager asked.

"Because I think the best cover story is if Langley pretends to be Wolf and uses his membership card from the Automobile Club to pose as conducting an informal club survey of suppliers who assisted motorists after the Run. I will accompany him as his wife," Tabitha answered.

"That seems a bit far-fetched if you ask me," the dowager replied with a sniff.

Isabella had arrived earlier, before the dowager had joined them, and Tabitha had already asked her if this was plausible. Now, the American weighed in. "Actually, from what I understand, the Club often gathers notes after such outings. Members like a handy list of reliable suppliers. Brighton was overrun with motorists, repairs, and lost items. An informal circular naming shops that helped would be welcomed, I am sure." The dowager sniffed again, this time injecting a little more grievance into it.

Before they set out, Tabitha gave Langley a detailed description of the glove she had discovered beneath Gustaf Freund's bed. "A right-hand driving glove," she said, holding her hands apart as if to outline its shape in the air. "Fawn-coloured, fine leather. The glove looked quite new. I noticed tidy hand stitching on the back. There was a faint mark on the button where a maker's stamp might have been. The size seemed much smaller than Wolf's, perhaps a seven. I think it might have fit me almost. That was all."

Given that seven was a small size for a man's glove, the group hoped that it was a distinctive enough feature to help them in their search.

Langley listened without interrupting before slipping Wolf's Automobile Club card into his pocket. Isabella already had her notebook ready. Since she was the one who knew where the stores were, she took charge from the moment the hall porter called their carriage.

"We will go along North Street first," she said. "If that fails, Western Road and West Street."

Langley looked somewhat abashed. "I confess I have never visited such stores," he said as the carriage rolled away. "My man, Ashby, usually attends to this sort of errand, or my tailor visits me."

"That may help," Isabella suggested. "If you look faintly lost, the clerks will try to be helpful. It will also explain why you felt the need to bring your wife and her friends with you."

It was another chilly, damp November morning, and everyone shivered as they left the hotel, pulling their collars up and tucking their hands deeper into their muffs or pockets.

Isabella had suggested they begin with the two largest department stores, Hanningtons and Vokins. "Vokins first," she said. "It is close and we can work our way towards Hanningtons."

From The Grand, the carriage turned up West Street toward the Clock Tower. The hill was short and busy, with carriages, omnibuses, and bicycles crowding the way. At the top, North Street ran left and right beneath the clock's gilt hands. Vokins stood close by on the north side. A few minutes farther along North Street, toward East Street, Hanningtons spread across several frontages, larger and grander. Coming from The Grand, one naturally reached Vokins first, then proceeded on to Hanningtons.

Vokins faced the Clock Tower. It was a grand building with a smartly dressed doorman at the entrance and tall, elegant windows offering glimpses of the bright counters within. Inside, the doors opened onto long aisles of polished cases, stylish displays of goods, and assistants eager to help the well-heeled customers who filled the store. Bells chimed softly as the doors swung open. Clerks in dark coats moved with practised ease, measuring tapes at their necks, pencils behind their ears. Langley paused, taking it all in. He looked somewhat lost and oddly impressed.

"So, this is a department store," he murmured. "Well, I never."

"Indeed," Isabella agreed. "Vokins reminds me of Marshall Field in Chicago, only on a smaller scale. Floorwalkers, a department for everything you might need to purchase; you should see it. Or Macy's in New York, or perhaps your own Harrods!" Langley appeared sufficiently impressed by the Brighton store and couldn't envisage an even larger, busier place.

The dowager, who had only shopped at Harrods on two occasions, nevertheless had no intention of attaching her name to Langley's as a department store neophyte. Instead, she said breezily, "Just stick close to me, Maxwell, and you will not get lost."

"I am not a small child," he murmured just a little too softly for her to hear. Tabitha caught his words and grinned.

"I am going to look at hats," the dowager announced. "I assume you are capable of managing while I am gone."

Tabitha assured her they would soldier on somehow. The dowager chose to ignore the sarcasm in her tone and went off to find the millinery counter.

Isabella asked a floorwalker where they could find men's gloves. The young man bowed and led them across the floor to near the lifts. A counter ran along one side, behind which were stacked drawers and tiered boxes. A young woman with a lace collar and a measuring tape around her neck approached.

"How may I serve you, sir," she asked Langley, then glanced politely to the ladies.

Langley produced Wolf's Automobile Club membership card. "I am Lord Pembroke, and this is my wife," he said, gesturing towards Tabitha. "I am a member of the Automobile Club and took part in the London to Brighton Run on Sunday. At the club's suggestion, we are noting which Brighton shops assisted motorists during the Run."

One question that worried Tabitha, although she hadn't voiced it during breakfast, was whether the name Pembroke would be recognised from the newspaper. Fortunately, when Gustaf Freund's death made headlines, the newspapers had barely mentioned Wolf and had merely stated it was the second death connected to the Run. She hoped this meant that the name, Lord Pembroke, wouldn't ring any bells. From the look on the young woman's face, it appeared that it didn't matter to her.

"The Automobile Club aims to compile a short list for the benefit of members," Langley continued. "Would you be so kind as to tell us whether you have sold men's driving gloves since Sunday? If it's not too much trouble, the date, size, and any relevant details, including names, would be helpful."

The young shopgirl looked uncertain and turned to consult a senior woman with an efficient demeanour and a pencil behind her ear. The senior examined the card, nodded once, and drew out a daybook from beneath the counter.

The woman then explained in an apologetic tone, "We only take names when a gentleman charges to account or asks for delivery. Cash sales go straight in the daybook without particulars. Repairs or alterations sometimes carry a name if the article is left and collected later. Otherwise, we note the size, colour, price, and the clerk's initials, nothing more."

She continued, "Having said that, we have sold two pairs of men's gloves since Monday," she said, then added, "Of course, we are closed on Sunday. Both pairs were plain, tan-coloured kid. One yesterday afternoon, size nine. One this morning, size eight and a half. No special entries. Both paid in cash."

"Thank you," said Langley. "You have been very helpful." Isabella pretended to make a note of the answer.

Isabella asked, "Do you keep an odd glove box for matching? I believe that some shops do."

"We do not for gentlemen's," the senior replied. "For ladies we sometimes have oddments after sales. Not for men."

No one questioned Isabella's request until they had thanked the two assistants and stepped away from the counter. Then, in a low voice, she said, "It is possible our man replaced only the missing glove. They are not a cheap purchase for everyone."

Langley, who had never shopped for himself or counted pennies, looked surprised.

"Some stores keep an odd-glove box, my lord," Isabella went on. "After sales and returns there are always singles without mates. For gentlemen they can sometimes find a near match in size and shade, then change the buttons to agree. It is quick work and cheaper than a whole new pair."

Tabitha, amused that an heiress knew such detail, raised a brow. Isabella smiled. "I like to see how things run. Shops are machines of a sort, in their own way. I ask questions, and I pay attention."

They collected the dowager and left Vokins without lingering.

"It is just as well," the dowager remarked. "There was nothing of sufficient quality."

Outside, Isabella glanced at her notebook. "Let us make our way to Hanningtons. We can try some of the smaller gentlemen's outfitters along the way."

Langley looked faintly relieved to be out of the shop. "These places are like mazes," he said. "Counters to the left and right, a bell every time the door opens, and people everywhere. It was rather overwhelming."

"It is all designed to keep you moving," Isabella said. "Hanningtons will be larger and busier still."

They visited two gentlemen's outfitters between Vokins and Hannington's, one with saddlery in the window and the other calling itself a gentlemen's repository. The first sold cycling gauntlets and had not sold fine kid gloves that week. The second had sold just a single pair of black gloves that morning to a clergyman.

By the time they reached Hanningtons, Langley had adopted a look of patient endurance. "I had no idea of my valet's stamina. I am beginning to wonder if I should increase the man's pay for his willingness to endure such places on my behalf."

"You did well," Isabella told him. "Let us hope we can find what we need at Hanningtons and be done with this excursion."

"Well, I still have not found a hat, so let us not wish the day away yet," the dowager informed them.

Hanningtons was indeed quite grand. They entered through revolving doors, an experience the dowager did not enjoy. "I will be finding a different way to exit," she stated.

A doorman at the entrance directed them to gloves, and a floorwalker escorted them along a long aisle to a wide counter.

A woman, a little past her prime, with a patient smile, stepped forward. "Good afternoon," she said. "How may I assist you?"

Langley displayed the Automobile Club card and reiterated his request. The woman listened attentively and respectfully, then nodded and reached for a daybook.

"We sold three pairs on Mondays; two size eights and a nine," she said. "Yesterday, one pair in the morning, size nine, and another in the afternoon. This morning, none so far. We also matched a single glove on Tuesday around five o'clock, not long before we closed."

The four of them maintained neutral expressions as Langley said, "Would you be kind enough to note the particulars of that last entry."

The woman ran a careful finger along the line. "Men's department. One kid glove to match. Buttons altered. Threepence. Cash. No name." She paused. "Size seven. Colour, fawn."

"Do you recall the buyer?" Isabella asked, maintaining a conversational tone. "We aim to compile a small list of shops that assist motorists, so any detail could be useful to the Automobile Club."

The woman did not rush her answer. If she wondered why their task required the names of drivers, she kept that thought to herself. "I was not at that counter for the sale," she said. "I can call the assistant who served him. If you would be so kind as to wait."

She left them and crossed the floor. After a minute, she returned with a younger woman, quite pretty and eager to please.

"This is Miss Keate," the senior said. "She served the gentleman."

Miss Keate folded her hands and took a breath, as if to ensure she would remember correctly. "The gentleman brought in a single glove," she said. "He asked if we could find a mate. The leather was quite fine, and the size, while small, was not entirely uncommon, so I fetched the odd glove box. We keep one for such occasions. I found a near match, but the buttons did not match, so our Mr Fawcett replaced both to suit."

"What time was this?" Langley asked.

"About five o'clock," Miss Keate replied. "Sir, if I may, the gentleman was very polite. He paid in cash and didn't give a name."

"Was he well dressed?" Tabitha asked, careful to sound merely curious.

"Not grand," Miss Keate said, "but respectable enough." Then, she considered the question and amended her answer. "Well, his clothes looked quite well made, but perhaps rather worn. I noticed that his cuffs were frayed. His coat had been brushed but it had seen wear. I remember wondering how a man who couldn't afford a new coat still had such fine gloves. Though, it did explain why he was hoping to replace the lost one rather than the pair. We price the odd gloves very cheaply, you see."

Tabitha asked Miss Keate if she could describe the physical appearance of the man. She was able to do so quite well; certainly, well enough.

"Thank you," Langley said. "You have both been very kind."

The senior clerk inclined her head. "If the Automobile Club prepares a list, we would be glad to be on it."

They took their leave and stepped back into the cool air of North Street. For a moment, none of them spoke. The traffic on the pavement swirled around them. At last, Langley said, "A single glove to match. Size seven. Buttons altered. Five o'clock yesterday. Do we think this is our man?"

"Not only do I think this is our killer, but I believe there is little doubt who it is," Tabitha informed him.

Langley looked at her expectantly. "Really?"

"You would not have recognised that description because he did not speak at the inquest, but I believe there is little doubt that the man who bought one glove was Ernest Wilcox." As she said this, Tabitha remembered noting how fine the gloves were when Wilcox accompanied them to Clayton Hill. She recalled him saying they were a gift from a satisfied client, which would explain how a man whose clothes had seen better days nonetheless was wearing such expensive gloves.

CHAPTER 33

Back in the carriage, the group discussed their next steps.

"We never considered Ernest Wilcox as the killer," Isabella pointed out. "Should we have?"

It was a good question, and one that Tabitha had been pondering since she realised who had bought the single glove. "It never occurred to any of us, including the police, I presume, because he was the person who reported finding the body. However, in hindsight, it was the perfect cover; he kills Havers, whether on purpose or by accident, then hails a cart and sends a boy off to call the police, while setting himself up as the Good Samaritan when they arrive. I wonder if he sent the boy so he would have time to arrange the scene as he wanted."

"But what of Gustaf Freund then?" the dowager asked.

"He must have stopped up ahead around the corner that was hidden by the hedge." Then, remembering that the dowager hadn't visited Clayton Hill with them, Isabella continued, "It is hard to describe, but once you see the road, it becomes clear that a car could have been pulled up there and that, perhaps hearing an altercation, Freund was drawn to a gap in the hedge where he might have witnessed the murder."

"And seen Ernest Wilcox dropping his glove," Tabitha pointed out. "At some point, Freund must have taken the glove, perhaps while Wilcox was talking to the boy with the cart, then he continued driving to Brighton. Later, he approaches Wilcox and tries to blackmail him."

"So, Ernest Wilcox murdered Freund as well?" Langley asked.

"It certainly makes sense," Tabitha agreed. Then, she made a decision. "I believe the time has come to lay everything we know, including the starting handle and the papers from Smithers's room, before Detective Inspector Maguire."

This was met with silence for a few moments before Langley added his agreement. "We probably should have done so earlier, but at this point, we have concrete evidence of who the killer is. It is already Thursday, and the murder was on Sunday. At some point, Maguire cannot force anyone except Wolf to stay in Brighton, and the opportunity will be lost."

When he expressed it in that way, the dowager and Isabella also concurred.

"Furthermore, I do not think we should waste any time," Langley suggested. "Let us stop by the hotel to pick up the starting handle and the papers Wolf found, then make our way to the police station immediately."

Fifteen minutes later, they were doing exactly that. They had paused just long enough to inform Wolf of what they had discovered and their plans. As frustrated as he was at not being able to join them then, he agreed it was time to share everything with Maguire.

The last time they had been in Brighton, Wolf, Langley, and later the dowager had visited Detective Inspector Maguire at Brighton Police Station; Tabitha had never visited it. Now, she looked with curiosity at the grand, imposing Georgian building with its array of neoclassical columns, which they had pulled up in front of. The dowager informed them that the police station was actually located in the building's basement.

Upon entering, they observed that the police station did not maintain the rest of the building's architectural grandeur. The ceilings were low, and the walls lacked windows. While police stations were seldom pleasant places, this one possessed an oppressive atmosphere.

Langley took the lead and approached the constable behind the desk, demanding to see Detective Inspector Maguire immediately. It wasn't even necessary for him to mention the Home Secretary's name; the sight of the group of toffs was enough to persuade the young policeman to nod and rush off to inform Maguire that he had visitors.

Within a few minutes, they were escorted into the detective inspector's small, dingy, rather depressing office.

Maguire's surprise at the visit was clear. "How can I help, m'lord?" he asked, as if they might be there to discuss anything other than Havers's murder.

There were insufficient chairs in the office, and no room to cram any others in. Tabitha and the dowager sat while Isabella and Langley leaned against the wall.

In the carriage, they had agreed that Langley would explain everything, with each of them contributing as needed. Well, Isabella and Tabitha agreed, and the dowager sullenly condescended to go along with the plan.

Now, Langley reviewed the main points they had deduced over the past few days: he asked Isabella to explain who Colonel Markham was and what his telegram had said. This resulted in the somewhat awkward explanation of how Wolf came to have Smithers's notebook and the other papers. He set the notebook, papers, and contracts on the desk. Langley then described how he found the starting handle in Felix Dubois's workshop.

Maguire said nothing, but a muscle in his cheek twitched, and his clenched jaw left little doubt about his feelings regarding their story. At Langley's suggestion, Tabitha and Isabella briefly explained what they had observed about the spot from which they believed Gustaf Freund had watched the murder. Finally, they recounted their morning's expedition and what they had discovered about a man, matching Ernest Wilcox's description, who had bought one glove.

When it was clear they had finished, Maguire took a deep breath before speaking in a cold, tight voice. "Let me make sure I understand you correctly. Lord Pembroke and Miss Hartwell broke into Mr Smithers's hotel room and rifled through his possessions. Then, Lord Langley took what you at least believed was potential murder weapon, from a crime scene and deliberately kept it from me and my men. Is that all correct so far?"

Without waiting for a reply, Maguire picked up the papers. "I don't know quite where to start. Why don't we begin with the fact that I cannot present these papers before a magistrate? You entered a man's room without leave. A court will not touch it."

Langley kept his tone steady. "Private trespass does not prevent relevance. Take possession now, seal them, and get a warrant to re-seize the same items from Mr Smithers's effects. Your chain is cured."

"The initials prove nothing," Maguire said. "G. S. could be anyone."

"They sit alongside supplier invoices that correspond with the notebook entries. You can compare them with Smithers's signature in the hotel register. Anyway, considering whose room we found them in, who else could G.S. refer to?" Langley argued.

Moving on from this point, at least for now, Maguire said, "These contracts are in French. For all I know, you have misread them."

"I speak fluent French. But feel free to fetch a certified translator. Better yet, ask the Patent Office to send an examiner. They will confirm immediately what a licence requires and whether it matches." Langley didn't raise his voice as he said this, but one look at his face should have told Maguire that he had chosen the wrong person to debate this with.

"If this is what you claim it is, then it is a trade matter. I am not inviting a civil suit," Maguire protested. "Moreover, this is fraud at most. It does not prove murder."

"It provides motive." Tabitha explained. "We also have a blackmail demand, and now we possess a probable murder weapon. All the threads come together and you are obliged to follow them. Initially, we thought that Smithers was committing fraud alone, but now we wonder if Wilcox is deeply involved and that, when Havers threatened Smithers, Mr Wilcox took the matter into his own hands and silenced him."

Remarkably, the dowager had kept her silence up until then. Now, she spoke in her most imperious tone, "Detective Inspector Maguire, surely even you can see how all this evidence is interconnected and leads to the obvious, logical, one might even say, the only conclusion: that Lord Pembroke is innocent and that Ernest Wilcox murdered Mr Havers and probably the German driver as well. Heavens above, the glove alone should be sufficient!"

"Why does the glove prove anything except that Mr Wilcox, who we know was at the scene of the murder because he discovered the body, dropped a glove which he then replaced?" This was said in a tone of such exasperation that Tabitha was afraid the man would throw them out of his office without further discussion.

In what she hoped was a calm, reasonable voice, Tabitha said, "Then why did Gustaf Freund, who we know was blackmailing the killer, have the missing glove?"

"How can we even be sure it was the killer he was blackmailing?" Maguire pointed out. "All the note said was: *I will tell what I saw on the road that day.* He could have seen many things. That a glove then ended up under his bed proves nothing. You cannot even be sure that it is Mr Wilcox's missing glove. This could just be a coincidence."

Suddenly, Tabitha had a dreadful realisation: "You are not going to do anything about this, are you? You remain convinced that my husband is the murderer and have decided that everything that we have presented to you is unrelated or purely coincidental."

Maguire hesitated for a moment. "I am prepared to question Mr Wilcox," he finally conceded. "However, nothing more at this time."

Tabitha could see that the stubborn policeman was digging in his heels. She stood and said without attempting to soften her tone, "I trust that you will."

CHAPTER 34

The group returned to The Grand, tired and frustrated. Tabitha didn't relish the thought of having to tell Wolf about their success in identifying Wilcox as the owner of the glove and their then unmitigated failure in persuading Maguire of its importance.

No one spoke during most of the short carriage journey from the police station. At last, as they pulled up outside the hotel, Langley told Tabitha, "Maguire is obstinate and beginning to veer into the realm of personal vendetta against Wolf."

"Well, no doubt he was not pleased by our apparent interference in his case against Robert Charles, even though we proved to be right in the end," Tabitha observed. "However, I am shocked that he would take that irritation so far as to ignore the clear evidence in front of him."

"If needed, I will speak to the Home Secretary and ask him to have a word with the Chief Constable."

The dowager sniffed. "One might question why you did not do that to begin with, Maxwell."

In a measured tone, he replied, "Given the current public sentiment against the upper classes receiving special treatment, I felt it prudent to let the investigation play out and Wolf's innocence to be proven beyond dispute. However, now that the proof is being ignored, it may be time. At the end of the day, if Maguire chooses not to see Wilcox as the obvious suspect, that is his business; our primary concern must be that he acknowledges Wolf's lack of involvement."

Tabitha pondered Langley's words. Of course, he was correct. Removing Wolf from the list of suspects was the most important thing. Nevertheless, the thought that Wilcox might slip away after committing two murders didn't sit well with her.

As they entered the hotel, the porter approached the dowager with a note. She read it and then informed the others, "It seems that Mr Dubois has woken up. I paid one of the nurses to alert me if and when this happened."

"Then, let us go immediately," Tabitha exclaimed. She then realised that this would keep Wolf on tenterhooks for even longer. "Langley, would you mind going and explaining everything to Wolf while Mama, Isabella, and I go to the hospital?" He nodded his willingness and moved towards the lift while the three women turned back to the carriage that hadn't even had time to pull away since they exited it.

The dowager instructed the driver to head to the Brighton Workhouse Infirmary. The carriage left The Grand on King's Road, went up West Street to the Clock Tower, continued along North Street to Old Steine, then up Grand Parade and across to Elm Grove. In front was the Workhouse Infirmary, a simple, functional-looking building with a tall central clock tower. A porter in a worn frock coat watched their approach with a bemused look, as if unaccustomed to fancy carriages stopping there.

The dowager descended and approached the porter. "We have come to see Monsieur Felix Dubois," she announced, offering her card. "He was brought from a workshop accident."

The porter hesitated. "Visiting hours are later, m'lady."

"I am sure they are for the masses. However, we will be visiting now." The dowager didn't give the poor man a chance to object before marching up the steps and into the infirmary. Isabella and Tabitha followed.

Inside, the entrance hall smelled strongly of carbolic. Its sharp medicinal smell made Tabitha involuntarily scrunch up her face. A ward sister met them, her apron and cap so starched that they barely looked like fabric. The sister did not look happy at their intrusion into her domain. She repeated the porter's words about visiting hours.

The dowager repeated her purpose, adding, "The police are concerned. Kindly take us to your patient."

The sister looked sceptical for a moment, but the dowager's voice and demeanour left no doubt that the woman would not be thwarted. The nurse gave a quick nod. "I will take you to him. You may have five minutes."

They were led down a corridor where doors stood open, revealing small wards with tidy rows of iron bedsteads, each covered with thin, grey blankets. At the far end of the corridor, the sister paused, pushed open a swing door, and led them into a narrow ward where Dubois lay propped on pillows, his eyes open and alert. He had one arm bandaged, and his hair was singed.

"You were lucky, Monsieur Dubois," the dowager said, taking the chair without asking. She introduced herself, then said, "We have questions. You will answer them."

She had spoken in French, but the man responded in serviceable English. With an embarrassed smile, he said, "I was a fool with a lamp and a petrol tin. I meant no harm to anyone, least of all myself." He looked at the dowager. "I remember that you and a gentleman found me, and I believe you called for an ambulance. Merci."

"Monsieur Dubois, when Lord Langley, the gentleman who found you, examined what was left of your workshop, he discovered your tool tray. On it was a starting handle with red paint on it. Do you have any idea why it was there?" Tabitha asked gently.

"Non. I saw it, but I do not know how it got there," Dubois said. "I mark my tools in blue. That handle had a red band by the socket. At Preston Park there was a crush. Spectators pressed in, a reporter asked for a word, then a constable told me to move the car along. While I answered, anyone could have set a piece on my tray. It happens. Drivers borrow, boys fetch and carry, and things are returned to the nearest bench. When I found it, I assumed that was what happened."

Isabella interjected, "Indeed, I know that is true." She hesitated for a moment before asking, "Do you know Mr Ernest Wilcox?"

"Oui. I know him."

"When you were at Preston Park, did you see him near your motor-car?" Isabella asked as casually as she could, but Dubois couldn't miss how pointed the question was.

"Yes, I saw Mr Wilcox hovering about. He mentioned he wanted to see how Peugeot arranged the throttle and asked if a tyre pump had gone missing. I thought nothing of it. Later, when I unpacked at the mews, the red-banded handle was among my spanners. I assumed a neighbour had put it down by mistake and meant to ask around in the morning."

Tabitha pondered how to pose the question they needed answered. "Monsieur Dubois, do you think it is possible that Mr Wilcox put the handle among your tools?"

Dubois frowned as he thought. "I was under the bonnet, checking the jet, when he appeared at my shoulder. I told him to look if he wanted and returned to my tools. Looking back, I do think he was holding a tool. But I thought nothing of it; a driver holding a starting handle isn't unusual."

"Did he touch the car?" Isabella asked. "Or your tray?"

"I could not swear to it. It was very busy. There was noise, questions, photographers. I saw him step away, then step back. He asked if anyone had seen a spare tyre pump left on the grass. He said a boy had borrowed his. He made a show of hunting for it. After that, I lost sight of him."

Tabitha glanced at Isabella, then back to Dubois. "Later, when you unpacked at the mews, did anything in your tools seem wrong?"

Dubois nodded slowly. "Yes. I saw straight away that there was a starting handle in the tray that was not mine. Heavier than my own, a little longer. It carried a band of red paint near the socket."

The three women exchanged a glance. Dubois continued with more certainty in his voice.

"I mark my kit in blue. Everyone working around me knows it. The handle I found had a red ring on it. I thought someone had played a joke, or that a neighbour had set it down by mistake. I meant to ask around the next morning."

"Did you keep it?" Isabella asked.

"I set it aside on the bench and thought someone might come by, asking. The day of the explosion, I finally put it back in my tool tray and thought I would take it back to London and ask around. Then I started to prise open a petrol tin and knocked the lamp. The blast threw everything. I do not know what became of the handle after that."

"The red ring is De Dion practice," Isabella said. "Thomas Havers drove a De Dion."

Dubois closed his eyes for a moment. "Then that is where it came from, you think?"

Tabitha kept her voice gentle. "One more thing. Just before you were taken away in the ambulance, you mentioned an Englishman. Who were you referring to?"

There was silence while Dubois thought. Then, a memory seemed to surface, and he said, "I was waiting for someone the day of the explosion. I was waiting for an English driver who owed me money for some work I'd done for him. I think I meant him."

"Well, that is quite disappointing," the dowager said with a pout.

Tabitha had to agree. Then, she had a thought. "Would you be prepared to speak to the police and tell them that the starting handle appeared in your tool tray after the Run and that Ernest Wilcox was hovering around your motor-car in Preston Park?" In all honesty, she wasn't sure that telling this to Detective Inspector Maguire would make a difference. Still, she hoped that at some point, the sheer volume of evidence would make it impossible to dismiss everything as a coincidence.

Dubois shifted against his pillows. "Madame, I am not a brave man, but I will say what I saw. I did see that man, Wilcox, linger by my tray with no reason to linger. If a strange handle with a red ring was found among my tools, someone put it there, and it was not me."

"Perhaps we should ask Monsieur Dubois to write a statement testifying to this," Isabella suggested. It was a good idea. Tabitha called the ward sister over. "Would you kindly witness Monsieur Dubois's written account?" The sister agreed and fetched a sheet of notepaper. Tabitha quickly wrote down what Dubois had told them, then he signed it, and the sister signed as a witness.

With that done, Tabitha exhaled. "Now Maguire must listen."

The dowager rose, satisfied. "Let us hope so."

As they stepped into the corridor, Isabella spoke first. "What do we do next?"

"I am not sure I can face the detective inspector again today," Tabitha admitted. "Let us return to the hotel, and I will send him a note and Dubois's testimony from there. I would imagine that he has not summoned Mr Wilcox yet, so perhaps this news will encourage him to do so."

CHAPTER 35

Tabitha, Isabella, and the dowager returned to the hotel and told Wolf about their conversation with Dubois. Then, they ordered lunch up to the room. They were expecting it any minute when there was a knock at the door. Assuming it was their food, Wolf opened it to find the hall waiter carrying a small silver tray on which sat a card, addressed to Miss Hartwell. Wolf thanked him. Isabella waited until the door had closed before she broke the seal. She read in silence, then passed the slip to Wolf.

"From my friend at the front desk," she explained with a knowing smile. "I asked him, as a special favour to me, to keep an eye on Mr Smithers."

"You have the young man quite in your thrall," the dowager observed, before adding, "Excellent job, Miss Hartwell. I admire a young woman who knows how to use her beauty to manipulate men." While there was no doubt that the dowager was entirely genuine in this praise, Isabella blushed. It was evident, at least to Tabitha, that she took no pleasure in wielding her loveliness in this manner and had merely done so for expediency's sake.

Ignoring the dowager's comment, Isabella said, "It says Mr Smithers left a note for Mr Ernest Wilcox. My friend at the desk copied the particulars into the message book before forwarding it: two o'clock at the tea rooms by the Clock Tower."

"How very enterprising of the young man," the dowager said dryly.

Tabitha glanced at the mantel clock. "It is already quarter past one. I assume we plan to listen in on this meeting somehow."

Wolf immediately stood up. "We must leave immediately. We cannot risk missing it."

"Wolf, my love. How are you planning to join this expedition?" Tabitha asked. "From everything Detective Inspector Maguire said this morning, there is no doubt he considers you still under house arrest at the hotel. And certainly, the constable was still loitering in the lobby when we returned earlier."

The dowager set down her teacup. "If you must go sneaking about, someone must keep an officious constable occupied, and who better than me?" Then, with the air of a martyr taking the higher path, she added, "Only recently, Tabitha, I was accused of refusing to accept that, in these affairs, one sometimes leads and sometimes lends support. Kindly observe that I am choosing to remain behind and forgo all the fun in order to play my part in supporting the investigation."

"Duly noted, Mama," Tabitha said.

Wolf cast a look of genuine gratitude towards the dowager. "Indeed, Lady Pembroke, you are as gracious as you are wily."

The dowager appeared very pleased with this remark. "Come down the stairs so that he is not alerted by the lift door opening. Keep an eye out and be ready to exit the hotel on my cue."

She stood up and left the room quickly. Tabitha, Wolf, and Isabella swiftly put on their outerwear and headed towards the staircase. Wolf wasn't pleased about Tabitha attending the tearoom rendezvous, but he knew better than to voice his objections.

As luck would have it, the constable posted in the lobby that afternoon was a very young man who had been with the police force for barely six months. While the dowager had never doubted her ability to cause a suitable distraction, when she saw how inexperienced the man was, she smiled and relished the thought of the scene she was about to create.

The dowager paused in the hotel lobby, prepared herself for the performance ahead, before patting her sleeve and skirt dramatically. "My reticule," she gasped breathlessly. "Gone. Vanished. Young man, you in the helmet, attend to me immediately."

The young constable sprang to her side. "What is missing, ma'am?" It seemed he didn't know who she was. Under normal circumstances, the dowager would have wasted no time correcting him and ensuring she was addressed appropriately. However, she decided to let the matter slide this time.

"A small black silk reticule with a silver frame and tassel. It contained my purse. We must establish a cordon before the ruffian can escape." She pointed at the vestibule. "You will secure that threshold, then take particulars. Name, hour, and errand of every passerby. It must have been snatched just as I stepped off the lift."

The constable looked with obvious scepticism at the very short distance the dowager must have walked from the lift. He was about to comment, then noticed the expression on the terrifying old woman's face and decided against it.

Instead, he glanced nervously around the lobby before saying, "Yes, madam."

"Good. Now we must do this methodically," she ordered. "Fetch that writing table." The dowager swept to the concierge stand and retrieved some notepaper and a pen. "We shall draw a search grid. Begin here at the door. We need to be sure where you have searched."

The constable did as he was told and fetched the small writing table and chair, placing them where the dowager directed. Then, she moved the chair slightly so her back faced the lobby, laid out the map, and insisted that the young, flustered policeman lean over her shoulder to see where she wanted him to search.

With his back also conveniently turned towards the lobby, she pointed at the rough map she'd drawn. "Square A is the vestibule. Square B the pavement to the carriage step. Mark the cigar counter as C. You shall proceed in rings. You will instruct the porter to walk the perimeter and report back at each quarter hour. This scoundrel must not escape."

The young man was so in awe of the dowager that he was quite dumbfounded, and any thoughts he might have had about the absurdity of the situation were certainly not ones he intended to voice.

Instead, he resumed listening intently as the dowager listed various locations inside and around the hotel. As she did so, she caught sight of Tabitha, Wolf, and Isabella lurking just beyond the lift by the door that led to the stairs. Almost imperceptibly, the dowager nodded, signalling they should cross the lobby and leave the hotel at once.

As they moved towards her, the dowager exclaimed to the constable, "Splendid, splendid young man. Now I need you to announce that no one may cross the vestibule until you have had a chance to sweep the area and interview everyone present. Speak with authority. I shall supervise."

The poor policeman was too absorbed in trying to explain why he lacked the authority to do that to notice the threesome, including Wolf, sneaking out of the hotel.

As they slipped out of the door and hurried away from the hotel front, Isabella couldn't help but laugh. "That poor young policeman. How long do you think Lady Pembroke will keep that up now that we've gone?"

"Knowing Mama, she is thoroughly enjoying herself and will likely keep the ruse going far longer than necessary," Tabitha replied.

Wolf suggested they hail a hackney cab; using the hotel carriage seemed far too conspicuous.

The cab turned onto West Street towards the Clock Tower. The tearoom at the corner was busy but not crowded. During the journey, they discussed how they should proceed. Smithers hadn't met Tabitha or Isabella, but Wilcox had. They were twenty minutes early, and it seemed best to wait inside the tearoom rather than outside.

"I suggest that we give a large tip to the waitress and ask her to seat us in a booth and to show Wilcox and Smithers to the neighbouring booth, with ours nearer the back so they don't pass us on their way in," Isabella suggested. It was an excellent plan.

Inside, the tearoom featured rows of small marble tables, a long counter with cakes displayed on stands, and three tall windows that overlooked the street. Along one side were booths that were more private and so likely to be Smithers's choice.

Wolf, Tabitha, and Isabella entered and approached a waitress. After quickly assuring himself that the two men they sought hadn't yet arrived, Wolf reached into his pocket for a shiny half-crown and made his request of the waitress. She quickly realised what they were hoping to do, pocketed the coin, and, without questioning why, led them to a booth that was shielded from view by someone entering the tearoom. Thanks to a gilt pier-glass angled along the wall, they had a clear view of the room's reflection.

Given that they'd left the hotel before their meal arrived, Wolf insisted that they order some sandwiches and tea.

Smithers arrived first. He looked worried but not panicked. He wore a coat that had been meticulously brushed and a tie that was more fashionable than elegant. He spoke to the girl at the door with an air of someone expecting special treatment and let her lead him to the booth next to Tabitha and Wolf's. He seemed more focused on watching the door than on observing his fellow patrons.

Five minutes later, Wilcox entered, hat brim low, collar up, trying to go unnoticed. Watching his reflection, Wolf noticed a tautness to his mouth and the way he carried his shoulders; it was clear the man was under considerable stress. Smithers gave a faint nod. Wilcox approached him. The two men sat close, heads inclined. A waitress came over. Smithers raised two fingers, ordered without checking with his companion, and then dismissed the girl with a pompous wave of his hand.

CHAPTER 36

Wolf angled himself slightly and caught the men's faces in the mirror. Luckily, because the tearoom was busy and there was a buzz of conversation in the air, Smithers didn't make as much of an effort to keep his voice down as Wolf had anticipated he might.

"That detective inspector called on me," Wilcox said. "He was asking a lot of awkward questions. Somehow, he knows about the starting handle, or thinks he does. It appears that the Frenchman's workshop exploded, and the discovery was made when he was rescued. I don't know exactly how they realised it was Havers's, but I'm guessing it has something to do with those busybody toffs. Then, he asked whether I knew Freund. He asked whether I had ever bought gloves at Hanningtons. I think they suspect me."

Smithers stirred his tea and took his time responding. "Well, you are guilty after all, old chap. Stopping was folly enough. Letting temper govern you was worse."

"Havers knew too much, or at least he guessed. He'd dropped some big hints at the start of the Run and started making more threats. When I saw him pulled over at Clayton Hill, I just wanted to try to reason with him."

"And yet, you ended up in a physical altercation with him which resulted in you clobbering him with his starting handle," Smithers pointed out.

"But it was an accident," Wilcox insisted unconvincingly. "I didn't mean to kill him."

"Then, perhaps the best course of action would have been to admit it to the police upon their arrival rather than playing the hero who stopped to help and called for the authorities." Smithers's voice was so condescending that Wolf almost felt sorry for Wilcox. He couldn't imagine how these two ended up as partners in villainy, but there seemed little doubt that Smithers was the brains of the team and barely tolerated Wilcox.

Snidely, Wilcox replied, "Are you aware that they suspect something about our operation? And not because I didn't keep my head. Someone has been at your papers. They have the French contracts." The man sounded almost pleased to have something to throw back at his partner.

Smithers's voice turned icy and fearful. "My papers? How? What?"

"I'm not sure how much or how. They know about Lefèvre. The police asked me about it."

Smithers tapped the spoon once, set it down, and appeared to compose himself. "Then you will do this," he said. His tone was calm, almost clinical. "Put your papers in order. If questioned, disclaim any partnership, and most importantly, keep your distance from me. If necessary, say that a French rival is trying to smear your name."

Wilcox leaned in. "And what will you do?"

"Nothing," Smithers said. "I was not involved in your quarrel with Havers. I was not involved with any German who found himself dead in a lodging house. I do not know what you did or did not do on Sunday afternoon. If you were foolish enough to let your temper strike sparks, that belongs to you."

Suddenly, Wilcox's voice dropped, and Wolf had to strain to hear. "He said he wasn't arresting me yet, but that I was not to leave Brighton under any circumstances. Now, I'm worried about the boy."

"What boy?" Smithers demanded.

"The boy with the cart," he said. "The one I sent to fetch the police. I think he saw the starting handle before I lifted it from the road. He might have seen me stow it under the rug in the back of the car. I can't be sure, but his cart came around the corner as my back was turned. He didn't say anything, but if the police show him the handle, I'm worried about what he might say."

Smithers sat still and stared for a moment. "You are saying there is a witness. Who is this boy?"

"Just one of the porter's lads from Devil's Dyke. He told the constable when he returned where they could find him later, and I overheard. He said he is an errand boy at the hotel. Apparently, they sent him from the Dyke Hotel to the Pyecombe smithy for a new horseshoe, and he was crossing past Clayton Hill when he came upon me. If they ask him about the handle, I'm finished."

In the mirror, Wolf saw Smithers press a fingertip to the rim of his cup, then wipe the moisture from his finger with his napkin in a gesture of disdain. "You will not go blundering after some child like a storybook villain. You will not drag me further into your panic. You will take a breath, you will tie off every loose thread that belongs to you, and you will sit quietly. If you run about, you invite further attention."

Wilcox's hand rested flat on the table, as if he were fighting the impulse to slap Smithers. "Sitting quietly is not an option. Maguire will have me back tomorrow. He asked whether I knew Hanningtons. He wouldn't have asked that if he hadn't heard about the glove. Someone has been to the shop. Someone asked questions. If the boy adds his piece, the picture is complete."

Smithers glanced towards the window and then back. "Destroy whatever remains. Deny the rest. That is my advice. As for the boy, if you approach him now and try to persuade him, you risk putting a noose around your own neck."

Wilcox shook his head. "I don't agree. If I hire a gig and go now, I can ask a simple question. A few coins may secure his silence. If not, an accident might happen by the cliff edge."

Smithers leaned back. "You are an even bigger fool than I thought. It's not enough that you've already killed two men; now you're going to find a boy, threaten and try to bribe him, and then what? Kill him too? I wash my hands of you!"

"Perhaps I am a fool," Wilcox said. "Or perhaps I am a man who refuses to be ruined by a child. Are you coming with me?"

"No," Smithers said immediately. "I do not follow men when they dig their own graves."

Wilcox's response was a sharp, mirthless laugh.

Smithers continued, "Do not write to me. Do not call on me. If you are questioned, forget my name."

Wilcox leaned in. "And what will you tell them if they question you?"

"I will say I knew Havers only as a face in a crowd," Smithers replied. "I will say I have never heard of Freund. I will say I spoke to you about tyres and pumps and nothing more. That will be true enough for a magistrate. Certainly, I will claim no knowledge, let alone involvement, in the deaths of Havers or Freund, because that is the truth."

Wilcox fixed him with a long stare, then rose. "You will find that the police and magistrates might not be as gullible as you believe."

"And you will find that I will not be standing beside you, regardless," Smithers said.

"Then, I will have to look after the boy myself this afternoon. I cannot risk the police questioning him further." With that, Wilcox stood, placed a coin on the table, turned, and departed. After a moment, Smithers shook his head in resignation at his colleague's folly, laid another coin down, and also left.

When they had gone, Wolf said, "I have to follow him to Devil's Dyke. I cannot allow him to hurt anyone else."

"What do you mean to do?" Tabitha cried in alarm.

"I will also rent a gig and follow him." He looked from Isabella to Tabitha. "You two need to go straight to the police station. Inform them that Wilcox is on the move and where he is headed. Tell them there is a witness at risk. Make them understand that this cannot wait."

"You must not go alone," Tabitha said. "Wait for Bear. Do you even have your revolver with you?"

"There is no time to argue about it," Wolf replied without admitting that he didn't have his gun with him. "If we all run to the station, we lose him. If I go now, I can try to save the boy. I will not try to grapple with a man on a ridge unless there is no other choice."

Isabella touched Tabitha's arm. "We can be at the station in five minutes if we take a cab," she said. "We will not leave him without help."

Tabitha took a steady breath and nodded. "Go," she said to Wolf. "We will bring Maguire."

Wolf nodded, kissed Tabitha, and rose. With his hat brim low, he followed Wilcox down Middle Street to a livery yard behind the shops. Wolf saw him speak quietly to the ostler and count coins into his palm. Within minutes, a bay cob was brought round with a light gig. Wilcox took the reins himself, adjusted the traces, and drove out towards West Street. Wolf waited a few minutes, then entered the yard and asked for the quickest gig they had. A chestnut pony and trap appeared. He paid cash, kept his hat low, left the yard. As he left, he heard a slight rattle coming from the gig. It occurred to him to turn back and swap the gig, but he didn't have the time. Instead, he prayed the rattle didn't mean anything serious, and set off two corners behind Wilcox, letting him climb towards Dyke Road while holding back in the traffic.

With Wolf gone, there was no time to lose. Tabitha settled the bill, and she and Isabella left the tearoom.

Tabitha paused on the pavement to orient herself before turning to Isabella. "Let us make haste." They hurried over to the cab rank and flagged down a hackney. Tabitha gave the address for the police station with a firmness that brooked no delay.

In the cab, Isabella said, "Devil's Dyke? What sort of name is that? If there ever was a name for a place in a penny dreadful, it would be that."

Tabitha simply nodded. Considering that the last time they visited Brighton, Devil's Dyke was where they apprehended a murderer after he had taken Tabitha hostage, she couldn't believe Wolf was pursuing yet another killer there.

At the police station, Maguire was conferring with a sergeant when the two women strode in purposefully. The desk constable stood upright. In a calm, clear voice, Tabitha relayed the conversation they had just overheard. She finished with the statement, "If you do not come now, Detective Inspector, you may lose both your suspect and your witness."

Maguire looked at them in amazement as Tabitha spoke. When she finished, there was a moment when she worried he might throw them out of the police station. Then, he turned to the sergeant and said, "Rig a light cart and gather some men. We need to head towards Devil's Dyke."

Tabitha seized his sleeve before he left the desk. "He is a desperate man, detective inspector. My husband is unarmed."

Maguire's jaw clenched. "We will stop Wilcox. I promise you." He tipped his hat and ran out.

The women had instructed the hackney carriage driver to wait. Now, as they got back in, Tabitha directed him to The Grand. "I am not confident in Maguire and his men. We need to alert Langley and Bear and have them go up there. With weapons," she added. Isabella nodded in agreement.

CHAPTER 37

As Wolf drove out of Brighton, the road inclined, and the chestnut pony leaned into the harness. The last time he had visited Devil's Dyke, they had travelled by train. When Wolf asked the ostler how long the journey should take, he said that with a brisk trot and a willing horse like Pansy, the chestnut, it should take only forty-five minutes. Of course, Wilcox had a head start, and Wolf wanted to stay far enough behind him so the other man didn't notice he was being followed.

While he had no desire to see the boy used as bait, Wolf realised that catching Wilcox in the act of terrorising the lad, hopefully with Maguire arriving in time to bear witness, might be the best way to prove his innocence once and for all. He assumed Maguire was heading for the Devil's Dyke hotel, given that was where he believed the boy to work. Of course, he might not find him there immediately. Wolf only hoped that there was enough delay to enable him to catch up with Wilcox and intervene.

Given the need for haste, Wolf felt a faint shiver through the shafts of the gig with a sinking heart, then heard a soft clatter from the near wheel. He eased the pony, listening closely. The clatter came again, sharper, followed by a sideways twitch of the gig. He pulled up immediately and jumped down.

He examined the near wheel, which he thought was the source of the noise. It showed a clear wobble at the hub. Wolf looked at the axle end and cursed softly; the linchpin was missing. Only a smear of grease and a bright ring on the iron indicated where it had been before it came loose.

Wolf had repaired a few gigs in his youth and knew what was needed. He scanned the hedge, found a straight green stick, and cut it with the knife he was relieved to find he had on him. He peeled away the bark, then shaved a taper until it fit snugly through the axle eye. A broken strand from the tug served for lashing. He hammered the makeshift peg in, turned it so it fit tightly, then wrapped it securely with the thong. Finally, he knotted it twice and tucked the end back under itself. All in all, he hadn't spent more than twenty minutes on the repairs.

Knowing that the gig still had some way to go, Wolf spun the wheel, testing it. The wobble had disappeared, but he had no idea how long his makeshift linchpin would hold. He checked the other wheel for caution's sake, then climbed up, took the reins, and urged the chestnut forward at a steady trot. He had lost more time and just hoped the delay wouldn't prevent him from saving the boy.

The chestnut had settled after the repair, and the gig was running smoothly as Wolf turned off Dyke Road and took the last rise towards the ridge. He drove into the yard by the hotel and pulled up. Another gig was already there, the bay cob blowing a little through its nostrils while a groom rubbed its neck with a grubby rag. The horse was the same colour as the one Wilcox had hired. The sight made Wolf's pulse quicken slightly and gave him hope.

Wolf climbed down, hitched the reins to the rail, and entered beneath the hotel's low signboard. The public room was filled with a scattering of men in working coats and a few visitors in city clothes, finishing a late tea. It was too late in the season for many day-trippers.

He crossed to the counter and addressed the barmaid. "I am looking for a young lad who works here. I am unsure of his name, but I believe he's your porter's boy."

The barmaid was a voluptuous woman who seemed dressed more appropriately for a woman half her age. "Sammy Turner? He's a popular one today, for sure. A gentleman was asking for him not twenty minutes ago." Then, the barmaid added lasciviously with a knowing wink, "Anything I can help you with, sir?"

When Wolf politely but firmly declined the offer, the woman nodded towards the door. "They stepped outside. The gentleman said he only wanted a word in private. From what I could see, they went that way, past the yard wall." She pointed in the direction she'd seen Wilcox and Sammy go.

Wolf thanked the woman and threw her a few coins before leaving the hotel. Outside, he caught the eye of the groom, who was still rubbing down the bay.

"The gentleman who came with this one," Wolf asked. "Which way did he take the lad?"

The groom jerked his chin towards the road. "They crossed and went towards the rim path, sir. I saw them pass the funicular ticket office. That way."

Another man, standing idly by the wall, added, "I glimpsed them near the hut, sir, then lost them behind the slope."

Wolf's gaze traced the line of the rim. The Dyke sliced through the hills in a wide, green scoop. Paths crisscrossed and branched, some leading to the main viewpoint with its benches and rail, while others descended lower and then curved underneath the lip. He had to decide immediately.

He crossed the road, skirted a cart with stacked crates of bottled ale, and headed for the most obvious path to the main outlook. There were a few people gathered there as a man with a battered guidebook in hand pointed across the Weald to a distant church spire. Wolf scanned every face and edge. He saw no boy and no Wilcox.

Doubling back at the fork, Wolf looked around carefully. Off to his right, the ground showed signs of narrow wheels. Between those wheel marks lay two sets of footprints. There appeared to be a distinct size difference, enough for Wolf to think they belonged to a grown man and a young boy.

Taking a chance, Wolf chose that path, only hoping he was correct. The Dyke's funicular hut stood closed for the season. He passed the first hut and took the slope that curled beneath the lip. Down here, the sound of voices echoed oddly. Wolf halted to listen. At first, he heard only the wind. Then, faintly, a boy's voice answered something he couldn't quite make out.

Wolf quickened his pace. The narrow path ran along a shoulder of chalk. To his right, the slope dropped away towards the bottom of the bowl. Wolf rounded a bend and saw them.

Ernest Wilcox stood across the path as if to bar it with his body. He held a rough-hewn stick that he seemed to be using as a cane in one hand and had his other hand half lifted, as if to keep the boy from passing. Sammy stood before him, chin raised, a cap pulled down tightly, and a worn jacket on his back. The boy must have been around ten or eleven years old. There was something about him that reminded Wolf of Rat. The two stood a little too close to the edge for Wolf's liking.

"Wilcox," Wolf called from twenty paces away. "Stand back from the boy."

Wilcox turned his head, his mouth tightening. "Lord Pembroke," he said in surprise, "This is not your concern. I'm just talking with the lad. I'm not sure what has brought you here, but I can assure you this is none of your business."

Sammy Turner glanced at Wolf, who saw relief flicker across his face. It seemed the lad had sensed the danger he was in. Sammy looked back at Wilcox and said, "I have to be back for the evening post."

"You will be," Wilcox said. "I only need a minute more of your time."

"Stand away from the boy," Wolf repeated. He continued along the path calmly, hoping not to startle either of them into a misstep, but not too slowly either.

Wilcox remained still. He casually lifted the stick and tapped it against the turf as if keeping time. "There has been enough lying about Sunday," he said, pitching his voice very low. "I would have the truth. That is all."

"You will not have it from a frightened child on a ledge," Wolf said. "Sammy, step this way. Come."

The boy moved to obey. Wilcox reached out quickly to catch the boy's sleeve. The lad jerked back, and Wilcox's fingers closed on the cloth. That slight movement caused the boy to slip on the loose gravel. Wolf moved instinctively. He covered the last steps, one hand extended for the boy, his other hand raised towards Wilcox's wrist. The stick came up, more as a reflex than a strike. It thumped Wolf's forearm and jolted him, then slid away and dropped to the ground. As the chalk slid under his heel, Wolf caught Wilcox's wrist and twisted enough to break the grip without breaking the arm. The boy darted behind Wolf's shoulder.

"Stand back, Wilcox. This is over," Wolf said, breathing heavily, every sense sharpened. "Sammy, go up the path behind me and keep to the inner side. Do not run. When you meet anyone, tell them you need the police."

Sammy did as he was instructed, slipping past and then descending the slope carefully, one hand brushing the bank as he moved. Wolf kept his body positioned between Wilcox and the edge until the boy had gone out of reach.

Wilcox looked at Wolf, and something mean and hard showed through whatever polish he had tried to present in Brighton. "You are a fine one to lecture, Pembroke," he said. "Playing at a motorist while the rest of us are trying to make a living. That's all I was doing, trying to make some money. Havers taunted me with what he thought he knew."

"And so, you killed him?" Wolf demanded.

"He fell and hit his head," Wilcox continued to insist. The man's jaw was clenched tightly. He had intended to resolve this quietly but had failed to do so. His eyes flicked to the upper path, then to the lower, and back to Wolf. He shifted one foot to the side as if trying to go around. Wolf mirrored the move and blocked him again. The turf was soft from recent rain, and the ground dropped away quickly. A misstep might be fatal.

"Do not be a fool," Wolf said. "This is over."

"Move aside," Wilcox said.

"No."

The two stood like that long enough for the wind to pick up again. Then Wilcox's face adopted an expression of resignation. He drew his hands to his sides and took a half step back, as if he would do as he had been told. However, Wolf noticed his eyes cut past him toward the lower path. Another man might have been fooled into expecting compliance, but Wolf had anticipated such a feint, saw the quick glance for what it was, and didn't relax.

Suddenly, confirming Wolf's instincts, Wilcox sprang towards him and bounded along the sheep track that ran beneath the lip and then curled round towards the saddle above the funicular hut.

Wolf pursued him immediately. He was no athlete and had lost some of his stamina since moving to Chesterton House. Luckily, Wilcox seemed even less suited for such exertion, and Wolf easily kept the man in sight as the path inclined upward. Twice, Wilcox glanced back, the fear on his face evident even from a distance. He tried to accelerate and steer towards the saddle.

There was far less light than just minutes earlier, and Wolf realised it was dusk. If he didn't catch Wilcox soon, the man might vanish into the darkness of night. No sooner had he thought this than lights appeared ahead on the ridge, followed by the shapes of men. Wilcox saw them as well and paused. The men ran towards him.

A voice carried on the wind. "Halt, Ernest Wilcox!" Maguire's voice was unmistakable. Another man held a lamp high, and the circle of light swung over the chalk and the grass and made Wilcox stand out against the pale surfaces. He had a choice now. He could try for the light, which meant the police, or he could try to throw himself through Wolf and past him. He stood, breathing hard, and stared from one to the other.

"Give yourself up now," Maguire demanded.

Wilcox did not answer. Instead, he looked down the slope and then up again, then moved. He did not run at Maguire. He flung himself at Wolf. He put his head down and charged like a man breaking a tackle. Wolf was ready. He didn't try to block him straight on but shifted half a pace and reached out a hand to try to grab Wilcox's jacket. As he grabbed at a lapel, Wilcox swung a fist and caught Wolf's shoulder, and they went side-on to the slope. The chalk under Wolf's heel slid. He went down on one knee and felt the ground shift slightly beneath him. He grabbed a clump of coarse grass with his free hand and held on, then used the lapel grip to turn Wilcox half round and check him.

Two constables approached rapidly down the last stretch of the slope with quick, sliding steps and reached them. Maguire followed behind. Wilcox swung once more, an ugly, wild blow, and grazed Wolf's cheek. He pulled to free himself and made a final push towards the open side. The nearest constable, a stocky man with meaty fists, placed one hand around Wilcox's upper arm and the other on his wrist, forcing it back. Maguire seized the opportunity, grabbed the free hand by the thumb, and bent it in. One handcuff clicked shut, followed by a second.

"You are done," Maguire said. "Take him up."

Wilcox's face twisted. He said, with more fury than sense, "It was an accident and you know it. And I never touched that Frenchman."

"Save it for the magistrate," Maguire said, calm again now that the thing was accomplished.

Wolf stood up. His knee ached as if struck by a plank, and his cheek stung, but nothing was broken beyond those knocks. He turned to look uphill. Sammy was there, pale and wide-eyed, with a constable's greatcoat around his shoulders. He had clearly run up to the road to meet the cart coming up and explained everything. Wolf gave the boy a quick nod, and the boy responded with a shy yet proud nod.

"Thank you," Wolf said to him in a level tone. "You were very brave."

"Yes, sir," the boy said. He ducked his head. "Thank you for coming for me."

"You are very welcome, Sammy," Wolf said.

Maguire issued a few sharp orders. One constable went to fetch the cart. Wilcox, hands in irons, gazed into the darkness then looked up at the lantern with an expression that flickered between rage and fear.

Detective Inspector Maguire looked at Wolf. "Lady Pembroke found me at the station," he said. "She bade me find you. We will take him in and hold him. The boy will be seen home. I will want his account again in the morning, clear and written down." Then, pausing, Maguire said, "I may owe you an apology, m'lord. It should go without saying that you are free to leave Brighton whenever you wish."

Wolf touched his cheek and found blood on his fingertips. He merely nodded in response.

By the time they reached the hotel, The Grand's carriage was pulling up, and Bear and Langley sprang out, followed by Tabitha and Isabella.

"Why did you come?" Wolf scolded Tabitha.

Rather more wryly, Maguire saw Bear and Langley with their revolvers at the ready, and said, "Did you not trust that I would do my job, Lady Pembroke?"

In an unapologetic tone, Tabitha answered, "I saw no reason not to be sure, just in case." Maguire inclined his head in acknowledgement of her scepticism.

EPILOGUE

By morning, the news had spread along the seafront. The *Brighton Gazette* carried a single column: **"Killer caught. The earl is innocent!"**

It reported that Mr Ernest Wilcox, a competitor in the London to Brighton run, had been taken into custody on suspicion of the murders of Thomas Havers and Gustaf Freund, and that Lord Pembroke had been thoroughly exonerated. The paper did not describe Wolf's part in Wilcox's capture, which suited him very well.

At midday, Detective Inspector Maguire furnished the coroner with a brief statement: "The suspect, when confronted with fresh evidence, made certain admissions regarding a quarrel with Mr Havers. No other party bears responsibility."

The verdict was accepted without question, and the press, finding no melodrama once the aristocrat was cleared, swiftly moved on to other topics.

For the first time in days, Wolf could step outside the Grand as a free man. While he would have been happy to pack their bags and return to London immediately, he realised that Tabitha felt guilty about how little time they'd spent with Rat and Melody since arriving in Brighton.

"I do understand your desire to be at home, and I share it," Tabitha told him that morning. "However, could you bear just one more day in Brighton so that we might eat fish and chips and all go and see the Punch and Judy show, if the weather allows?" Wolf didn't have the heart to refuse her.

Both Tabitha and Wolf felt strongly that they also needed to thank Isabella properly. There was little doubt that the case would not have been solved without her help.

"How do you think she would feel about joining us for a fish and chips lunch?" Wolf asked.

Tabitha chuckled. "If it were anyone other than Isabella, I might worry that it would all feel far too common, but I have a sense that she will relish the chance to try some working-class food."

There was a heavy pause, and from his wife's expression, Wolf could guess what she was thinking. "I am happy to ask only Isabella and not extend the invitation to Arlene," he assured her. "Anyway, I am not sure I can imagine her sitting in a seafront restaurant sprinkling malt vinegar over her fish and chips." Even Tabitha had to laugh at this image.

This left one question outstanding: how would the dowager feel about such an outing?

After sending a note to Isabella with the invitation, Tabitha and Wolf went into the dining room for breakfast. They found Langley and Bear already seated at a table. By the time pots of tea were brought to the table, the dowager had joined them, and Wolf had told her about their proposed luncheon.

"Fish and chips? What sort of proletarian fare is that?" she declared.

Although no one believed the old woman had never heard of fish and chips, none of them felt equal to entering into battle with her over something so trivial.

Instead, Tabitha said, "We have asked Miss Hartwell to join us, but will understand if you feel the outing beneath you."

Given the dowager's well-known fondness for cheap pies and beer in dingy public houses, they didn't expect her actually to turn her nose up at such a meal. Still, she amused herself by pretending to consider the invitation before finally deigning to join the outing.

Isabella sent a prompt reply accepting the invitation, so the plan was to meet her at the restaurant at one o'clock. It was a sunny, if slightly chilly day, and everyone agreed that a walk along the seafront would be pleasant, if rather bracing.

Tabitha wasn't sure what the dowager would think of the sunlit establishment with red-checkered tablecloths and its cheery owner. However, as soon as they entered the fish and chip restaurant, the dowager abandoned any pretence that she wasn't excited about the meal. Whatever judgement the dowager might have been inclined to pass was forgotten at her first bite of crisp batter and flaky cod. When Tabitha explained how the malt vinegar enhanced the food, the dowager sprinkled it so generously that it seemed she might have overdone it.

Luckily, that didn't seem to be the case. The woman's eyes lit up as she took her first bite. "Are we able to get this fare in London, Jeremy?" she asked.

"Yes," Wolf replied with a smile. "Fish and chips are readily available if one knows where to look."

"Then, why have we not partaken of it yet?" the dowager asked, as if there had been a conspiracy afoot to keep her from the food.

Isabella appeared to enjoy the meal almost as much as the dowager. "I've never eaten anything quite like this before," she admitted.

Once everyone had satisfied their initial hunger, Tabitha brought up a topic she had been wondering about all morning. "Isabella, how long do you plan to stay in Brighton?"

The woman smiled. "I will be driving back to London tomorrow. I love Nene, but a little bit of her goes a long way."

"Then, might I offer you accommodation at Chesterton House while you are in town?" Tabitha asked to Wolf's surprise. Not that he minded, as she knew he wouldn't. It was rather that, with the imminent arrival of the baby, he was surprised she was so willing to have a houseguest.

Perhaps Isabella had the same thought. "That is so kind and generous of you, Tabitha. However, I am very comfortable at the Savoy and don't want to impose on you as you near your time." Before Tabitha could insist she felt up for guests, Isabella continued, "However, I hope we can see much of each other whilst I am in town. Despite the circumstances, it has been delightful getting to know you all, and I hope to continue the acquaintance."

Whatever Tabitha was about to say was brushed aside as a commotion arose at the end of the table when Melody argued with Liam over who had eaten more chips. Mrs O'Leary resolved the dispute before it ended in tears, and the adults' conversation then shifted to the investigation.

"All I can say," the dowager declared, "is that, as far as I am concerned, the whole business was sufficient proof that the motor-car will be the ruin of civilisation."

It didn't seem like the right time for Wolf to continue claiming that the vehicle was the wave of the future. Instead, he finished his fish and chips and looked forward to his drive back the following day with pleasant anticipation.

As the group walked at a leisurely pace along the seafront, Wolf remembered his promise to Rat and realised he now had to persuade Tabitha, and indeed Langley, to allow the boy to drive back to London with him.

Unsure how best to broach the topic, Wolf turned his head slightly to look at his wife. "Tabitha, there is something I forgot to mention..."

∾

To access a bonus epilogue to this book, sign up for my newsletter at sarahfnoel.com/newsletter/

∾

Want a sneak peek at book 14, A Lyrical Woman? Keep reading...

When the dowager receives an unexpected invitation from Queen Victoria herself to attend a grand concert at the Royal Albert Hall, she suspects there's more at stake than music. A foreign dignitary's sudden death soon confirms it.

Confined to bed after a health scare, a very pregnant Tabitha must lend her sharp mind from afar, guiding Wolf and their new friend, the indomitable American heiress Isabella, through a maze of coded messages, vanished guests, and diplomatic whispers.

The trio must tread carefully as rumours swirl of anarchists, spies, and scandal within the highest circles. One wrong move could spark an international incident. They must act quickly, but discreetly, mindful of their reputations and of the trust placed in them by their sovereign.

Elegant, witty, and full of intrigue, *A Lyrical Woman* reunites readers with Tabitha, Wolf, and the formidable Dowager Countess of Pembroke in a tale of courage, cunning, and devotion to both family and Crown.

∼

Coming Soon: An Impertinent Heiress, book 1 in The Isabella Hartwell Society Mysteries. Preorder now and meet your new favorite sleuth.

London, 1899. American heiress Isabella Hartwell came for adventure, not a coronet. But when a young lord dies at a country house party moments after quarrelling with her, suspicion turns her way.

Refusing to be sent home in disgrace, Isabella begins an investigation of her own. With the indomitable Dowager Countess of Pembroke at her side, she soon learns that beneath silk gowns and polished manners lie secrets worth killing for.

AUTHOR'S NOTE

The London to Brighton Emancipation Rally happened in 1896. The Motor Car Club's Commemoration Run didn't start going to Brighton until 1899, but I took some creative license and started it in 1898.

Afterword

Thank you for reading A Conspicuous Woman. I hope you enjoyed it. If you'd like to see what's coming next for Tabitha & Wolf, here are some ways to stay in touch:

SarahFNoel.com
Facebook
@sarahfNoelAuthor on BlueSky
sfnoel on Instagram
@sfnoel on Threads

If you enjoyed this book, I'd very much appreciate a review (but, please no spoilers).

ABOUT SARAH F. NOEL

Originally from London, Sarah F. Noel now spends most of her time in Grenada in the Caribbean. Sarah loves reading historical mysteries with strong female characters. The Tabitha & Wolf Mystery Series and its spin-off, The Continental Capers of Melody Chesterton, are exactly the kind of books she loves to curl up with on a lazy Sunday.

Visit Sarah's website (sarahfnoel.com/) to join her mailing list, connect with her on social media, and see what's coming next!